LOVE AT *Second* SIGHT

Potions and Passions
Book 4

CATHERINE STEIN

ISBN: 978-1-949862-25-6

"1831-1893 Plan of Edinburgh & Leith with Suburbs," which appears in the cover design, is reproduced with the permission of the National Library of Scotland. *https://maps.nls.uk/index.html*

Book cover and interior design by E. McAuley: *www.impluviumstudios.com*

To Erin, for pushing me to be my best
and making my books shine. Enjoy your favorite trope.

I

Memory Lapse

September, 1882

"UGH."

She twisted, stretching limbs that had been too long in one position, trying to loosen her muscles and awaken her brain. Mornings were the worst.

Her movements sparked a sickly churning in her stomach. Damn. Was she ill? Had she had too much to drink last night? Her head didn't seem to be pounding.

She cracked her eyelids. If she were truly suffering the bottle-ache, the sunlight would spear into her brain like a randy john into a two-penny whore.

Nothing.

No stabbing, no headache. Which meant she really was sick.

She groaned and rolled over, reaching for the warm body and strong arms that would comfort her. She would snuggle against his chest and he'd stroke her hair and tell her everything would be all right.

Her arms grasped nothing but air. The other half of the bed was empty.

She blinked and opened her eyes fully, trying to clear her sleep-fogged mind. The room sharpened into focus. Where was she?

Unadorned wood-paneled walls surrounded her. The bed and the small dressing table looked to be fixed to the walls and the floor. A shaft of sunlight slanted across the bed from the single, round window.

A boat. That explained the queasiness. She was seasick.

What it didn't explain was why she didn't remember any of this. Or why moments ago she'd been so certain she always woke beside a man. Who was he, she wondered. For that matter, who was *she*?

"Bloody hell!"

She bolted upright, jerking any remaining sleepiness from her mind. She was awake. Fully. And remembered… nothing.

She threw back the covers to get a look at herself. The filmy, pale green nightgown didn't conceal much. It wasn't entirely transparent, but she could clearly make out the dark circles surrounding her nipples. The fabric clung to plump breasts and a slightly rounded belly. What skin she could see was pale and unblemished, save for an inch-long, crescent-shaped birthmark on her left wrist. She seized a lock of hair. Black, shot through with brown highlights.

She clambered from the bed and examined the stranger that stared back at her from the mirror. Moisture glistened in eyes the color of amber. Tingles of fear raced along unfamiliar skin. How could she not know her own body? How could she not know her own name?

She choked back an upwelling of nausea. Lost, alone, with no memory, and seasick on top of it all. She had risen from her dreams into a waking nightmare.

She clutched the table with both hands, steadying herself.

"It's only a problem. Problems have solutions."

There. She was good at this sort of thing. Analyzing problems. Finding the solutions.

Her whole body twitched. How did she know that? That was a good sign, wasn't it? If she could remember a detail like that, then there was hope she would remember other things as well.

Unless whatever had caused this also caused false memories.

"Well, there's only one way to find out," she told herself sternly.

And the first thing to do was to look for clues to her identity. Beginning with herself.

"This nightgown I'm wearing is of quality material and workmanship, which suggests a certain amount of money at my disposal. The fact that I'm staying in this cabin reinforces that idea. While it isn't large, it's well-appointed and carefully maintained. First-class accommodations. I speak with a Mayfair accent, so I must be from that part of London. My use of bad language and indecent thoughts, however, suggest that I might not be entirely a lady. Perhaps I was born to the aristocracy and have fallen from grace. Or perhaps I was born elsewhere and have learned to mimic an upper class woman."

Her eyes dropped to her hands, fixing on the gold band on her left ring finger.

"I'm wearing a wedding band. It's simple and..." She paused to pull it off and inspect it. "Not engraved. I might be married, but then where is my husband? Is he the man I expected in my bed?"

She took another look around the room. Her trunk—at least, she assumed it was hers— stood in a corner, opened wide to display its contents.

"There is only a single trunk, and it has only a woman's garments inside. Clearly no man is sharing this room. Perhaps my husband is in a separate room? Or perhaps I'm not married and the ring is only to allow myself the freedom of a married woman or a widow to move about unchaperoned. Maybe I'm a courtesan."

She wondered what it said about her that she would prefer the life of a courtesan to a marriage where her husband didn't wish to share her bed.

"Moving on."

The trunk was her best hope for clues. She began with a survey of the outside and was rewarded when she discovered a tag bearing a name and a destination.

"I have a name!" she squealed. "I am 'A. Harper,' and I'm on my way to Es—Esbj—no, no, the j sounds more like a y. Esbjerg, Denmark."

Neither the name Harper nor the city of Esbjerg triggered any new memories. Still, she knew more than she had before the investigation began.

"I wonder what my given name is. Agnes? Ugh, I hope not. Arabella? Augusta? Angelique sounds like a courtesan, I think."

She turned to the contents of the trunk, removing each item carefully and mentally cataloging it. Her memory didn't seem to be lacking now. It simply had certain, rather significant, holes in it.

The two traveling dresses were simple, sturdy, and well-made. Good fabric, neat stitching. The single evening gown was a lovely, deep-orange silk, with a daring, scooped neckline and a tidy bustle. All the clothing of a wealthy woman.

Eight pairs of gloves in different lengths and colors accompanied the dresses, but no hats, scarves, or other accessories. The only shoes were a single pair of dancing slippers to match the evening gown and a pair of black ankle boots.

The underthings intrigued her. Her corsets were made of beautiful, shimmery fabric, with fancy ribbon trimming. Embroidered patterns ran up the sides of every pair of stockings. Even the drawers and chemises had pretty ruffles or bits of colored trim. These undergarments were made to be seen. Perhaps she really *was* a courtesan.

Setting the last of the clothing aside, she turned to the few other items packed inside the trunk. Angelique, or whoever she was, possessed a pretty silver hairbrush, a matching hand mirror, and a small bag of other personal grooming products. A little stuffed bear in a pink tutu and a jaggedly-sewn green waistcoat with mismatched buttons had been tucked in a corner—a relic of the childhood she'd forgotten along with everything else.

"Ooh, these look fun."

She lifted out the stack of penny dreadfuls and thumbed through them. A brass bookmark in the shape of a tiny dagger jutted from the bottom book. She withdrew it carefully, marking the place with a finger. Perhaps if she read the book, she might remember something.

The little knife-bookmark had been stamped on one side with the maker's mark. She flipped it over and gasped. On the reverse were engraved the words, "To Anna. Stay Fierce. Love Nick."

"Anna." She tested the name on her tongue. It felt right. She could be an Anna. "But who is Nick?"

Her husband, perhaps? It was difficult to imagine a husband who didn't share her room using such intimate forms of address. Or telling her to "stay fierce." Most men didn't want a fierce wife.

Maybe Nick was her protector. Or had been in the past.

"And we're back to the courtesan idea again." It made sense for a woman who read penny dreadfuls and swore and drank.

She pulled out the last item in the trunk—a mostly-empty, unlabeled whisky bottle. She popped the cork and took a sniff. Yes, definitely whisky, and high quality too. If she'd drunk it all, it had been over a span of time. She had already established that she was not the worse for drink this morning. She recorked the bottle and set it aside. Her stomach was still protesting, and whisky would only make things worse.

"But if I'm a courtesan, where are all my jewels? And my cosmetics? I haven't any of either, and that seems terribly peculiar."

It seemed terribly peculiar for any woman of means to lack jewelry, in fact. Had she been robbed? Had she sold off her trinkets to pay for this journey? And why Denmark? What Englishwoman had business in Denmark of all places?

Anna's chest rose and fell in a heavy sigh. So many questions, and few answers. Still, she had more knowledge than she had possessed only a few minutes prior. She would repack the trunk and go out exploring. Perhaps her fellow passengers or a crew member could help jog her memory. At the very least, she could request an anti-seasickness potion. Some steamers stocked them for the first class passengers.

Another random fact. She knew so many random facts and so little about herself.

Anna restored her possessions to their prior locations, keeping everything neat and tidy. As she packed things into drawers, she spied a small bottle that she had missed among her personal items. Made of glass, with a rubber dropper cap, it appeared to contain some sort of medicine or potion. She lifted it out to read the label.

Jenson's Original Fetal Health Tonic –
Safe and Effective Daily Potion for Mother and Child

Anna's jaw went slack. For several seconds she sat, frozen, gaping at the bottle.

She wasn't seasick. She was pregnant.

II
A Dark and Stormy Day

"FOR GOD'S SAKE, man, come back inside."

"Not until I see that steamer." Quinn Harper tugged on the collar of his overcoat. Cold rain dribbled down the back of his neck, soaking into his already-damp shirt. "I'm not moving until I know she's safe."

"Don't be foolish, mate." Wilhelm Petersen, one of Quinn's warehouse managers, rubbed the bridge of his once-broken nose and tapped his foot impatiently. "You'll either catch your death or get washed out to sea."

As if to prove a point, another wave crashed over the pier, puddling around Quinn's rubber wellingtons. The ships anchored in the Esbjerg harbor bounced in the churning water. Out past the breakwater, the sea heaved and roiled, lashed by the wind and pounding rain. Tendrils of lightning forked across the sky.

"If that ship goes down, it'll destroy me. It's carrying the most important person in my life, do you understand that?"

The *two* most important people. They weren't talking much about the baby yet, because Anna was nervous. Early bouts of bleeding had scared her. Her daily drops of health potion were helping, as far as he could tell, but he hadn't seen her in two weeks. In the nine months since their Christmas wedding, this was the first time he'd been away from her for more than a day. He wanted nothing more in the world than to hold her and know that she was well.

"I understand that you're off your head," Petersen grumbled. "You can't help her out here. Come back to the tavern and have another drink."

"I've had enough. I only get drunk with Anna." The whisky he'd had earlier had already left him woozy. Not enough food or sleep and too much tension made for a poor head for spirits, it seemed.

"You *are* off your head. What kind of man wants to lush it up with his wife and not his mates?"

The flood of memories brought a smile to Quinn's face. "We do tastings together. Sample the merchandise. Sometimes we get carried away and it leads to… other things." Let it sound like he was talking about bedroom antics. He didn't want to share the way it truly led to silly games, private jokes, and hours of laughter. That was too personal, too intimate. Quinn had never in his life had a friend so close as Anna and he didn't want to let anyone else encroach on that world.

"Newlyweds." The word carried the casual disdain of a man who didn't know what he was missing. "You realize any sensible man would've left her safe at home and scratched any itch with a sweet little Danish girl, right? Now get your daft, romantic self back inside before we both freeze our arses off."

"You go. I'm waiting."

"Her ship's fine. Our cargo boat made it here in one piece. I'm living proof of it."

"Storm's gotten worse since then." Quinn turned his face to the wind, welcoming the sting of the rain on his cheeks. The physical discomfort provided relief from his raw emotions. "It's a bad one and it came on suddenly. We've lost ships in less than this, and you know it."

He rubbed his temple with fingers stiff from the cold. The dizziness was growing worse. Maybe he *was* crazy to be out here. But this helpless feeling of knowing Anna was out there was driving him mad.

"At least have another sip of whisky. Warm yourself up."

Quinn felt the nudge of a liquor flask against his arm, but waved off the offer. "No. That drink at noon went right to my head."

"That so?" his companion inquired.

"Aye. Feeling a bit off. Might be coming down with something."

"You don't say. How's the memory? You know why you're standing out here in a bloody downpour?"

"What? Of course. For..." The image of her flashed in his mind. Dark hair tumbling around her shoulders, her rosy lips curved in a coy smile. The tinkle of her laughter echoed in his ears. "For Anna. My... wife."

Why did his brain seem so sluggish? He could still picture her in his mind's eye, but the words came slowly and sounded strange.

"You don't have a wife," said the man standing beside him.

"What? I do. A-Anna." Did she really exist? Had he just imagined her?

"I think it's about time we left this godforsaken port behind and walked back to the tavern, don't you?"

"I, um..." He rubbed his temple, trying to wake himself up or shake off the confusion, or anything really. Where was he? What was going on? Why was he out in such a storm?

The stranger next to him took his arm and steered him away from the shore. "You don't have a wife."

"I don't?"

"No. No wife. Your name is Smith and you're a warehouse manager."

"I am?"

"You just lost your job. You're looking to head back home to England."

"England. Home. London."

"No! Not London. Somewhere else."

"Scotland? Edinburgh?"

"No, dammit. Somewhere we don't… Newcastle."

"I don't live in Newcastle."

"Yes. Yes, you do. You're Mr. Smith, an unmarried man from Newcastle."

"Smith. Newcastle. Right."

Why did that sound wrong? Quinn squeezed his eyes closed, stumbled, and opened them again. He was ill. That was it. He was ill and his head was swimming and nothing made sense. He'd go inside, out of this storm, and have a lie-down and wake up feeling better.

"Don't worry. I'll keep repeating it until you remember."

Quinn nodded weakly. God, did he feel awful. The whole world seemed to be spinning, and he didn't think he was drunk. Drunk was more fun. Drunk was bawdy jokes and laughter and a dark-haired angel.

"Wasn't I waiting for something? Someone?"

"There is no someone. Come along, Smith. Let's get you inside and get another good dose of whisky in you."

"Aye."

Whisky sounded right. He knew all about whisky. But damned if he could remember why.

III

In a Strange Land

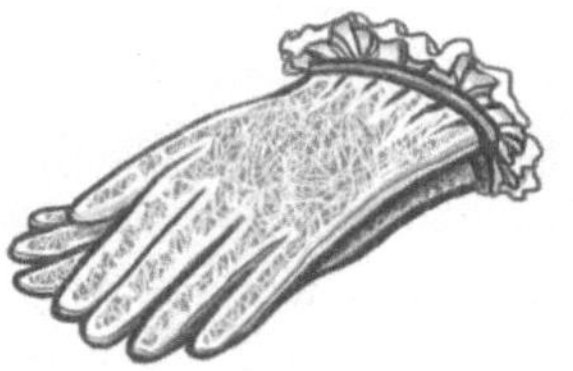

ANNA HUDDLED UNDER HER CLOAK, sheltering from the rain that hadn't entirely relented. She stood along the rail of the steamer, a good distance away from the disembarking passengers. The sun had long since set, but potion-fueled lamps lit the deck and the gangplank descending to the pier. Beyond that, a trail of small lanterns led out into the darkness. Five anxious men hovered near her, victims of the same strange ailment that had wiped her memory.

The remainder of the twenty-five passengers appeared to be unaffected, and had been pronounced entirely fit and healthy by the overbearing Dr. Bullard, who now stood tutting and contemplating the small amnesiac group.

"It is best that we keep you all quarantined until the cause of the contagion can be determined."

A couple of heads nodded.

"Arrangements are being made to place you all into the same portion of the hotel, where you can remain apart from the other guests while we investigate."

Anna rolled her eyes. Contagious memory loss? More likely they'd all been poisoned, though any explanation for how that could have happened accidentally or why anyone would do it on purpose eluded her.

"Why didn't you just run up the black and yellow plague flag?" she muttered.

"Is there a problem, Miss…" Dr. Bullard consulted his sheet of paper. "Ah, what was your name, again?"

"Harper. Mrs. Anna Harper."

"Yes. Let me note that down, Mrs. Harper."

The way he said her name made it plain that he didn't believe her. She had doubts herself. She wasn't listed on the passenger manifest. Passage for "one lady, traveling solo" had been booked for her by Messrs. Stewart and Lachlan. Her solicitors, she assumed, or those of whomever had sent her here.

Still, she liked the name Anna Harper and had determined to use it as her own unless other proof of her identity surfaced.

Dr. Bullard looked back up from his notes. "And you had a problem?"

"Yes." Her belly was her problem. It quivered and grumbled, protesting the lack of food. She'd eaten no breakfast because of her morning sickness, little lunch because of the storm that had made even some of the crew seasick, and nothing since. It was past time they were eating dinner, and she didn't just want food, she needed it. Her baby depended on it. "I'm feeling weak from hunger and you are making us stand here and wait when we could be disembarking and heading into town for a meal."

Not that she had any idea how far town was or what sort of meal awaited her there. She knew nothing of Esbjerg, and the little lanterns didn't provide enough illumination to see what lay more than a few dozen yards away. Somewhere, though, there was a hotel. With food.

"Now, my dear," one of the men said, his tone that fake-soothing condescension so often directed at women who dared speak their minds. "Surely the good doctor knows best. And you are certainly overwrought, thinking yourself to be this Mrs. Harper traveling all alone."

"I *am* Mrs. Harper traveling alone, and I'm not overwrought, merely hungry." And growing more irritable by the second.

The man—Eglamore, his name was—gave a sad shake of his head. "You poor dear. You are not alone, I assure you. It is clear, from the location of my stateroom directly beside yours, that it is I who is truly your husband. So, you see, even though we do not remember the details, you have nothing to fear. I am here to protect you."

For a moment, Anna could do nothing but stare at him. "You are *not* my husband!" she blurted at last.

Eglamore was sixty if a day and the way he leered at her made her skin crawl. She would never have married a man such as he, not of her own free will. She could imagine being forced into such a marriage to save a beloved family, perhaps, but if such were the case she would have found herself a good contraceptive potion—and, if possible, one to cause impotence—well before any vows were recited. That man was absolutely not the father of her child.

Who is? she wondered for what had to be the millionth time that day. Did she love him? Or was he merely a good romp? Was he her real husband? An illicit lover? Would she ever remember? Would he ever know he had sired a child?

"Come, my dear," Eglamore crooned, reaching to take her arm. "Allow me to assist you and all will be well, I promise."

Anna didn't bother with a reply, or even a false smile. She spun on her heel and marched off, following the trail of men who hadn't lost their memories. Thank God she couldn't remember the rest of the journey. It had probably been hour after hour of random men treating the one woman on board as if she were an unruly farm animal.

"Mrs. Hatcher!" the doctor shouted after her.

"Harper," she muttered, not breaking stride. Anna Harper was a sensible woman. The sturdy boots and the simple dress made her getaway a breeze. She flew down the gangplank, following the trail of lights into the city.

Or, well, something resembling a city. Town. Village. Maybe it was just the darkness playing tricks on her eyes. Was that really an empty field pushed right up against the hotel? Were all the buildings as low and austere as they seemed? She could find only two that rose more than a story above the ground. Why was there no street lighting? She jogged after a man with a hand lantern who looked to be escorting the other passengers. Perhaps he could answer some basic questions.

She stopped in her tracks. Did she know how to speak Danish? She thought for a moment and couldn't come up with even a simple "hello."

Why was she here? It appeared she wasn't Danish, so it was unlikely she was meeting family. A friend? In this small, foreign town? A lover? Perhaps she was running away with a tall, blond, Nordic scoundrel.

"Mrs. Hatcher!"

Anna rolled her eyes once again, picked up her skirts, and hurried off toward the hotel.

A blazing fire and dozens of mirrored candle-lamps assailed her the moment she stepped inside, and she squinted in the sudden brightness. Hotel staff scurried about, lugging trunks and assisting the newly-arrived passengers. The scent of a hot meal pricked her nose, setting her belly to growling with even greater vigor. She wormed her way up to the front desk.

"Do you have a room reserved for a Mrs. Harper?" she asked, hoping the man would speak at least some English.

He consulted his books and shook his head. "Only rooms under the Harper-Douglass company, and I believe they are all filled."

"Oh. Um." Harper-Douglass company? Did she have some connection with that? It seemed too wild to be a coincidence. But how was she to find out? "Anything reserved by Messrs. Stewart and Lachlan?"

Another shake of the head. A shiver of apprehension raced down Anna's spine. She had no room? She'd found no money among her possessions. What would she do if she had no place to stay and no way to pay for… anything?

"Mrs. Hatcher!"

She spun around, hands going to her hips. "Harper. It's *Harper*. Like someone who plays a harp. Except I suppose that would be a harpist… Never mind! I have no interest in whatever it is you have to say, Dr. Bullard."

"Doctor?" A lanky man with a thick Danish accent jumped into the conversation. "You are the doctor from the ship? You must come with me. We have two men here who have also lost their minds. Quickly."

Dr. Bullard allowed himself to be dragged from the lobby. Anna followed behind, curious. This malady wasn't confined to the steamer. Peculiar. The cause could be something native to Esbjerg. Some poison that had made its way both onto the ship and into the hotel. A poorly made potion, perhaps? Not that potions looked to be in much use here. Back home in London, the hotels were all potion-lit, especially now that prices were dropping at last.

She started. Was that a memory? Home in London. Potions at hotels. She filed it away for later processing and slipped into the room Dr. Bullard had just entered.

Two men waited in the room, one pacing nervously, just as the men on the ship had done. The other sat at a table, writing. Anna's gaze fell on him. And stuck fast.

Something tightened in her chest and her belly. Her breath caught in her throat. If any man was her Nordic scoundrel, it was he. He wasn't the absolute most handsome man in the world—if one measured handsomeness by such foolish notions as symmetry and perfection—but he drew her to him as if they were a pair of magnets. North and south. Opposite and complementary.

There were small crinkles at the corners of his blue-gray

eyes, as if he smiled often, and his bow-shaped upper lip looked pink and kissable. His strong, slightly-pointed chin was dusted with a day's growth of beard. His hair was not the pale, Nordic blond, but a darker shade with a slight reddish tint.

He rose to greet the doctor, giving her a good look at the whole length of his body. Slightly above-average height, with strong arms and broad shoulders. Plain black trousers and a tidy, white shirt topped with a charcoal-gray waistcoat. No jacket or tie. A man who worked for a living, she guessed. The precise tailoring of his clothing suggested he was successful at whatever he did.

"I'm pleased to meet you, Dr. Bullard," he said. "I hope you can resolve this matter as quickly as possible for all our sakes."

An Englishman. Another Londoner, by his accent. Covent Garden, she guessed. She seemed to be good with this business of placing people by their accents. Another thing to add to her list of "Who is Anna Harper?"

So, he was not Nordic, not especially tall, and only somewhat blond. If he wasn't a scoundrel, either, she was going to be terribly disappointed.

And how disappointed will you be if he isn't your mystery lover?

The captivating man shook the doctor's hand, but his gaze was fixed on her. She wished she were close enough to get a better look at those stormy eyes. Even at this distance they had her bewitched. He stared back at her with such heated intensity her heart began to race and her palms to sweat.

He ignored whatever Dr. Bullard was saying and took a step toward her. "Excuse me, miss? Do… Do I know you?"

IV

Names and Places

"I'm sorry," he apologized immediately. That had been rude, especially when she already had that stunned look on her face. He ought to have waited to be introduced. It was difficult to remember manners, it seemed, when one couldn't even remember oneself.

"Oh, no, it's quite all right," the black-haired beauty replied. "I don't even know myself entirely." She walked over and held out her hand. Wrist-length red gloves made a striking contrast with her simple brown dress. She wore no hat, no jewelry, and no discernible cosmetics. Her hair had been twisted into a tight chignon. Even so unadorned, she shone like a diamond. "Mrs. Anna Harper."

"Smith." He resisted the urge to kiss her hand, settling for a firm handshake. She was married. Damn.

"It's a pleasure to make your acquaintance, Mr. Smith. I understand you are suffering from the same memory affliction as several of us just arrived on the steamer?"

"Aye." Was he Scottish, perhaps? His accent was English, but he had a definite preference for "aye" over "yes." Another thing for his notes.

He moved toward the table and picked up his pen. Mrs. Harper followed.

"What are you writing?"

"Everything I can remember. Even flashes of memory. I'm putting it all down in the hopes that maybe I can make some sense of things."

"Very logical. I approve. I've been making a mental list, but perhaps I will commit those things to paper, in case my memory falters again. It has seemed quite robust today. I haven't forgotten a single name, and I can recall conversations I have had throughout the day, perhaps not perfectly, but well enough."

"I can't remember much of anything. My mind seems to have gone blank sometime this afternoon. I found myself sitting at the tavern down the street, a drink in my hand and no memory of how I had come to be there. My memory of myself was vague, at best. I had to look in a mirror to know the color of my own eyes."

"Yes. It was the same for me." She took a seat at the table. "Let me see your list. Perhaps I can help you."

The list wasn't long. A few words that had been rattling around in his brain, bothering him. Smith. Newcastle. Whisky. A few indistinct thoughts or memories.

"So Smith is your name?" she asked.

"Aye, as far as I know. It's one of the few things that's been in my head the entire time."

"Interesting. I didn't remember my name. I had to find it written among my things. For all I know it might not be my name at all."

A burst of excitement shot through him. Maybe she wasn't married after all. His gaze dropped to her hands. He couldn't tell whether she wore a wedding ring underneath her colorful gloves.

One red finger tapped at the paper. "Why Newcastle? You're not from there."

"I'm not?"

"Well, I suppose you could live there now. But you speak like a Londoner. I would guess you were raised in the Covent Garden area."

He scribbled "Covent Garden" on his paper.

"So I'm a working class man, then. I suppose I knew that already."

"Yes. Just look at your hands and your muscled arms. You're someone who does things for himself. And the quality of your clothing suggests that you've made a good living at it."

"You have a keen eye and a sharp mind, Mrs. Harper."

"Why, thank you." Her lush, full lips curved into a man-killing smile. "It's nice to meet a man who realizes I have a brain."

"Well, I can see how your multitude of charms might addle a man's brain, but so much so that he overlooks yours? Absurd."

Stop flirting, you bloody arse. She's married, for God's sake.

He stared resolutely back down at his notes, considering adding "dissolute cad." *He* could be married, for all he knew.

The thought of forgetting his own family sent a stab of pain through his gut. Was someone, somewhere waiting for him? Or perhaps thinking him dead, not knowing the truth was possibly even worse.

A sudden gurgling noise shook him from his maudlin musings. Mrs. Harper put a hand to her belly.

"Excuse me. I haven't eaten since lunch, and…"

"What?" he interrupted. "You, there, Bullard! What kind of doctor are you to leave an ailing woman to go hungry?" He hopped up from his seat. "Wait right here," he said to her. "I'll take care of everything."

He rushed from the room, glad of an occupation that

would do some good and take him away from her for a time. This was all he needed. A little bit of distance to get his mind settled. Then he could stop obsessing over those wild, amber eyes that were unlike anything he'd ever seen. As far as he remembered.

His hopes were dashed the moment he returned with a plate of fresh fish and a pot of hot tea. Her eyes lit up like fireworks on Bonfire Night and she tucked in with such enthusiasm that he found himself envying the damned fork every time it slipped between her lips.

What the hell was wrong with him? Why was every muscle in his body twitching with the desire to haul her into his lap and kiss her senseless? Was he really such a Lothario? Or was it something about this woman in particular?

She swallowed another bite of fish and tapped his notes again. Her red gloves had been set aside, revealing the soft, unmarked hands of a woman of wealth and privilege. Far too costly for a Mr. Smith from Covent Garden.

"This," she said. "'Dark-haired.' Is that why you thought perhaps you might know me?"

"Yes. It was the vaguest flash of memory. I think a dark-haired woman, but I'm not certain of that. I only had a sense that I knew a person with dark hair and there was some significance to it. Friend, family, enemy. I couldn't say."

"Interesting. And what is this, here, at the bottom of the page? Q-u?"

"My name, or what I know of it. I thought if I signed my name, letting my hand write as it has done thousands of times, perhaps it could break through this cloud around my mind. But that is as far as I can get before my thoughts intrude."

"Well, what given names begin with Q? I hope it's not Quincy. I don't think that would suit you at all. Quentin, perhaps? Or Quinn?"

A jolt shot through him, and he flinched so hard the chair rocked beneath him. "Quinn feels right."

"Excellent. Well, it's a pleasure to meet you, Mr. Quinn Smith."

She favored him once again with that devastating smile. She had swept into the room and in a matter of minutes had given him back more of himself than he'd thought possible. He had hope now that his condition would be temporary. Perhaps a good night's sleep would restore still more memories.

Regardless, he needed to take his leave of her, before the urge to lean in for a kiss became overpowering and he earned himself a good, hard slap to the face. The chance that she might allow a taste could be worth the risk, though.

Quinn shoved himself away from the table. That was quite enough. Maybe it would be better if he didn't have his memories restored. Maybe it wasn't worth knowing what kind of scoundrel he was. This could be his chance for redemption. To become a better man.

He executed a hasty bow. "Please excuse me. It has been a trying day and I believe it's time I retired for the night. Pleasant dreams, Mrs. Harper."

"Pleasant dreams to you, too, Mr. Smith."

He hurried away. He had a horrible feeling he knew what would haunt his dreams all night. He'd heard a scientist theorize once that dreams were formed from the day's memories. And Anna Harper was his only real memory.

V

Unnecessary Arrangements

UGH. NAUSEOUS AGAIN . Anna sat up. Again. That was a nice word. She took a moment to get her bearings. The hotel room. Small and plain, but nice in its own way. Because she knew where she was. She hadn't forgotten yesterday. Thank God.

She took her pregnancy potion—three drops precisely, as per the directions on the bottle—and lay in bed for a time, mulling over all that had happened the day before.

No additional old memories had sprung up overnight that she could determine, but her new memories were clear and just as she expected them to be. Her spirits buoyed by this fact, she read over the notes she had made the night before, and jotted down a few more things.

1. *multiple victims = likely potion-caused*
2. *ingested via food or drink?*
3. *2 sources of exposure; 1 the night before on the boat, 1 that morning in Esbjerg?*
4. *if accidental: what food or drink would be in both places?*
5. *if intentional: how did poisoner get potion to boat and to Esbjerg?*

6.   *check to see if any reserved rooms were not taken last night,*
     in case I am not Anna Harper

Good questions, all of them, and she was glad she had thought to ask about the room. She could do that when she went to probe into the Harper-Douglass company.

Too bad it wasn't the Harper-Smith company. She'd liked Quinn Smith's notes and his logical approach to things. They would make a good team. At the very least, she intended to speak with him again. Even small details about the Esbjerg poisoning would help her investigation, and he seemed to have clearer flashes of old memories than she did thus far.

She chose the gray dress today, with peacock blue gloves. She really did have excellent taste in gloves. Not only was this particular pair a pretty color, but it was made of a soft, supple leather that protected her hands without impeding her movements.

Picking up her notes and her pencil, she headed for the stairs, determined to discover more clues to her mystery ailment.

A different man stood behind the front desk than had been there when she'd arrived last evening, but she discovered to her relief that he also spoke excellent English. Esbjerg was small, but the port town clearly knew how to handle the influx of foreigners.

"I know this is somewhat of an odd question," she said, "but did any of the reserved rooms go unused last night? I had expected to find a room waiting for me, but there was none, and then, of course, arrangements were made to locate me with the other... ailing people."

Talking about her memory loss to a stranger, even in so oblique a manner, made her tense. She disliked giving anyone a reason to think her in any way infirm, unintelligent, or incompetent.

The man didn't so much as frown at her peculiar question,

but simply consulted the books. "No, madam, all reservations were accounted for."

"Thank you."

Anna touched a finger to her lips. It made no sense that someone would have arranged for her journey without also arranging for a room or providing her money to pay for one. The only sensible conclusion was that someone had expected her to share a room. Her husband or a lover, then. Or was she to have immediately boarded a train to another town?

"And what of the Harper-Douglass rooms?" she asked. "I believe I may have some connection to their organization, and I would like to consult with the men, if possible."

"I'm afraid they have already departed, madam."

"What?"

"Three rooms for one night for the men overseeing the delivery from their ship. They left this morning. I am very sorry, madam."

"The ship has gone?" She spun around, as if she could see the vessel through the wall behind her.

"I expect it has."

"And what of the ship I arrived on?"

"I expect that has sailed also. The sea was calm this morning and the captains wished to sail in the fine weather."

"But..." Her fallback plan if she found no further clues to her identity was to return to Edinburgh, where the ship had originated. Surely someone there could help, such as Messrs. Stewart and Lachlan. But she had expected a day or so and some warning before the ship departed. Now she would have to wait a week for the next opportunity. And she had no money to pay for her room and board.

There was nothing to be done for it. Her investigation would have to continue.

"Could you tell me if any of the Harper-Douglass men remain here in Esbjerg?"

"I do not believe so. I am sorry. I have seen them in the

past. They unload their shipments quickly and without fuss. They may have drinks at the tavern, but they keep to themselves and depart promptly. Very focused on their work."

"Hmm. And do you know anything about what their work is?"

"Of course, madam. They deliver Scotch whisky."

Anna blinked. Whisky. One of the words on Quinn Smith's list of memories. Another vague link between the Harper-Douglass company and the memory loss.

She nodded to the man behind the desk. "Thank you very much. You've been very kind to answer my questions."

"My pleasure, madam."

She turned back toward the stairs, thinking to head up to the hall where all the afflicted guests had been housed. She could knock on doors until she found Mr. Smith and interrogate him about the whisky connection.

Before she reached the staircase, a voice called out, "Mrs. Hatcher, there you are!"

"Oh, for God's sake," Anna muttered. For a moment she considered fleeing up the stairs, but she forced herself to turn and meet Dr. Bullard with what she hoped was a polite smile.

"I was just on my way to fetch you," he said, grabbing her arm without a by-your-leave and tugging her toward the dining room.

Anna twisted her arm, trying to free herself, but the man was surprisingly strong. "Let me go."

"Now, now, my dear lady, you must join the others. You were not at breakfast and we had begun to fear you had run off. Terribly dangerous for a woman in your situation. Can't have that happening."

"I didn't run off. I was feeling unwell."

"What? Have you fallen ill? You appeared in perfect health last night."

Anna wriggled once again and finally managed to slip his grasp. "I'm not ill."

"And yet you were this morning?"

"Yes. No. It's not an illness. Merely a passing discomfort."

He paused and frowned at her for a moment. "Oh! But, of course. You are increasing. Your husband will be pleased to hear it."

Anna almost stumbled. "What husband?"

"Egglebert or whatever his name was."

"Oh. Him." She rolled her eyes.

"You ought to have informed him of your condition. Now, allow me to give you a tip for staving off your nausea. It is a proven cure. I used it on the ship and you will recall that I was never seasick."

"I recall very little of the voyage, sir."

"Yes, yes. But here is the remedy: I have a special solution of water and laudanum, which is to be injected into the rectum and held there overnight. I can provide both the solution and a special cork for keeping the liquid in the body."

"Eew." Anna struggled against a new wave of nausea. "That is revolting and surely not good for the baby." Drat. She shouldn't have confirmed her pregnancy. It was no one's business but her own. She would take care not to mention it again.

"Nonsense. It is perfectly harmless. I will see that you are provided all you need. Then you will not suffer further bouts of this morning sickness on our journey."

"Journey?"

Dr. Bullard entered the dining room, and she followed, wanting to know what he was talking about and hoping Mr. Smith would be among the "others" he had mentioned.

"Yes. I have begun arrangements to escort all of you forgetful people to Copenhagen for further evaluation and treatment."

She stopped in the doorway. "I haven't the means to travel to Copenhagen." She hadn't the means to travel anywhere. Or even to remain here, really. She would have to search through her trunks for anything she might sell for passage back to Scotland. "And shouldn't we remain in Esbjerg to investigate the source of our condition? That seems to me the best way to effect a cure."

Half-a-dozen pairs of masculine eyes lifted to the ceiling. Probably imploring the heavens to open up and smite her for daring to disagree.

"Do you know of potion makers in Copenhagen who might be able to craft a medicine to restore our memories?" she continued. "Because I believe this must have been caused by some pernicious potion. Nothing else makes sense."

"I will be the judge of that, Mrs. Hatcher," Dr. Bullard replied, his haughty nose in the air. "In consultation with my colleague, Dr. Knudsen."

Oh, no. No way would she subject herself to the ludicrous advice of two such persons. She gave the doctor a resolute shake of her head.

"I'm afraid I must decline to accompany you. I don't have the money to pay for a train ticket to Copenhagen. Good day, gentlemen."

She turned and strode from the room. A flurry of footsteps sounded behind her, but she refused to look back, not even to see if Mr. Smith was among those following her. She would abandon her plan of talking with him and instead go out seeking more information on the Harper-Douglass company. She could consult with Smith at a later time. And if he joined the others on the inane journey to Copenhagen, well, then he was not a fit collaborator.

She quashed the flutter of disappointment that accompanied the thought. She hardly knew him. She would lose nothing if he turned out to be a fool.

Only my one potential friend.

"My dear, do not fret!" Eglamore called after her. "I will pay your ticket. You must drop this ridiculous notion that you are anything but my wife."

Anna spun around and glared at him.

He rushed to her side, his eyes lingering on her bosom, and said in a low voice, "I will put you in my very own compartment this time and see to all your needs."

"I will go nowhere with you," she snapped. "Can you honestly think I would accept your absurd idea and submit myself to your repulsive attentions? What would happen when we did recover our memories? Suddenly you would have absolute proof I was not your wife. Then what? I can't imagine you would even bother to apologize for raping me. Instead, you'd tell me I deserved ruination for being an obstinate whore."

Eglamore, Bullard, and two other men from the ship gasped in unison.

"Oh, what? Did I say a bad word? But that's what you think of me, isn't it? That's all you think women are good for."

Eglamore coughed, composing himself. "I will give you one last chance to reconsider, my dear. You know full well no woman would be traveling to this place alone, and there is no other reason to place you at the end of a hall with only my room beside yours. We must be married."

"Interesting reasoning." Quinn Smith's quiet, but firm, voice carried from somewhere behind the other men. A path cleared and he stepped between Eglamore and Dr. Bullard. "By the same token, I am now her husband, as I have a room currently beside hers. As does Mr. Marshall, I believe. Mrs. Harper, I'm afraid you shall have to choose between us."

Anna favored Mr. Smith with a genuine smile which tightened as she let her gaze rove over the rest of the assembly.

"I choose divorce. Good day, gentlemen." She whirled around and marched away, leaving the pack of scandalized men to fend for themselves.

VI

Qualified Victory

QUINN CHEWED ON THE END of his pencil as he stared down at his notes. The dream had been so vivid, but by the time he'd risen from his bed it had faded to almost nothing. Just these few lines.

"This isn't a game, a lark, or a casual fling. Not for me."

"What is it, then?"

"Love."

He didn't even know who had said those things. Had he been the one speaking of love, or was some poor woman in love with him? Was this a memory, or merely nonsense conjured up by his disordered brain?

He forced himself to flip back to his other notes. He could do nothing more about the dream unless it came to him again. He was almost certain it had been erotic in nature, so there was a chance it would. He seemed to have sex on the brain altogether too much. Regardless, he would keep the notebook beside the bed from now on to give him a better chance to scribble down further dreams before they faded.

For now, the best thing he could do was investigate the situation here in Esbjerg and try to track down the cause of his memory loss. Mrs. Harper was absolutely right about that.

As if conjured by his thoughts, she swept into the dining room, still attired in her gray dress and blue gloves. Her gowns were unfussy, almost austere, but well-made and cut to flatter her figure. She was a woman of means.

Which made him wonder what she was doing all alone in a small, foreign town, with no money or jewels. Had someone abandoned her? Had she sold all her possessions in order to run from someone? Or *to* someone?

"You're still here!"

He looked up at her face. Her eyes had widened in surprise, and her lips were parted. His heart beat faster as he imagined kissing her. Again.

Bloody hell.

"Won't you sit down?" he asked. "I have a fresh pot of tea, and this wienerbrød is excellent. I intend to have my fill, as it comes with the room and I have time remaining before I must vacate the premises."

She slipped into the chair beside him, which only intensified his desire. He was a fool.

"Why are you here?" she asked. "I thought Dr. Bullard took all the others to Copenhagen. You declined to accompany them?"

The note of pleasure in her voice caused a flutter of happiness inside Quinn. Aye, definitely a fool.

"Correct. My decision was only in part because the man is cracked, however. Like yourself, I find myself without funds."

Her bright, amber eyes grew round. "What? Oh, no. I'm very sorry. How did you come to be here without any money? Or were arrangesbnts made for you, much as they were for me?"

"I seem to have had no arrangements at all." Quinn rubbed his temple. "I don't even know how I arrived in Esbjerg.

Boat? Train? Steam car? Donkey cart? If evidence existed, it has been erased or stolen. Last night when I retired to my room, I found my trunk—or what I'm told was my trunk—in disarray. Anything I may have had of value is gone and the charred remains of burnt papers lay in the hearth. I could find nothing personal or sentimental, no travel plans or tickets, and no money. Nothing but my clothing and a few grooming implements."

"Damnation," muttered Mrs. Harper.

A muscle twitched in Quinn's jaw. Her swearing amused him. Interesting.

Mrs. Harper drummed her fingers on the table. "The culprit doesn't want your memory restored. *You* are important, somehow. No one else had papers destroyed or money stolen. Given the two separate poisonings, someone on the ship must have been a target as well. Me, I wonder? No one ransacked my room, however. Could that have been an oversight by the villain? Or perhaps lack of opportunity? It could be that being a woman helped me in this instance. He could draw unwanted attention sneaking around a woman's room."

Quinn ripped off a piece of pastry and chewed it slowly, considering her words. "You're quite good at this investigation business. You notice details and come to logical conclusions."

"Possible conclusions. There is always the chance that I've missed or misinterpreted a clue, so I try to keep an open mind."

"Perhaps you were targeted because of this talent of yours. Maybe you were investigating our villain and discovered something he didn't want you to know. So he used his pernicious potion."

She smiled at his use of her earlier words. "Possible. I seem to be unconventional enough for such a career. But why were you targeted? Are you also an investigator? Or perhaps you were my contact and I was meant to pass information to you. It makes me wonder if I'm actually Anna Harper at all, or if that is merely an alias. It feels too much of a coincidence that a Mrs.

Harper and a Harper-Douglass company would both arrive here on the same day. You listed the word whisky in your notes, Mr. Smith. Are you familiar with Harper-Douglass Whisky?"

Quinn laughed. "Everyone who is anyone in London is familiar with Harper-Douglass Whisky. It's what all the toffs drink." He blinked rapidly. "How do I know that?"

"My memories have been much the same. Seemingly random details that I can't connect to anything else."

"Damned frustrating."

"Yes, it is." She pulled off her gloves and picked up a bit of wienerbrød. The band of gold on her left ring finger mocked him.

Quinn let his eyes drift to the serving girl who was cleaning up a nearby table. She had a pleasant figure, a cheerful demeanor, and a beautiful smile. Kissing her would be enjoyable, certainly. Why, then, didn't he feel the same compulsion to do so that he did every time he looked at Mrs. Harper? Was it that nebulous memory that he'd known some dark-haired woman? Or did her unavailability appeal to him? It would be appropriate, he supposed, for the cad he feared he may have been.

"You are absolutely correct," she said. "This bread is delicious. And I will be happy to eat it all, because I haven't the foggiest notion how I'm to pay for dinner tonight. What do you plan to do when we've been booted from our rooms for our lack of ability to pay?"

"I don't know. Find work, I suppose. Surely someone in town has odd jobs that need doing. The next ship bound for Newcastle leaves in five days, and I hope I can be on it."

"Isn't the London ship a day earlier?"

"Yes, but you will recall that Newcastle was one of the things I remembered. Those words stuck in my brain, like Smith and whisky."

"So you hope it will be relevant or that the people there will know you and help?"

Quinn nodded.

"That makes sense. I was hoping to return to Edinburgh, since that's where my ship arrived from. I intend to track down these Messrs. Stewart and Lachlan who arranged my journey. I must wait a week, though, and I can't pay my room and board, let alone my passage, so I suppose I, too, must seek out work."

"Absolutely not!" Quinn flinched, startled by the vehemence of his own words.

Mrs. Harper's amber eyes blazed with fury. "I beg your pardon? Did you just attempt to tell me what I can and cannot do?"

"My apologies. It's not my place…" His words trailed off. For whatever reason, the thought of her needing to work for her keep made his every muscle tense. "It's only that I doubt you've ever worked a day in your life."

"I wouldn't know," she snapped.

"Yes, you would. Look at your hands." His eyes followed his own directions, taking in her perfect skin and the interesting birthmark on the inside of her left wrist. It was almost a crescent moon shape. "You wear beautiful, fancy gloves. Your skin is flawless. No lines, marks, scars, et cetera. You come from wealth and have never done manual labor."

"True. But that doesn't mean I can't work."

"Genteel work," he conceded. "Befitting a lady."

She glared at him. "My needlepoint is atrocious."

"How do you know?"

"The same way you know that everyone in London drinks Harper-Douglass Whisky, I imagine. Bits of old memories. And since the rest is lost to me, all I can rely on is who I am now. And who I am now is a woman who intends to earn herself some room and board and a trip back to Scotland."

"You cannot simply go out and start plowing fields!" He was going to win this argument. He had no idea why it mattered so much to him, but every protective instinct in him had awakened, and he wasn't about to let anyone treat her as anything other than a lady.

"Of course not. It's harvest season, not planting season."

"You know what I meant."

"Yes, I do know. You meant that I can't take care of myself because I'm a woman. And this after you praised my investigational skills. I'm disappointed in you, Mr. Smith."

I'm disappointed in you. Good God Almighty, had any words ever cut so deeply? If they had, Quinn didn't want to remember them.

"You are the most capable woman I know," he babbled, suspecting he was only digging himself a deeper hole, but unable to stop himself.

"I'm the only woman you know."

"And you will remain so until I can get my memories back." A smile tugged at his mouth as a solution presented itself. Appeal to her logical mind. "Which is why you must continue investigating."

The angry slant of her brows softened into an expression of suspicion. "What are you on about?"

"You can't simply go out and start washing dishes or threshing wheat. Not only are you not accustomed to that type of work, but it would be a waste of your abilities. You should use your mind instead. Keep investigating. Discover all you can about our condition and its causes. Seek out a cure, if you can. Meanwhile, I'll work for the both of us. I've done manual labor before."

"Not for some time. Your clothes are too nice and your hands bear no recent scars. You worked your way out of that life, and you might find yourself quickly regretting delving back into it."

Not as much as I would regret letting you delve into it.

"I will cope," he replied.

She ate another chunk of pastry and sipped her tea before replying. "I will allow you this victory, because I do have a great many things that I still want to investigate. This will give me the time and means to do so. But don't think I don't know exactly what you're doing."

Quinn tore out a sheet from the back of his notebook and scribbled on it.

IOU
Mr. Quinn Smith to Mrs. Anna Harper
One unconditional surrender

"Will that suffice?"

She read over the note, folded it, then unbuttoned the top two buttons of her bodice and tucked the paper down her décolletage. Quinn's mouth went dry.

"Yes," she replied. "That will do nicely."

VII

Detective Work

A GRUNTING NOISE dragged Anna from a sound sleep. She tried to roll over, only to find her progress hampered by cumbersome and confining garments. Was she sleeping in her clothes? And where was she? This was her new normal, it seemed, waking in a strange bed without a companion.

A masculine groan came from somewhere below, startling her fully awake. She did have a companion, after all, though he wasn't sharing her bed.

Anna sat up, surveying the room in the early morning light and sifting through her memories from the night before.

It was a serviceable room they'd been given, though small. The residence of a young man who now worked on a merchant vessel and would be away from home for some time yet. His mother, who didn't speak a word of English, had bustled them into it last night, calling them Herre og Fru Smith. Anna hadn't even tried to correct her. It had been difficult enough finding someone who could provide Mr. Smith a temporary job and a place to stay. Their condition had presented a greater problem than she had anticipated. People seemed to fear it might be catching, and the language barrier made it especially difficult to plead her case.

Her nose wrinkled at the scent of fish and seawater. This single bed in a fisherman's hut near the docks was hardly ideal, but it was tolerable.

Smith groaned again. "Damnation," he mumbled.

Tolerable for one of them, at least. Though he had slept on the floor by his own insistence.

"I beg your pardon," Smith said, wincing as he struggled to his feet.

"What for?"

"The swearing, of course."

"Oh. It *was* rather prosaic. You could have said 'bloody hell and buggery!' or 'by the devil's flaming arsehole!' or something of that sort."

He rubbed his temple as if he were in pain. Which perhaps he was, considering the unforgiving wooden planks he'd slept upon. "Who *are* you?"

"Mrs. Anna Harper. Have you lost your memory again?"

He sighed and shook his head. "No, I haven't. Please excuse me. I'm going to the washroom."

"There is no washroom. I'm not even certain there's an outhouse."

"No matter. I can piss off of the dock if necessary." He didn't apologize for the vulgarity this time, but simply strode from the room, calling back to her, "I will see you for breakfast."

The mention of food made Anna's stomach flip-flop. She soothed it with a glass of water and three drops of her potion, then set about tidying herself as best she could manage. Her dress was rather wrinkled, but she wouldn't be going anywhere her appearance would matter and she wasn't about to attempt to wield a flatiron in any case. She would probably burn herself or the gown or both.

She pulled her hair into a tight knot, donned her sturdy

black gloves, and set out with notebook in hand to begin the day's investigations.

On her way out the door, she nearly collided with Mr. Smith, who was rushing back into the house. He looked upset, and it wasn't only that his red-blond hair was mussed or that he had dark circles under his eyes from a poor night's sleep. His brow was furrowed, his complexion pale.

"I beg your pardon," he said, the words pouring out one atop the other. "I must change clothes and leave immediately. I'm late, apparently. It seems I was supposed to be up at dawn. Please excuse me." He darted into the house.

"Well."

Anna opened her notebook to the page with her notes on Mr. Smith and added, *Ordinarily punctual. Flustered by tardiness. Oddly cute when in a panic.*

Not very professional, that last bit, but she declined to cross it out.

The docks were busy at this time of day, full of fishermen setting sail for their day's work and hefty men hauling crates onto cargo ships for overseas transport. Anna sprang back as a man hurried past her, leading half-a-dozen cows on ropes. She had considered inquiring whether any of the merchant ships were bound for Edinburgh, but if she did, she would make certain to ask what the cargo was. A few days more at the fisherman's house was preferable to a ship full of seasick bovines. Who imported cows, anyhow?

She spent an hour familiarizing herself with the town beyond the docks and the hotel, making note of any places that might be of use during the days before her ship arrived. To her great delight, she discovered a chemist's shop advertising potions made in-house. Someone with potions knowledge might be able to give her some insight into the poison that had robbed her of her memories. She found nothing that looked as if it might cure her during her brief scan of the shelves, and the proprietor of the shop was occupied with a talkative customer, but Anna jotted a few notes and made plans to visit again the next morning. Today she had a different objective in mind.

It took half an hour of language difficulties and salacious jeers from dock workers to discover which warehouse contained the shipment of Harper-Douglass Whisky. Anna found it locked tight, and the only ways to see inside were the clerestory windows well above her head.

Undeterred, she circled around to the back of the building, out of sight of anyone else, and constructed a scaffold of broken crates and discarded planks. The makeshift assembly teetered as she climbed atop it. Planting her feet in a wide stance for balance, Anna cupped both hands around her eyes and peered into the darkened interior of the warehouse.

Nothing appeared obviously amiss. Crates were neatly arranged and not stacked overly high, and the warehouse space was clean and well-maintained. A desk and filing cabinet in one corner served as the office space for the small operation. No papers or books lay out in the open. Anna recorded all the details in her notebook, from the layout of the room to the number of crates.

In the middle of her climb down, her scaffold collapsed, leaving her with a throbbing knee and a small tear in her sleeve, but she gritted her teeth and limped about, scattering the evidence of her snooping.

"Hmph. And Quinn thinks I'm not capable of manual labor."

She tossed aside the last bit of planking, then jotted in her book, *Do not call him Quinn to his face.*

Satisfied with the results of her investigation, Anna headed back to her temporary residence, pausing only briefly to examine the front door of the warehouse along her way. Neither of her hosts was about when she arrived home, but she found the door unlocked and a small luncheon waiting on the table. She sat down and ate her fill, ignoring the gnawing guilt over what she intended to do while the generous family was out.

. . . ✎ . . .

"What's all this, then?"

"Hmm?" Anna sat up, yawning. She had only meant to close her eyes for a moment, but the candle illuminating the room had burned down to a stub while she slept. This business of carrying a baby was exhausting. Plus, she had filled the chamber pot far too many times during the course of the day. It was a wonder the whole world didn't know of her condition already, what with her inability to eat breakfast, her ravenous appetite in the afternoons, and her ever-expanding waistline. One of her corsets had ingenious little side-ties for expansion, and she was certain she would need to use it before long.

"I'm sorry, did I wake you?" Quinn—Mr. Smith—asked.

"I was merely resting. How was your day?"

He shrugged. "What is all this?"

"Ah. My tools."

Anna climbed out of bed and gathered up the remains of her work. She had bent every single one of her hairpins, some several times over, until she had settled on several useful shapes for opening basic locks. They were now all sorted and tied into bundles with little bits of thread. Her long hair tumbled about her shoulders.

"Do you mean to pick locks?"

"Excellent deductive reasoning, Mr. Smith. I intend to have a look inside the Harper-Douglass warehouse, as a matter of fact."

The corners of his mouth turned slightly downward. He wasn't a man given to frowning. His smile was far more natural. Another thing for her notes.

"Perhaps I was too earnest in my encouragement of your investigations," he said. "Surely there is another way to see inside the building? Some way less likely to land you in prison?"

"Ah, but if I enter the warehouse in a public fashion, then anyone can see, and our villain might know what I have done.

Now, he might well anticipate that I wish to look around the warehouse, but if I do it by stealth I prevent him knowing if and when I have done so."

Smith shook his head. "When we recover our memories, I won't be surprised if it happens that you work for Scotland Yard."

"Oh, I doubt that. I had to spend hours practicing to learn to open the lock on our door here." She pulled her watch out of the small pocket in the front of her bodice and checked the time. "I really ought to be getting back to bed. I would prefer a bit more rest before I set out tonight."

"Tonight?"

"Well, I can't very well go breaking into a warehouse in the middle of the day, can I? You are welcome to come along if you would like."

"No, I wouldn't like. I don't want you doing any such thing."

Anna sniffed. "I believe I have mentioned before that you don't get to tell me what to do."

"I remember."

"Good. Don't worry. I'll be back before dawn, and I'll be sure to wake you so that you will be on time tomorrow."

"Absolutely not. I'm going with you. I won't leave you to take on such a dangerous task yourself."

A smile touched her lips. "Excellent. You can carry the other tools, then."

His brows drew together. "What other tools?"

"The hammer, screwdriver, and pry bar. I intend to borrow them from our hosts in case we need to open anything that the hairpins cannot manage."

He rubbed his temple. "Why is it that I both admire your tenacity and daring and hate it at the same time?"

"I believe you have certain protective tendencies. Perhaps you are a soldier or an officer of the law or some other sort of person tasked with seeing to the safety and welfare of others."

"Perhaps we are both detectives and that is why our enemy wanted to wipe our minds." Smith heaved a sigh. "Let me see what I can do with those lock picks."

Nothing, as it turned out. Smith struggled to open even the simple lock on their bedroom door, so Anna had the privilege of unlocking the warehouse while he stood and held the lantern.

"Someone is bound to see us," he hissed.

"Hold still. I will only be a few more minutes."

"This is insane."

Anna adjusted the tension on the lock. "There is something about this company that is relevant to our troubles. We need to know more or we may never get our memories back."

"They might come back gradually," he argued. "I remembered something from my childhood this morning. My grandmother. She was blind and she would sew by feel. I have no idea why I remember that, but I'm certain it's true. I think she was Scottish. She used to call me 'laddie.'"

"That's very sweet and an encouraging sign, but not especially useful to our current undertaking. A little to the left, please. Yes, perfect, thank you."

Anna felt the last pin slip into place an instant before the lock sprung open. She let the door swing wide and gestured at Quinn to enter, giving him a smile of triumph. A slight nod of respect was his only reply.

She closed the door behind them, and Quinn opened the lantern wider to illuminate the room. Several of the crates had been moved since that morning. Anna made a quick count. No crates missing, but about half were out of place. She moved in closer.

"These have been opened, and recently."

"Aye. That's not unusual if someone wanted to check that everything arrived safely or transfer the goods to smaller containers for distribution. I see no such boxes anywhere, however." He lifted the lid off of one crate. "Whatever they were doing, they're not done, or they would have nailed the crate shut again." He pointed the lantern into the box. "Well, that's interesting."

Anna peered inside. Nestled among sawdust padding were rows of neatly stowed whisky bottles, each about three-quarters full. She lifted one out.

"I know this bottle!"

"Of course you know this bottle. I told you all the fashionable people in London drink this whisky, and you are obviously a lady of some means."

Anna turned the bottle about in the lantern light. The square shape and patterned glass were unmistakable.

"No. I mean I have a bottle just like this. In my trunk."

"In your trunk?"

"Yes. I had it on the ship. It's nearly empty." She continued to scrutinize the bottle. "Why is there no logo?"

Quinn picked up another bottle and flipped it upside down. "Here. It's on the bottom. You can see it best by looking down the top when the bottle is empty."

"I wonder how you know all this."

He shrugged. "I must drink a lot of whisky."

"Maybe you work for the company. A distributor? Or perhaps a customer. Or a competitor. Maybe you've been trying to steal their secrets and they're getting back at you for it."

"I think what we need to be asking is why are all these bottles partially empty?"

"Someone was thirsty. Obviously." Anna placed her bottle back into the crate. "Theft of whisky. A small amount from every bottle. But the bottles must be full when they arrive at their destination or someone would notice."

"Exactly. Someone is siphoning off a portion of the whisky and then passing off a diluted product as the genuine thing, I'd imagine."

"Open another box."

They checked three more crates with loose lids, finding more partially-drained bottles in each one.

"Try this crate," Anna suggested, tapping a crate that had been moved since that morning but was fully sealed.

Quinn examined it for a moment, then went to work with the pry bar, carefully easing the crate open in such a way that it would be simple to nail it closed again.

Anna grinned at him. "You've done this before. You must be a packager or distributor or something. A warehouse owner, perhaps."

The lid popped off. "Full bottles," Quinn said.

Anna plucked one from the sawdust. "In that case, there's only one thing to do." She uncorked the bottle and lifted it. "Slàinte!" She took a small sip, then passed the bottle to Quinn.

"Do dheagh shlàinte," he replied. He examined it in the light for a moment, took a careful sniff, and then sipped. Anna watched his mouth, telling herself it was merely part of the investigation. He held the liquid for several seconds before swallowing, then repeated the entire process.

"Terrible," he said at last.

"I agree."

"It's been diluted with some foul liquor. Would have tasted better with water." Quinn recorked the bottle and shoved it back into the crate. A few whacks of the hammer, and he had the lid secure enough that their tampering wouldn't be immediately obvious. "Let's get out of here. I think we've seen enough."

Anna picked up the lantern and walked toward the desk. "One moment. I'd like to take a quick look at any books or papers." She pulled open the bottom drawer of the cabinet and angled the lantern downward. Her fingers had just closed around a small leather-bound volume, when a rattling at the door sent a jolt of fear down her spine.

The book slipped from her fingers. She doused the lantern

and shoved the drawer closed. As the warehouse door opened, a strong arm wrapped around her waist.

"Don't make a sound," Quinn hissed, and hauled her behind the stack of crates.

<h1 style="text-align:center">VIII</h1>

<h1 style="text-align:center">Hide and Seek</h1>

AWHISPER OF A SIGH *escaped her lips and she relaxed into Quinn's embrace. He smoothed one hand over her belly as his other arm tightened around her, just brushing the underside of her breasts. Holding her this close, he could smell the subtle rose scent of the soap she used to wash her glossy, black hair. Her head dropped back against his shoulder, tilting just enough to allow him access to the column of her throat. Here in the dark she was little more than a shadow, but he didn't need his sight to savor her body. He pressed a kiss to her neck, her skin soft and smooth against his lips.*

The sound of two men arguing in Danish jerked Quinn out of the memory. He held Anna Harper snugly against him, his lips a hair's breadth from her delicate flesh. His head spun with the hint of rose that had triggered the memory. Her unbound hair fell across her shoulders and brushed his cheek. Was it her he had kissed, sometime in his unremembered past? Or another woman entirely?

The voices moved closer. Anna pressed back into him. Tingles of desire slithered across his skin everywhere their bodies touched. If she didn't stop wiggling, he was going to find himself in a Situation. At least it provided a distraction from all his aches and pains.

What had he gotten himself into? This entire day had been one disaster after another.

Not only had he arrived late for his temporary employment, but he'd proven himself the most incompetent fisherman in all of history. He had no sea legs, he couldn't tie more than a simple knot, and it had been so long since he'd done any heavy lifting that his back felt like someone had taken a hammer to it. He ought to have been trying to sleep off some of his discomfort, not snuggling a woman he wasn't supposed to be touching, while in danger of being caught trespassing.

Sounds of moving and opening crates joined the voices. Quinn didn't know how to speak Danish, but some of the antagonism had gone out of the voices, replaced by a grudging cooperation. Bottles clinked. Corks popped. There was a bit more shuffling, then the gurgle of pouring liquid.

Anna turned in his arms. Whatever lanterns the whisky diluters were using gave off just enough light that he could see her face tilted up to look at him. Her expression was indistinct, but Quinn guessed it was one of excitement. They had caught the whisky thieves in action.

He didn't dare let her go. Bold as she was, she could very well decide to scale the stack of crates to take a look, or even storm out into the open to confront the thieves.

Her hands settled on his shoulders. That trace of scent and the warmth of her body intoxicated him. He needed only to dip his head to bring their mouths together for a kiss.

Dammit, Smith, stop fantasizing.

Just because he'd once ravished some other dark-haired

woman who smelled of rose-water while hidden in a closet didn't mean he could do it to Mrs. Anna Harper behind a stack of crates in a warehouse. Even if she seemed interested.

She's excited by the adventure, not by you.

Quinn forced himself to put a bit of space between their bodies without relaxing his grip. He stared at the blank gray nothing of the wall beside him and listened to the men at their illegal work. Nothing helped. He could still smell her and hear her soft exhalations. He could feel the grip of her fingers on his coat and the pounding of his own heart. The aches in his back had tightened into spasms. He tried to focus on the pain and not on Anna.

Some indeterminate amount of time later, the sounds of pouring and filling ceased. The men hammered lids back into place and began to move the crates.

Anna's fingers dug into his shoulders, and it took Quinn several seconds to realize he was gripping her equally tightly. If those men began to take more crates down from the stacks, Quinn and Anna would lose their cover. The door was too far. If they ran, the men would cut them off.

The thieves struck up another conversation that he couldn't follow, but after several minutes of talking, their footsteps retreated towards the door.

Quinn's fingers unclenched from Anna's dress. The door opened and closed, the lock clicking into place. For several minutes he didn't move.

Anna spoke first. "Before we leave, I want to take a peek in one of these crates." She tapped the box beside her. "I have a hunch I want to confirm."

Now? After a near disaster? "We're lucky we weren't discovered. We ought to leave immediately."

"You can leave. I'll meet you back at the house."

Dammit.

Quinn sighed, picked up the tools, and set to work.

"Aha!" Anna exclaimed when he lifted the top from

the crate. "The bottles here are also only three-quarters full. They're arriving in Esbjerg already partly emptied. This means the initial robbery is happening back in Britain. The whisky is stolen and then the tampered bottles are shipped here, where they are diluted and sold as the genuine product. Thank you, Mr. Smith. You can close this crate while I take a look at the books."

Quinn worked quickly while Anna shuffled papers. The sooner they left here, the better. The criminals could return for the next round of filling at any time, and he didn't want to find out if they were capable of more than theft and fraud. He secured the box, checked that he hadn't left anything out of place, and crossed the room to the tiny office space.

"We need to leave before those men return."

She nodded. "There's nothing here. The papers are all in order. One log book with dates and shipments, and signed papers detailing numbers of crates delivered and distributed. These thieves are tampering only with the contents." She tucked all the papers back into the file cabinet. "Also, they only date back two months. This is a relatively new distribution site."

"Good to know. Let's go. Please."

She nodded and handed him the lantern. "Shine this on the door for me while I lock it back up."

They stepped outside and she produced her set of hairpins from somewhere in her skirts. Quinn closed the lantern to a narrow beam and aimed it at the lock, looking away to let his eyes adjust to the moonlit night.

"One thing is certain," he mumbled. "I'm not a detective. I'm not enjoying this, I'm not good at it, and I have no desire to do it ever again. You on the other hand…"

"I was rather terrified for a moment there that we would be caught. The remainder of the night, however, has been a rousing success."

Quinn answered with a grunt.

"You don't do surly very well," Anna chuckled. "Even your grunts are half-hearted."

"I'm merely tired. It's been a long day."

She yawned. "It has." A short time later, the lock turned and she straightened up. "Done. Let's go to bed."

He stared at her stupidly for a moment. She looked ghostly in the moonlight—a black-and-white apparition sent to haunt him. She was certainly good at it.

"To sleep," she clarified. "Because we're tired."

"Aye. Bed."

He followed her in silence back to the fisherman's house, where they crept carefully into their bedroom so as not to wake their hosts. Not only was he a poor excuse for a fisherman, but he was an embarrassment of a guest. The sooner he left town, the better.

Quinn removed his boots and coat and attempted to situate himself on the floor in order to cause as little pain as possible. Lying flat would help his back, he hoped.

"You don't have to sleep on the floor, Mr. Smith," Anna said, repeating word-for-word her offer from the night before. "The bed is large enough for two and I don't mind."

"*I* mind. It's inappropriate."

"As is breaking into a warehouse and holding me like a lover behind a stack of crates."

"I meant only to protect you from detection."

"Oh." She slipped off her own boots and lay back on the bed. "Goodnight, then."

"It's not that I don't find you desirable. In fact, I find you much too desirable."

Now what the hell was he doing? His brain wasn't functioning. He needed to shut his damn mouth and go to sleep. Which meant, of course, that he kept talking.

"I can't be so close to you at night. You might wake up to find me committing unspeakable acts upon your person."

She sat up abruptly, her amber eyes wide and almost

glowing in the dim light of the lantern. "Is this a common occurrence for you?"

"I certainly hope not, but I'd rather not chance it."

"Or perhaps you have it all wrong and you're merely shy of women. Perhaps you're still a virgin!"

Quinn snorted. "I'm almost certain I once pleasured a woman in a closet, so I think not."

"A closet? That sounds rather… awkward."

"I think we were hiding and took advantage of the opportunity."

"Interesting. I will have to add that to my notes about you." She lay down, pulled the blanket up over herself, and doused the lantern. "Goodnight, Mr. Smith."

Quinn yawned, his eyes drifting closed. It had been a hell of a day. "Goodnight, Mrs. Harper." Her earlier words penetrated his tired brain just as he was drifting to sleep. "Wait. You have notes about *me*?"

Her only response was a sleepy sigh.

IX

The Chase

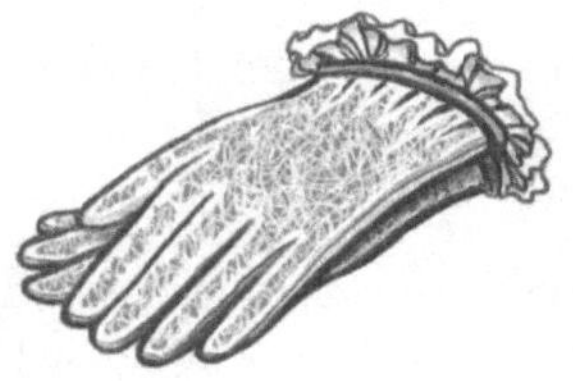

ANNA OPENED HER EYES just wide enough to watch Quinn struggling into the ill-fitting fisherman's clothing. He was late again, apparently, because it was past dawn and he was muttering invectives as he yanked on the garments. She had missed much of the dressing, but caught a good glimpse of him without his shirt. He had a nice chest, sprinkled with dusty-blond hairs, that tapered to a narrow waist. He was slenderer than most of those who worked the docks here, but he was fit and strong nonetheless.

She shivered at the memory of his arms clutching her last night, holding on as if he feared to lose her. Twice during the course of their midnight adventure she had been certain he was about to kiss her. The intensity of her disappointment when he hadn't had surprised her. It had seemed so right. So inevitable. Perhaps she *was* his dark-haired lady. If she was, it annoyed her that she couldn't remember the closet tryst.

"That bloody boat to Newcastle can't arrive soon enough," Quinn grumbled. "Two more days and we can get the hell out of here."

"We?" Anna jerked upright and Quinn whirled to face her.

"You're awake?" He quickly did up the last of his buttons and stepped into his tall rubber boots.

"*We* are not going to Newcastle."

"I have to go there. It was one of the only things I remembered when this all started. It must have some significance. Look what we've discovered about the whisky."

"You can go to Newcastle if you'd like. I'm going to Edinburgh. It's where the Harper-Douglass cargo came from and where my passenger steamer came from. It's the obvious choice for learning more."

He frowned quizzically at her. "But the next Edinburgh boat is five days off. How will you earn your keep once I leave for Newcastle?"

Anna smirked. "I will take up an occupation, obviously. It should be a simple task without you around to hassle me about it."

Why did the phrase "without you around" cause a sick feeling in her stomach? She didn't need him. What use did she have for a man who wouldn't let her work and kept almost-but-not-quite kissing her? It was only her pregnancy making her queasy. She hadn't yet taken her daily drops.

"We work better together," he argued. "Come with me to Newcastle. We will investigate my background, hopefully trigger some new—old—memories, and after a few days we can take the train to Edinburgh. You'll be there almost as quickly as if you wait for the boat."

A good argument. A damned good argument, in fact. Anna didn't have any answer except to say she thought Newcastle irrelevant to her investigation. Somehow the question of the whisky had taken precedence over regaining her memories, though she still believed the two were intermingled.

Solve the mystery of the thefts and you'll solve the mystery of yourself.

"I don't have time to argue about it," Quinn said, plopping an ugly hat down over his reddish-blond locks. "I have to go to work. I might be back in time for dinner tonight. We can talk again then." He started to leave, but paused just outside the door, glancing back over his shoulder and saying, "Good day to you, Mrs. Harper."

Anna stared at the door a moment, puzzling. He was a fascinating man. Frustrated with his situation and unused to being frustrated. She suspected he would be perfectly happy with a straightforward problem with a clear solution, no matter the difficulty. He wasn't averse to hard work. But definitely averse to feeling helpless or useless.

She climbed out of bed and changed into her brown dress, tucking everything she thought she might need into the numerous pockets she had discovered. The IOU from Quinn went into the slender pocket inside her bodice, her watch into the pocket on the outside. She tucked a set of lockpicks into the long, narrow pocket hidden in the waistband of her skirt. If she'd had any money, she would have stashed it there as well. Her dagger-shaped bookmark went into the small slit pocket at her right hip, and her notebook into the larger slit in front of it. She really was a very practical and prepared sort of person. Whoever Anna Harper had been before the memory loss, she would certainly get along splendidly with current Anna Harper.

On her way out of the house, she discovered a nice breakfast laid out on the table in the main room. Not quite ready to eat anything, she wrapped it all up in a cloth and took it along with her. She'd be glad for the food later in the day.

A brief walk carried her to the Harper-Douglass warehouse, where she discovered a small contingent of men loading the whisky crates onto a wagon. Startled, she stopped and stared. Had the criminals finished diluting all the bottles? She and Quinn had visited shortly after midnight, leaving plenty of time for the men to return and complete their underhanded work. What were they using to fill the bottles and where it was coming from? They didn't simply drive up with a cart full of the stuff, because then they would have filled all the bottles at once. They were sneaking it in, bit-by-bit, possibly carried by hand.

A tall, thin man at work loading the wagon asked her a question. She didn't understand, of course, but it brought her attention to the fact that she was still staring at them and they were staring back at her.

"Headed to the train station?" she guessed. "For distribution?"

The man said something else. He sounded annoyed now. Was his voice one she had heard last night, or was it only the language that sounded the same?

Anna bid the men farewell and walked on, as if out for a casual stroll, not looking back. A bead of sweat welled on her neck and trickled down her back. If any of those workers were her villains, they were certainly watching her. Did they know she was on to them, or did they merely suspect?

The moment she was out of sight she quickened her pace, not slowing again until she had reached the tiny shopping district where the chemist's shop was located.

"You're being paranoid," she told herself. "No villain is going to attack you in broad daylight in front of a crowd."

Not that there was much of a crowd. Most people in the small town were busy at their work, fishing, manning the docks, or out in their fields tending to their crops and animals.

Anna sat herself down on the stoop of the general store—the most populated place she could see—and unwrapped her breakfast. She munched on her bread and meats, keeping an eye toward the docks in case any suspicious persons had followed her, or in case the wagon full of whisky passed by on the way to the train station.

A pair of teenaged scorchers on bicycles flew down the road, shouting at one another as they jockeyed for position. Anna grinned and watched them race back and forth along the street, their antics a welcome relief from her worries. By the time the chemist down the road popped out of his shop to scold the youths, her belly was full and her heart was light. It was time to make progress.

A small bell tinkled as Anna pushed the shop door open. The chemist, who had been scowling at the bicycle racers, smiled when he saw her and greeted her in Danish.

"Hello," she replied. "Do you speak English?"

He held his thumb and forefinger slightly apart. "Little English."

"Oh, excellent." She wouldn't have to employ her desperation plan and beg someone at the hotel to come and translate for her. "I'm afraid I don't speak any Danish at all and haven't had any opportunity to learn."

The chemist nodded, understanding her meaning if not all her words. Probably he had guessed why she was here. In a town this size, surely everyone had heard something of the Englishwoman who had lost her memory.

"I arrived here by boat a few days ago," she said. "Several of us on the ship had lost our memories suddenly. Two men here in town had the same trouble."

He nodded again. "Yes. I hear this."

"It cannot be a sickness. I think it must be a potion that caused it."

"Ja." He rubbed his chin. "Maybe a bad potion."

"I think we must have been drugged. Could such a potion be put into food or drink?"

"Klart. Yes. You drink bad potion and…" He touched his head, then waved his hand as if something was floating away.

"Exactly. How does one find a potion like that? I assume you cannot buy it at any potion shop."

"In Esbjerg, nej. I am only potion maker. No bad potions here."

"But in a large city, like Edinburgh, there would be people making such things. Selling to criminals."

"In big city, I think yes."

Anna tapped a gloved fingertip on the counter. "So it seems our villain bought his pernicious potion in Edinburgh, then arranged to drug us during the voyage. But how did he drug Mr. Smith and the other man at the tavern? He would have needed to arrive before my ship did, or send the drug or drugged product ahead…" Her words stuttered to a halt as her brain put the pieces together. "The whisky! I have that mostly empty bottle of whisky, and the Harper-Douglass cargo arrived that morning."

Most likely she had brought along the whisky as a medicinal, in case of headache or other ailment. Sharing the bottle with her fellow passengers would have been a common courtesy on a days-long voyage. And Quinn knew enough about Harper-Douglass Whisky that having a drink of it when a shipment arrived was entirely plausible.

Anna addressed the chemist again. "If I bring a drink here can you look at it and tell me if it has any potion in it?"

"Ja. I can smell and taste potion."

"Huh. I wonder if I noticed anything unusual when I drank it."

"Is hard to taste potion for you maybe."

"But you can do it?"

"Ja. Yes."

"Wonderful! Do you have anything that might cure it? Some health potion that could help us remember?"

He pursed his lips. "Maybe. This…" He touched his forehead. "Hard to heal."

"I understand. Anything that might possibly help would be appreciated. I have no money, however. Is there work I could do around the shop to pay for the potion? Clean or organize, maybe?"

He rubbed his chin again. "I think of work for you."

"I will come back and bring the drugged whisky. Later today? Or tomorrow morning? Then if you have any work that needs to be done, I will do it."

"Ja. Good. Tomorrow."

"Wonderful. Thank you so much." She held out a hand to him and they shook firmly.

Pleased with her success, Anna stepped out the door and into the sunshine with a broad smile on her face. Tomorrow she would have more answers, and perhaps some small amount of improvement in her memory. For the rest of today she would try to find herself a simple job that might earn her a few coins. With Quinn busy, there was no one to tell her not to get her hands dirty.

She wandered slowly up and down the street, considering the shops and what she knew of her own skills. She could organize things, certainly, or do inventories. Perhaps there was some sort of clerk about that could use help sorting and filing.

"You! English lady!"

Anna whirled around. Her heart leapt into her throat. Coming at her was the man from this morning. The one whose voice she had thought sounded familiar. She backed away, looking for an escape route and anyone she might call to for help. The street was deserted, the only people inside the shops where they might not hear.

The man stalked toward her, his brows pinched together in a scowl, his fists clenched. Her body vibrated with the need to flee. She could expose his crimes and who knew what he was willing to do to stop her. Confronting him was too great a risk.

Anna's eyes flicked back and forth. Run toward the chemist's shop and beg for help? No. She'd never make it in time. Her pursuer had a long stride and she didn't think she could outrun him. Her gaze fell on the bicycles now propped up against the side of the general store.

She was moving before she had even consciously processed the decision. Her sturdy boots pounded on the packed dirt, racing for the vehicle that could carry her to safety. She knew how to ride, apparently, because she grabbed a bike without breaking stride, set it in motion, and vaulted up into the seat.

Her skirts bunched up, exposing a good potion of her leg and hampering her movements, and she had to yank at them to allow her legs the necessary freedom to pedal. These contraptions were meant for a man in trousers. This one was also meant for someone several inches taller than herself. Even as far forward as she could sit in the seat, she nearly had to pedal on tiptoe. Still, it was much faster than running. She tore down the street, her legs pumping like a well-practiced rider.

It took only moments for the buildings to give way to farm land. Anna raced down the dirt lane with no better idea of where she was headed than "away."

A clatter of wheels behind her made her dare to glance back over her shoulder. The lanky whisky thief had grabbed the second bicycle, and he looked to know how to ride it.

"Fuck!"

She really did know quite a lot of bad words. If she managed to escape this villain, perhaps she'd write them all down in her notebook. She swerved to the left, taking a narrower path between two fields of some sort of grain. Wheat? Barley?

The path deteriorated with alarming rapidity. Her bicycle bounced over pits and humps. Anna clung to the handlebars, struggling to keep the wheel straight as she pedaled with all her might. The violent storm on the day she had arrived had flooded the low-lying areas enough that wet patches still remained along the narrow path, and her tires splashed through puddles, flinging mud across her stockings and skirts.

A pretty little thatched-roof cottage marked the end of the lane. A lone goat harnessed to a long rope gnawed on a small shrubbery near the front door. It lifted its head at the sound of the approaching bicycles, deemed them unimportant, and returned to its repast. Anna saw no other creature, human or animal.

With her enemy gaining ground and no help in sight, she made another sharp left turn, taking the bike off-road, through a wide swath of field that had already been harvested.

She stood up on the pedals, giving herself a better push across the uneven terrain and softening any jolts to her body to protect herself and her baby. Her thighs had begun to burn, but she didn't dare slow down. Out here, that man could do anything to her, and all she had to defend herself was a dagger-shaped bookmark not sharp enough to do much more than open a letter.

Up ahead, Anna could see the buildings of Esbjerg proper. She hadn't gone far out of town, but the rough ground made every yard feel like ten. Her massive front wheel hit an unseen obstacle, lifting the back wheel off the ground and nearly throwing her up and over the handlebars.

She yelped and clung to the bicycle, fists clenched to prevent her sweat-slicked palms from losing their grip. Her heart pounded and her breath came in great, heaving gulps. Her adversary crept ever closer, powered by his longer, stronger legs. She fixed her gaze on the town ahead and pedaled with all her might.

I can make it, I can make it.

The litany repeated over and over in her head, powering her exhausted muscles. If she could reach town before her pursuer caught up, she could ride for the docks. It was a populated area all day, and if she were very lucky, Quinn would be working on shore today and not out on a boat.

A fence marking the boundary of the farm spelled the end of her hopes. She looked left and right, but could see no end, no gaps, only fields of taller, thicker crops in both directions. Seeing no other choice, Anna aimed straight at it.

"Give up, English lady," the man shouted at her. "You have no escape. I will not harm you, only turn you in for a thief."

He was the thief, and she wouldn't trust the word of such a man when her life was at stake. She sped toward the fence, lifting her feet from the pedals and hooking her legs over the top of the handlebars.

Even prepared as she was, the impact tore the air from

her lungs. The bicycle stopped dead, while Anna kept going, flying several yards past the fence. She hit the ground feet-first, tucked and rolled to a stop in a patch of thick grasses. Who was she and how had she acquired these skills?

No time to contemplate now. Behind the fence, her enemy cursed in Danish, swerving and pulling his bicycle to a stop. She couldn't outrun him if he hopped the fence. Anna darted back to the fence, reached over it, and grabbed the bicycle with both hands. Giving a grunt of exertion, she hauled it up and over, thanking God it was a slender, light-weight model. The sturdy machine was blessedly undamaged. She rolled it into motion and clambered back on.

A stab of pain shot up her left leg. Damn. She'd tweaked the same knee that she'd banged up when snooping around the warehouse. She bit her lip against the pain and pedaled on as best she could.

Another minute and the docks were in sight, but her legs were near to giving out and the lanky man was almost upon her, still screaming words she couldn't understand. Seeing people up ahead, she shouted for help, but to a man they sprang back in surprise, gaping at the wild woman on the bicycle.

"Quinn!" she screamed, praying he was somewhere on the docks. "Quinn Smith!"

Anna barreled past ships and warehouses, calling for him as dock workers pointed and shouted all around her. A few reached out and tried to snatch her right off the bicycle.

The meaning of her enemy's words became clear. *Stop her.* She was a foreigner, throwing respectability away by riding and shouting and exposing her legs to the world. Every man here was on the side of the villain.

Up ahead, a beefy man hefted a narrow, wooden plank. Anna swerved, afraid he meant to hit her with it. Too late, she realized he had an entirely different plan in mind. He threw the board like a javelin straight through the spokes of her wheel.

The wheel jammed, freezing the bicycle and catapulting Anna headfirst into the air.

She screamed.

X

Acute Reactions

"ANNA!"

Her name erupted from deep in Quinn's chest, an inhuman howl of impotent terror. He raced toward her, helpless to do anything but watch as she hurtled through the air. For a few horrifying instants he was certain she was going to die in front of him and it would end him.

And then, somehow, mercifully, she cleared the dock, plunging into the icy water with a tremendous splash.

By the time he reached her, she had hauled herself up onto dry land, where she sat, hugging her belly and rocking back and forth. He couldn't tell whether the rivulets of water streaming down her cheeks were tears or runoff from her dripping hair.

He dropped to his knees beside her. "Anna, oh, God, Anna."

A choked sob broke from her lips.

He reached for her, stopping just shy of embracing her. Moments ago she had been his entire world, but everything else was crashing back in and he remembered he had no right to touch her. Whatever memories had inspired his utter terror were lost, but some lingering sensation of them warred in his mind with his current reality. He rubbed his temple in an attempt to ease the growing headache. Whatever woman or women had been in his past, he couldn't conflate them with Anna Harper.

"Are you hurt?" he asked, desperate to help however he could.

She only sobbed harder.

"Anna. Mrs. Harper." He settled his hands lightly on her shoulders. Bad idea. His fingers automatically clenched tighter, and it took all the force of his will not to haul her into his lap. "It's Quinn Smith. Are you hurt? Do you need help?"

She shook her head. Droplets of cold water sprayed from her hair. Her clothing was soaked through and her body trembled beneath his hands. He needed to get her someplace warm at once.

"My b-b-baby," she wept.

"Huh?"

He had no idea what she was talking about. Did she have a child? Had the crash jarred something loose from her forgotten memories? Or was she speaking in some sort of metaphorical terms? She could even be babbling nonsense. If she'd struck her head, it could have done untold damage to a mind already hampered by amnesia. She was sitting up, however, and she wasn't swooning. Both good signs.

"Mrs. Harper, are you well? Are you hurt in any way?"

"N-no. Th-that man…"

Quinn looked past her toward town. The second bicycle had vanished, along with the man who had been chasing her. Quinn had never even gotten a good look at him.

"He's gone. You're safe. Let's get you out of here. Can you walk?"

"He could've k-killed…" she mumbled, not looking up.

"I know." Quinn brushed his thumb across her tear-stained cheek, then jerked abruptly away, curling his fingers into a fist. "I was terrified for you. I can't even imagine—"

"No. Not me. My b-baby." A new torrent of tears began to fall. She said something else, but she was shaking and weeping so hard that Quinn couldn't decipher her words.

"Enough of this. I'm taking you home and propriety be damned." He hooked one arm beneath her legs, wrapped the other around her back and scooped her off the ground. "Let's get you someplace warm and dry."

She nuzzled against his chest, dampening his shirt. "I'm s-sorry. I c-can't stop cr-crying."

"Shh. Everything will be all right." He wasn't at all certain that was true, but it seemed like the thing to say.

Anna only burrowed closer, saying nothing as he carried her down the docks to their temporary home.

The house was deserted, their host still out fishing and their hostess at the laundry down the street. Quinn set Anna down in front of the fireplace and began to unbutton her dress. Water dripped from her hair and clothing, and she was shivering badly. It may have been entirely indecent of him, but he had no qualms about stripping her naked to save her from hypothermia.

She made no protest as he divested her of several layers of garments. By the time she was down to her corset and shift, she at last began to perk up. She gave him a little half-smile.

"This is not how I envisioned you undressing me, Mr. Smith."

Quinn froze. The thought that she had envisioned any such thing momentarily stalled his brain. Several seconds of awkward silence ticked by before he asked, "Can you handle the rest on your own?"

"I think so, yes. I will go change."

"I'll hang these wet clothes on the line for you."

"Thank you. If you could remove my things from all my pockets, I would appreciate it."

"Of course."

Quinn didn't realize quite what she meant by "all my pockets" until he began to look for them. Did most women even have pockets? He didn't think so, but Anna appeared to delight in them. Her watch in the little watch-pocket was obvious, but then he discovered the hidden pocket on the inside of her bodice, his IOU carefully folded and tucked inside. Her skirt had large pockets on either side, one of which held her notebook. He fanned out the pages and set it in front of the fire to dry, fighting the urge to flip through and see what notes she had written about him.

A lump in the skirt's waistband revealed a narrow pocket that held her lockpicks. He removed them and patted down the skirt, searching for anything he might have missed. Something sharp jabbed into his palm.

"Ow!"

It took him some fumbling to find the small pocket inside and behind the larger front pocket. He slipped a hand into it and pulled out the object that had poked him.

A dagger-shaped bookmark. Laughing a little, he turned it over in his hands. How like her not only to have such a thing, but to carry it on her person as an improvised weapon. He tipped it toward the light to read the inscription.

To Anna. Stay Fierce. Love Nick.

"Well, shit," Quinn muttered. He dropped the bookmark beside her other things and snatched up the clothes to take them outside.

This Nick was probably her husband. He would be furious that another man was handling her underthings. Clearly he loved her. The bookmark was the gift of someone who both understood and appreciated her.

Quinn draped her things over the line and stomped back inside to feed the fire. Angry at the unwarranted jealousy building inside him, he tossed a log carelessly into the flames, sending a shower of sparks skittering across the hearth.

This was absurd. He'd known she was married, known she was off-limits. But every moment spent with her had drawn him deeper into the fantasy that he stood some chance with her.

This is not how I envisioned you undressing me.

"Goddammit."

"Something wrong?"

He turned toward her voice and immediately wished he hadn't. From where he knelt beside the fire he had an unobstructed view of bare feet, bare ankles, and several inches of bare calf beneath a pale green nightgown so sheer he could see the shape of her legs clear up to mid-thigh. A heavy blanket draped around her shoulders cut off his view at that point, to his immense relief and disappointment.

"Never mind me," he said, his voice embarrassingly low and gruff. "How are you? Here, sit." He jumped up, pulled a chair in front of the fire, and helped her into it.

"Thank you." Anna adjusted the blanket around her shoulders and wiggled her bare toes toward the fire. "I'm feeling better. I'm sorry for… before."

"Think nothing of it. You had a terrible fright and could've been killed. You were rightly distraught."

"Yes, but I'm not a hysterical sort of person. It's not that I never cry, but it came on so suddenly and then I couldn't stop no matter what I did. Even now when I try to think about what happened I can't be logical about it. I simply start to—" She choked up and blinked away tears, one hand clutching protectively over her belly again.

She was pregnant. Of course. No wonder she'd been so terrified. She hadn't been the only one at risk in the bicycle crash.

"I, uh, I understand a tendency for strong emotions is common for women in your, er, condition."

Her eyebrows shot up. Quinn cursed under his breath. Mentioning a pregnancy was in the top ten Things a Gentleman Does Not Say. Maybe even in the top five. Right up there with, "You look tired," and, "I hate your new hairdo."

"I'm sorry," he said. "It's none of my business."

"No, it's quite all right. I've been carrying on about the baby, so it's not as if it were a secret. I'm actually a bit surprised you didn't notice the other night when you had your hand on my belly."

He shrugged. "It doesn't seem especially obvious yet, and who has a flat belly, anyhow?"

She looked directly at his abdomen. Damn. How much had she seen this morning?

"I, uh, take regular exercise, apparently."

Anna made a little half-snort, half-laugh. "Well, Mr. Regular Exercise, you ought to take that flat belly of yours and go back to work."

"No. You're still shivering a bit, and your legs are covered with goose pimples. I don't know if you've sustained any injuries from your crash. I can't in good conscience leave you alone without being certain that you're dry, warm, and in need of no immediate medical attention. You stay here by the fire. I'll hang the rest of your wet things and then I will see about cooking some dinner. That way I'll have done something to earn our keep. I doubt I'm wanted back on the docks in any event."

"Do you even know how to cook?"

"We'll find out, won't we?"

He did, in fact, know how to cook, because an hour later the delicious aroma of simmering stew filled the small house. The scent said "home" to him, even if he couldn't remember where that home was.

Anna had made a full emotional recovery from her ordeal, though she kept flexing her left knee and rubbing her right shoulder. He would keep an eye on her, because he suspected she would push on through any injury rather than admit to the pain.

She sat in front of the fire, engrossed in a penny dreadful, running her bookmark down the page as she read. Even knowing what was inscribed there didn't stop Quinn watching her. A shiver of trepidation ran down his spine at the thought of what he might discover when he arrived in Newcastle.

Ah, yes, he could imagine someone saying. *Quinn Smith, famous philanderer. Seducer of other men's wives.*

Thank God Anna insisted on going to Edinburgh instead. It was better that way, for both of them. She had a husband and child to think about. He was better off anywhere else.

She closed her book and turned to look at him. "How long before I can eat? It smells wonderful and I'm growing quite hungry."

"I meant it to simmer for a few hours yet. But I'll fetch you some bread and butter. You need to keep up your strength."

"Yes. I've been thinking."

He paused half-way out of his seat. "Oh?"

"It seems Esbjerg may not be safe if the villains know we are on to them. I can't put my life and that of my child at unnecessary risk. I think you are absolutely right and I should leave with you on the boat to Newcastle."

Quinn stared at her. "You should?"

"Yes. Don't you agree?"

Fuck.

"Aye," he said. "Absolutely."

XI

Morsels and Fragments

Anna tucked the vial carefully into one of her small hidden pockets. The potion maker had verified that her whisky had been tainted, after which she'd promptly disposed of it. She'd then spent five hours sorting, cataloging, and relabeling every potion and ingredient in the chemist's shop. But she had earned her potential cure.

She shivered in anticipation. In a few short minutes, she might have her memories back.

Anna pressed her face to the glass, looking for any suspicious persons outside before opening the shop door. Behind her, the chemist coughed impatiently. He'd been polite to her and had honored his promise to assist her, but with none of the good cheer he'd shown the day before. The scandal of the bicycle chase had destroyed her reputation, and he wanted her gone.

Two people were walking down the street in sight of the shop, so Anna stepped outside with only minimal worry that the events of the day before might repeat themselves. There would be no bicycles, at least, and if she did need to flee, she would aim straight for the docks instead of taking whichever path looked nearest and easiest. Lessons learned.

She rolled her shoulder. She wasn't certain whether she had hurt it hefting the bicycle or flying off into the water, but it still smarted. Not enough to need medical attention, but just enough to annoy her.

She'd gone no more than a few yards when she caught sight of Quinn Smith, moving down the street at a blistering pace. He slowed a bit when he saw her, but continued in her direction, his stride no less determined. Anna couldn't deny the relief his presence brought. If an enemy happened by, she would have a partner at her back.

"Mrs. Harper, there you are," he said, turning to walk beside her and offering his arm.

Anna curled her fingers around his biceps, the bright blue of her gloves making a striking contrast against the black of his coat. Was this electric sizzle every time she touched him something she experienced with other men, or was he somehow exceptional? Perhaps she would soon find out.

"Did you learn anything at the chemist's?" Quinn asked. "You were gone so long I'd begun to worry. You missed lunch entirely, and I was imagining you locked up somewhere for indecency or dead in a ditch."

"I was busy doing organizational work in exchange for this." She plucked the potion from her pocket and held it up for him to see. A thin red liquid sloshed inside the vial, glinting in the sunlight. "A medicinal potion to help us regain our memories. The chemist did caution me that they might be gone forever. But if they aren't, this could help us access them."

"It's certainly worth trying. Shall we drink it?"

"He said it's best taken with food." She tucked it away.

"Well, then let's have a good meal before we leave town. I have enough coins to buy us dinner at the hotel."

Anna stopped walking and turned to face him. "How did you get coins? I thought no one wanted to hire you any longer. That you were tainted by association because I had made a spectacle of myself." She made no attempt to curb the bitter sarcasm in her voice. It was grossly unfair the way people placed all the blame on her.

"I did what I could to smooth things over this morning. One of the best English speakers in town helped with translation, and the official verdict is that it was all a misunderstanding. You thought he meant you harm, he thought you were stealing the bicycle, and the situation spiraled out of control."

Anna huffed. "Good enough, I suppose, since we're leaving town. Assuming you were able to book our passage?"

"The ship bound for Newcastle arrived a few hours ago. I think even without money, the local people will make certain we depart with it in the morning. But I've already taken care of the matter. I sold my watch and my best suit and that gave me enough to pay the fare for both of us. Our things have already been loaded onto the ship. We'll be sharing a room again, but there are two bunks, so we needn't worry about sleeping arrangements, and we can simply take turns changing clothes and washing up."

"I think we can survive three days of that."

"After sleeping on that rock-hard floor, I feel I could survive anything."

Anna started off again, tugging on Quinn's elbow to drag him along with her. "I offered the bed. You have only yourself to blame."

"True. But it was a small price to pay to save you from ravishment."

She sniffed. "Rubbish. I'm quite convinced you aren't the ravishing type."

"Perhaps I simply fear being stabbed with your bookmark." Mischief sparkled in his blue-gray eyes, and a smile tugged at the corners of his mouth. "It makes me wonder what other dangerous things you conceal on your person."

"Well, I suppose you will never find out, since you are never going to ravish me."

"Indeed."

Quinn fell silent, then, looking away from her. *What might he be thinking?* she wondered. She knew he was attracted to her, but fighting it. She wouldn't call him a proper sort of man—he was far too at ease with her unladylike tendencies for that—but certainly an honorable one. He wouldn't act on his desires with so little still unknown about both their pasts.

Anna reached into her pocket and fingered the potion. How would their relationship change if the potion restored their memories? Her hand twitched. A part of her would rather pour the potion out than risk their friendship. Still, they had to know. The shadow of their pasts haunted them, and the only way to be free of it was to shine a light on it.

The staff at the hotel greeted them with the same cool politeness the chemist had exhibited—all courtesy, but no cheer. They were tired of the chaos in their midst, and Anna lamented that she was a part of it. These were good people, and they didn't deserve to have trouble brought to their pleasant little town. The villain who had drugged her had much to answer for.

A serving woman set a plate of aromatic fishcakes and colorful vegetables in front of Anna, and her stomach growled in response. She tugged off her gloves and set them aside. The meal smelled divine. She speared a flaky bite of the fried fish and lifted it to her mouth, only to pause when she noticed Quinn staring at her and smiling, his own fork still on the table.

"What? Did I do something funny?"

"Oh, no. Pardon." Was she mistaken, or was he blushing now? "I was only smiling at your enthusiasm for your food. You made a delightful little sigh just now, and… This is becoming inappropriate. I apologize."

He was definitely blushing. How oddly adorable. He dove into his own meal and didn't look up again until he had demolished half of what was on his plate.

Deciding the lack of conversation had dragged on quite long enough, Anna asked, "Are you ready to try the potion?"

He gave a nod and she filled two empty glasses from a pitcher of water, then poured half the potion into each.

"To your health," she said, lifting her glass.

Quinn clinked his glass against hers. "And yours."

Anna drained her entire glass. The potion had a cool, minty taste, and left a tingly sensation on her tongue and in the back of her throat. Her eyes locked with Quinn's. They stared at one another, the silence heavy with anticipation.

"Do you remember anything?" he asked at last.

"I'm not certain. You?"

He shrugged. "We should talk. Ask one another questions. See if that will bring some memories out."

"Good idea. I was unclear about how quickly the potion was supposed to take effect." Anna took a bite of her remaining food, thinking as she chewed. "This is delicious. Have you ever had it before?"

"Not that I recall."

She laughed. "You are a resilient man, Quinn Smith. I can tell because you're tolerating your situation well enough to make jokes about it."

A single blond eyebrow twitched. "I was perfectly serious."

"Now you're teasing me. Do you flirt this way with all the women?"

"Only the audacious ones." His brows narrowed suddenly, and he blinked. "That was a memory. Those words. I said that exact same thing to the exact same question once."

"To whom?"

"I don't know. It's all very hazy. But the words came out, without a thought, and I knew immediately that I was repeating something I'd said before."

Anna leaned across the table, her muscles tensing with excitement. "Maybe it's working, then. What else do you remember? Your dark-haired woman? The closet?"

"No." He squeezed his eyes closed briefly. "When I try, I get nothing. I think I need it to come more naturally. Let me ask you something. How do you like your food?"

"It's excellent, as I already said. I've had no complaints about any of the food here. And your stew was exceptional, so we know you know how to cook. I don't think I do, though."

"What's your favorite food?"

She paused to think about it, and to her surprise the answer seemed obvious. "Biscuits. Chocolate ones. Especially served with a pot of bracing black tea." She closed her eyes, concentrating on the memory of the tastes and smells. "Our cook makes the best chocolate biscuits. He says they were among the first things he learned to make when he came to England. He's from India and he makes the most amazing curries. My brother adores all types of Indian foods, so we often…" Her eyes flew back open. "I have a brother!"

"Apparently."

"He is very tall, and his hair and eyes are just like mine."

"What's his name?"

"I don't remember. I can picture him and the curry and the tea and biscuits, but nothing beyond that." She shook her head. She felt slightly dizzy and she didn't know if it was from the potion or from the sudden influx of old memories. "Your turn again. You said you have a Scottish grandmother."

"Aye."

"What of other relatives? Mother, father, siblings?"

"I don't remember."

She tried the same line of questioning that had worked for her. "Any foods you particularly enjoy?"

"None that spring to mind."

"What about drink? You are very knowledgeable about whisky. Is it your favorite drink, or do you have another?"

He stared off at nothing, turning his empty glass slowly in his hand. "I hate gin. It tastes how I imagine gnawing on a pinecone would taste."

"Yes? And?"

"I will try most anything once. I giggle when I'm drunk. It was mortifying as a youth, but I don't care any longer. And it doesn't bother h—her." His eyes snapped back to Anna.

"Her? The dark-haired woman? Or the woman from the closet?"

He leaned back with a sigh. "I don't know. I had a flash of laughing and—I think—playing a board game. But it faded in an instant, the way dreams do."

Anna pursed her lips, considering the situation. The potion was helping, it seemed, but the effects were irregular and gradual. Perhaps it was best to wait and see what memories popped up over the next hour or two rather than trying to force them.

"Why don't we finish our dinner and then you can show me the ship and we can check that our things have been loaded. Give the potion some time to work. Then maybe once we're settled we can try again?"

"It's as good an idea as any. I don't know that I'm ever going to get anything more than these little flashes."

Without thinking, Anna reached across the table and laid her hand atop his. Something jolted through her. Not a memory, precisely, but an awareness—a sense that she had touched him this way before. He stared at her, storm-colored eyes wide, lips slightly parted.

If it weren't for the table separating them, she might have been foolish enough to kiss him. Instead, she withdrew her hand and turned her attention to her food.

She knew him, from somewhere, sometime in the past. Whatever that meant.

Anna tried to put the matter out of her head and keep up a casual chatter, but as the evening wore on her thoughts kept drifting to the heat of that skin-to-skin contact and the almost-memory it had conjured up. Perhaps she should have kissed him after all. If mere hands meeting could cause such a reaction, imagine what lips could do.

Her body twitched. What if a kiss brought forth a memory of the same activity with a different man? How humiliating.

I'm so sorry, Mr. Smith. I thought perhaps there might be something between us, but as it happens, there's someone else.

And what if she remembered this someone else but now preferred Quinn? Awkward, to say the least. No kissing, then. With her gloves on she had some measure of protection against accidental touches, as well.

Aboard the ship, she opened her trunk, taking a quick inventory to be certain nothing had been stolen during the move from the fisherman's house to this cramped cabin where she would spend the next three nights.

"All in order?" Quinn asked.

"I believe so. All my clothing is here, and my books, and this little…" She gasped as her hand closed around the toy bear.

"What? What's wrong?"

"I remember!" She bolted upright, thrusting the toy in his direction. "I have this bear and my brother has a rabbit. We had adventures and tea parties with them, and even though I was younger and a girl he never minded playing with me. We would dress them in pretty clothes and take them exploring around our house. I remember the house! The rugs, the curtains, the furniture. My mother telling me that even adventurous ladies don't stand on chairs, even if they can't reach something." She crossed the cabin in only two steps, placing her left hand flat against Quinn's chest and gazing up into his eyes. "Oh, Quinn, I remember my mother!"

She felt, rather than heard, his sudden intake of breath as his chest rose and fell beneath her hand. His hand closed over hers. To remove it from his person, certainly. She had no business touching him so intimately, yet in her excitement it had seemed the thing to do.

"I remember too." The soft, deep tones of his words sent

a chill down her spine. His thumb pressed up beneath the edge of her glove, tracing the birthmark on her wrist, his gaze never leaving hers. The tickle of his light caress started a frisson of desire that raced from one sensitive spot to the next, each stroke of his thumb a new wave pulsing through her. "I remember this."

"Quinn." She inched closer. He lifted her hand, replacing his thumb with his lips.

"And this."

Anna could only gasp, trembling as he sucked gently at her delicate skin. His kiss sparked no memories, only sensations, but she knew one thing for certain. She wanted those lips everywhere.

Quinn pulled back, letting her hand slip from his grasp. His eyes had darkened and he drew several deep breaths before speaking.

"Please excuse me. I need a moment alone to… consider things." He gave her a quick nod and rushed out the door.

Anna sank down onto the bottom bunk, still shivering with unfulfilled lust.

"Bloody hell, Quinn Smith. Who *are* you to me?" Because if he wasn't her lover, then he needed to be. And if he was, then she wanted those memories back. Now.

XII

Exchange of Knowledge

"**E**XCUSE ME, SIR? Are you in need of assistance?"

Quinn paused in his pacing to address the crewman. "I'm fine," he repeated for the third time in the last hour. He must look like hell, because everyone seemed to think he was one big wave away from casting up his accounts.

In truth, the only thing troubling him was the burst of new memories brought on by Anna's potion and that rose-scented soap.

I think I will wash off the smell of the ocean and then pay a visit to the chemist.

He'd had no idea when he'd left her the morning before that those parting words would turn his world upside down. Ever since she'd fed him the potion with dinner, memories had been flitting through his mind, triggered by tastes, smells, sounds. The recollections were mostly vague or non-specific. Foods he'd prepared or eaten, sights and sounds of places he'd visited, several flashbacks of his childhood home, including the smell of pine boughs and Christmas pies.

Only when Anna had inflamed multiple senses at once had any detailed memories appeared. With her hand pressed to his heart, her orange-gold eyes large and luminous, and the rose-scented soap wafting from her freshly-washed hair, he'd found himself transported once again to those amorous moments in the closet.

He remembered it all. Ducking into the tiny room full of linens to avoid a belligerent fellow guest who couldn't handle losing a game of billiards to a woman. Becoming trapped there when someone else wandered into the hall and struck up a conversation. Laughing at their self-inflicted imprisonment, their bodies crushed close together.

Her seductive whisper.

I quite like it here.

He'd held her, breathed her in. Traced the moon-shaped mark on her wrist, just under the edge of the pretty gloves she always wore. He knew it even in the dark. He'd lifted her wrist to his lips and kissed her there, because he knew it was a ticklish spot and he loved the way she shivered in his arms. He'd kissed her neck and her shoulder. Peeled the evening gown from her body to expose more of her to his touch.

Quinn had hardly slept last night, tossing and turning in the small bunk as he relived the memory and wrestled with its implications.

Anna Harper was his dark-haired woman. They were lovers, or had been in the past.

As vivid as the memory was, he could recall little useful information regarding the circumstances of the encounter. He could see the hall with the closet in his mind. He knew what Anna had been wearing that night. He even had the vague notion that the house belonged to an earl. Though how mere Quinn Smith had enough social standing to be invited to the home of an aristocrat, he had no idea.

None of that gave him the answers he wanted. How long had their affair gone on? Had it all happened before Anna had wed? Or had she come to him to escape an unhappy marriage? He couldn't imagine her betraying a husband she cared for, but if he were cruel or neglectful she would do all she could to gain independence and happiness.

"Damn, damn, damn," Quinn muttered. He had to tell her. Perhaps it would trigger the memories for her. Even if it didn't, she deserved the truth.

He found her in their cabin, engrossed in one of her penny dreadfuls. She sat on her bunk, her legs tucked up beneath her, one stockinged foot peeping out from the edge of her pooled skirts. He quashed the urge to wrap his fingers around her slender ankle and slide his hand the length of her calf.

"Are you ready to talk?" she asked, glancing up only briefly.

"Er... yes. I think I ought to tell you everything I've remembered. I hope it might trigger more of your own recollections."

She finished the page, then slipped her bookmark into place. "Shall we swap notes?"

Quinn's brow furrowed. "Pardon?"

"I will give you my notes to read, and you give me yours."

"Oh. I suppose that's a sensible way not to miss anything."

"I thought so. Here." Her leg stuck out even further when she bent to reach her notebook. Knowing he'd touched her before only intensified his desire. He very nearly turned around and went back to pacing the deck. Anna stopped him by tossing her mangled journal at him.

Quinn caught the book out of the air reflexively and opened it. She made her notes in pencil, and her neat handwriting was still legible, despite the dunking in the ocean. The notes had been carefully organized into sections.

About me. About him.

Unable to contain his curiosity, Quinn handed over his own notebook and began to read everything Anna had written on the "about him" page. Mixed with random information, such as his name and probable place of birth, were observations on his personality, most of them complimentary. She believed him smart and logical. The words, "doesn't underestimate women," were followed by a series of excited exclamation points.

Oddly cute when in a panic.

His heart skipped a beat. Suspecting her attraction to him and seeing it written in her own hand were two very different things.

Does he want to kiss me?

More and more every second. Hoping to ease some of his frustrated lust, Quinn turned to the page where she had written about herself. The second line on the page nearly made him drop the journal.

"You think you're a courtesan?" he blurted.

She glanced up from her perusal of his notes. "It seems logical."

"Not to me. I think you're a Lady. With an uppercase L."

Anna poked at his journal. Today's gloves were bright red and molded to the exact contours of her hands. "It says right here that you now believe I am your dark-haired woman. Of course, you also seem to believe yourself a scoundrel who seduces innocent women, so your conclusions are somewhat suspect."

"We had an affair, you and I. I don't remember much outside of the closet incident, but whether it was before your marriage or after, I had no business dallying with you."

"Nonsense. I was a willing participant, was I not?"

"Extremely willing. Eager, even."

"Well, there you have it. I am obviously a courtesan. I use a married name to give myself greater independence."

He couldn't deny that it was a possibility. His knowledge of her body suggested their affair had been of some duration. She could have been his mistress.

"What about Nick and the bookmark?"

"What of him?"

"He obviously loved or loves you. He could be your husband."

She snorted. "Now you're being ridiculous. Men don't praise their wives for fierceness."

"Why not?"

Anna blinked at him, her pretty face scrunched into a tight frown. "Wives are supposed to be demure and obedient."

"Says who?"

"Everyone. There are whole books written on the subject."

"Women are plenty fierce where I come from. Even without specific memories, I can tell you my mother and grandmother were not demure and obedient. But that's Covent Garden. You're from Mayfair, correct? The neighborhood of a proper Lady."

"Ladies don't have trysts in closets. They also don't drink whisky, swear, read penny dreadfuls, pick locks, ride bicycles, conduct investigations, and any number of other things that I've surely done."

"I think you'd be surprised."

Anna's mouth twisted in a scowl of annoyance. "Why are you insisting on this? Do you really want me to be a Lady? Do you want me to be married to some stuffy Lord?"

"No. I don't. But I need to remind myself why I shouldn't touch you. You might not be what people expect of a woman, but I don't believe you flit around from man to man, trading your favors for money. You are a respectable married woman, Anna Harper."

She stared at him for a long moment, her face and posture attesting to that fierceness the mysterious Nick had praised.

"Well, maybe I don't want to be." She pushed past him and rushed out the door, but not before he caught the trickle of a single tear down her cheek.

XIII

High Stakes

"The tea is quite good," Quinn remarked, "even if they do insist on serving it alongside absurd little sandwiches. A man needs to eat about fifty of them for a proper meal."

Anna nodded and made a sound that came out something like, "Mmphh." She swallowed her bite of sandwich and tried again. "Yes, the tea is excellent."

The ship to Newcastle was neither large nor fancy, but it was comfortable. Simple sconces on the dining room walls glowed with yellow potion light, illuminating a serviceable carpet, sturdy tables, and a simple afternoon tea to fuel the passengers—English men of business, most of them.

"It looks as though it might rain," Quinn remarked, casting a glance out the window.

Anna nodded behind her teacup. Yesterday had been one of those warm and sunny autumn days, and she had spent some of the day outdoors. Today, however, a gray drizzle kept everyone inside.

"Perhaps," she replied.

They had been reduced to this. Talking about food and the weather. She'd suffered through a full day and a half of nothing but food and weather and the occasional question as to her comfort. And one business-like read-through of both their notes, which had resulted in no new memories and complete avoidance of discussion of their shared history.

Quinn picked up another tiny sandwich. He'd eaten sixteen of them, by her count. Something to record in her journal, perhaps. It wasn't as if she had any useful information to add. The potion had helped her conjure up memories of childhood and the sights, sounds, and smells of London, but the effects had since worn off, and nothing new was forthcoming.

She grabbed a sandwich for herself. Number ten. They were ridiculously small, she had to admit. She wished she could find the humor in it, but currently all she could feel was frustration. She hadn't slept well since she could remember, and it left her both tired and cranky. The first day at sea had aggravated the morning sickness she had previously thought was improving. The combination made her a terrible companion.

Anna hated the awkwardness that had grown between herself and Quinn. She hated the strange mixture of knowing and not knowing. Most of all, she hated that she still wanted to kiss him and had no idea whether she should or not.

The memories she had regained since drinking the potion hadn't clarified her situation. Why had she gone to Esbjerg? Had she intended to meet Quinn there, or possibly confront him? Had she planned to run away with him? Did she have an angry husband who had sent her away? And how did it all connect to the whisky thefts?

She gulped down the last of her tea before it could go completely cold. What if Quinn had been the whisky thief and he'd simply forgotten? A giggle burst out as a whole scenario coalesced in her mind.

"Something funny?" Quinn asked.

"What if we are our own enemies?"

"I don't follow."

"I am Mrs. Harper, correct? What if I have betrayed Mr.

Harper of Harper-Douglass and joined you—a competitor or a disgruntled employee—in a scheme to steal whisky? We colluded and set up the entire operation, using the new distribution site in Esbjerg. We arranged to meet there, presumably to both continue with our nefarious adventure and to resume our illicit affair. But something went wrong. Either we were discovered and deliberately poisoned, or our own plan to use the poison on someone else backfired and we mistakenly drank the tainted whisky. Now we are investigating our own misdeeds and our minions don't know how to handle it."

Quinn stared at her for a moment, then burst out laughing. "Part of me wants that to be the absolute truth. But you're much too good a person, Mrs. Harper."

"Maybe I wasn't always a good person. After all, if I am married as you believe, then I should never have been with you in that closet."

"I have reached the conclusion that that particular incident must have taken place before you were married."

"So I left you for another man."

"I expect so. Someone your family approved of, no doubt. A man of wealth and rank. Perhaps a duke."

Anna had to cough to avoid choking on her last tiny sandwich. "You think a duchess could simply vanish and no one would come looking for her?"

"Who would look for a duchess in a small Danish shipping village?"

"Someone would make the connection to the solicitors who arranged my passage and would have sent telegrams at the very least."

He shrugged. "Yes, well, I suppose it's about as plausible as your theory that we are villains who wiped our own memories."

"Exactly. No one has come looking for me. If I have a husband, he either deliberately sent me away or he can't be bothered to look for me. And if that is what I find upon reaching Edinburgh, then Messrs. Stewart and Lachlan will be drawing up divorce papers citing abandonment. But I still believe I'm merely pretending to be married. Probably for the sake of my baby."

Quinn gave a little shake of his head. "I'm sure the baby is your husband's."

"The husband who abandoned me? Ha!"

"The husband who loves you and is frantically searching for you."

"Well, he's not doing a very good job at it." Anna pushed her plate away and rose. Quinn immediately sprang to his feet. "I'm finished, and I think I shall go somewhere else. I don't want to argue about this anymore. I wish this boat had a billiard table. I'd like to know if I really can play well enough to beat uppity men."

"There may not be a billiard table, but I did spy a stack of board games in the lounge area."

Anna jumped in excitement. "I love board games!"

"Yes, I know. It was in my notes about the dark-haired woman. Why don't you get settled in our cabin. I'll fetch some games and join you momentarily."

"We can't play in the lounge? It would be more comfortable."

His eyebrows twitched. "It would also hamper your ability to call me vile names and play in the cutthroat style to which you are no doubt accustomed."

She grinned at him. "Which would be no fun at all. Very well. To spare your sensitive feelings and allow you to avoid public humiliation, we shall play in the cabin. I'll request a fresh pot of tea to be sent to the room."

"Of course. Must keep it a civilized humiliation, after all." His eyes gleamed. They appeared bluer today, almost a match for the steel-blue waistcoat he wore. "I shall see you shortly, prepared to accept a thorough drubbing."

Anna gave him a nod and headed for the room. He was flirting again. What did that mean? The back and forth of teasing and withdrawing was enough to drive anyone mad.

She returned to the room and arranged a small seating area, using her bed and her trunk as the chairs, and Quinn's trunk as the table. She was still fussing with the exact placement when Quinn arrived, games in hand.

"Gaming appears to be a popular pastime on this ship. We were left with the choice of backgammon and Mansion of Happiness."

Anna eyed the pair of games. "Mansion of Happiness is a silly game. I can't take all that moralizing seriously. It would be much better played drunk."

"I'm sure we could arrange to add a bit of something to our tea."

"No, thank you. I'm already worried that the tainted whisky could have hurt the baby. I am trying to take care with what I drink."

"Backgammon it is, then." He opened the board, arranged the checkers, and handed Anna a pair of dice. "Ladies first."

"Don't be ridiculous. We roll for first turn. What stakes? A pound per point?"

"A pound? Are you mad? We haven't any money."

Anna began pulling pins from her hair, setting them beside the game board. Most of them were still slightly bent from when she'd crafted her lockpicks. "We can use pins as markers. Money payable upon retrieval of our memories and our bank accounts."

"Very well." Quinn divided the pins into two equal piles. "The most expensive hairpins in history, I wager."

"Another wager? How much?"

He leaned toward her, his elbows on the makeshift table and his eyebrows arching as he gave her a wicked smile. "Trounce me, Anna Harper. Take me for all I'm worth."

Her skin prickled. Had he meant for that to sound so sexual, or was he merely trying to rouse her competitive spirit? Her eyes fixated on the bow curve of his upper lip.

"One match, to ten points," she said. "And if I win, I want a kiss."

He sat back, and for a moment she feared she might have gone too far. But then he picked up his dice, shook them in his hand, and rolled.

"I accept."

XIV
Winner Take All

QUINN ROLLED THE DICE and moved two of his checkers. Nine points apiece. One final game. Winner take all. The longer the match went on, the more tempted he was to lose on purpose and pay his forfeit.

But he couldn't do that to her. She was a damned fine competitor, and she wanted to win fairly. If he let her win, she'd be more likely to slap him than kiss him. Which probably made it the smartest thing he could do.

He had already established, however, that Quinn Smith didn't always do the smartest thing.

Anna's dice rattled. Double fives. She moved three more checkers into her home board. Quinn's fingers tightened around his own dice. He ought never to have agreed to this. As much as he longed to kiss her, he didn't want to cause any trouble, and every kissing scenario he could imagine led to trouble.

Option one: We have a torrid affair, she regains her memories, remembers husband she loves, is crushed and heartbroken, marriage possibly ruined. Most likely scenario.

Two: Torrid affair, regain memories, I'm a scoundrel and she remembers why she left me and is angry and disgusted by what we've done regardless of any husband or lack thereof.

Three: Torrid affair, regain memories, her husband is a cruel blackguard who has abandoned her and his child, I thrash him as he deserves and go to prison, she's trapped in a terrible marriage. Should I kill him, instead? Still prison, but she's free.

Four: Torrid affair, regain memories, she really is a courtesan and soon tires of me and moves on to someone else. Depressing.

Five: Torrid affair, we never regain memories and things continue on indefinitely? Quit dreaming, Smith.

Six: One kiss, she remembers everything, hates me and never speaks to me again. No torrid affair. Best option?

Seven: One kiss, she remembers nothing, but finds me boring and unsatisfying.

Anna's voice pulled him from his maudlin contemplation. "It's a six and a three, Quinn, there aren't that many possible moves. Simply pick one."

"Sorry. I was distracted for a moment." He picked up a checker and moved it around the board.

"Because you're about to lose and will owe me a kiss?"

Exactly.

"Because I'm plotting my strategy for a triumphant comeback."

She chuckled. "I'd like to see that." Her dice bounced across the board. She scowled at the two and three that turned up.

"See? My luck is turning."

He didn't expect the words to be prophetic, but suddenly every roll seemed to go his way. Anna inched her checkers from point to point, while his whizzed around the board. She rolled, swore, rolled again, accused him of cheating, and swore some more. One-by-one, Quinn's checkers disappeared from the board. He tossed the dice one final time, rolling a five and a three, enough to remove his last two checkers.

"Fuck," she muttered.

He plucked two hairpins from the pile. "Eleven to nine. You owe me two pounds."

She sighed. "I don't suppose you'd like a kiss instead?"

I'd love one.

"Not a chance," he said. A good, sensible reply. Stay out of trouble. "I'm afraid we must remain platonic former lovers."

"You're no fun at all."

He reached for the other game board. "Or perhaps we can make a new wager."

Idiot.

Her eyes lit up. "Wager on Mansion of Happiness? A game that uses a teetotum because dice are a tool of Satan?"

He plucked one of the dice from the backgammon set before closing it. "Let's be rebels."

Anna's eyebrows twitched, and her lovely mouth curved into a broad smile. "You're going to find yourself in the pillory." She gestured at a square on the Mansion of Happiness game board.

"That's for perjurers. I'm aiming for the Summit of Dissipation, personally."

"A noble goal. To help you achieve it, let's say that every time you have to pay one of your counters as a fine, it equals one pound, payable to the victor."

"Better yet, each fine is a pound to the pot. Loser pays winner the amount of the entire pot."

"You're on the Road to Folly, Mr. Smith." Anna placed a player marker on that square as she spoke. "But I accept."

Quinn plucked the marker from the board and moved it to back to the start. "No cheating, Mrs. Harper. We all begin at the beginning. Ladies first."

"For this game, I will accept your chivalrous offer." She rolled a three and moved her marker.

Quinn rolled a four. "Haha! Honesty! Six extra spaces to my oh-so-virtuous self."

Anna raised her eyes to the ceiling and tossed the die again. "Four. Audacity."

Quinn scanned the instructions that had come with the game. "You do possess that quality in abundance, but as much as I admire it in you, I'm afraid that according to the rules you must return to your 'former situation' and, I quote, 'not even *think* of Happiness, much less partake of it.'"

"I will move my piece back," she retorted, "but audacious as I am, I will be thinking of happiness the entire time. Because, even with an opponent as impertinent as you, I'm exceptionally happy to be playing games just now."

"We are both bound for hell."

"Undoubtedly."

They continued around the board, taunting one another for each vice or virtue landed upon. Anna made a mumbling comment about closets when he landed on Chastity, and he applauded her when she reached the Summit of Dissipation—which came with a fine of three, adding nicely to the growing pot. They both crept nearer to the Mansion, threw over twice, and had to return to the beginning.

"This could take forever, you know," Quinn said, landing on Honesty for the second time. "I can see how a few drinks could speed it along."

"A few drinks and we'd be even rowdier than we are now." She rolled a six and hopped over him, stopping on the space marked Passion.

"Whoever gets in a Passion," Quinn read, "must be taken to the Water, have a dunking to cool him, and pay a fine of one."

"I refuse." Anna folded her arms across her chest.

"You can't refuse."

"Nevertheless, I refuse. I won't treat passion as a vice. It's a natural and healthy emotion, whether one is passionate about an interest, a cause, or a…" She trailed off momentarily, then looked him straight in the eye. "Or a lover. I will not be ashamed of it."

Quinn's entire body tightened. Was anything in the world more tempting than this audacious, passionate, beautiful woman? He'd fallen for her in the past, and he teetered now on the cliff's edge. One little nudge and he would fall again.

He rolled the die, putting his mind back to the game and the monetary wager. The small cube hit the board, hopped, spun, and came to rest with four black dots winking up at him.

His heart pounded. He leaned over the board. Square-by-square, he moved his piece until it came up flush with hers. Anna leaned in as well, watching, her shoulder nearly touching his, her delectable lips a mere turn of the head away.

"And what happens when two players 'get in a Passion' together?" he asked, his voice nearly a whisper, low and thickened with desire.

She shoved the makeshift table aside, flung her arms around his neck, and kissed him.

XV
The More We Know

ANNA REMEMBERED. Not the Closet Incident, yet, but this. The way he tasted, the way he felt. Scattered pieces of board games surrounding them. It had been different, that other time. Slower, gentler. As if they had all the time in the world.

Today they were ravenous. Starved. It had been so long, so very long, since his lips had last brushed across hers, since his tongue had last slipped inside to drink deeply.

The memories had no frame of reference. It could have been mere weeks they'd been apart, or months. Even years. All she knew for certain was that she'd been craving this. Craving him.

Quinn scooped her up and set her on his lap, one arm curving around to hold her, the other weaving through the long strands of her loose hair. He tipped his head at just the right angle to seal their mouths together.

This was no exploratory kiss. No searching, no testing. His lips and tongue mets hers with practiced sweeps, greedily reclaiming territory he had possessed before. Though she had begun it, he swiftly took charge, pushing the kiss deeper, wetter, then drawing back, teasing her with soft nips before plunging in again.

After a time, he relented, ceding the lead to her, letting her lick that perfect curve of his upper lip and drag kisses along his stubbly jaw. He groaned when she moved to his neck and sucked hard at the skin just above his collar. She would mark him there, where everyone could see it.

"Anna." His grip tightened, his fingers squeezing her hip, dragging her closer. The bulge of his growing erection pressed against her thigh. "God, Anna."

"Quinn."

She tugged at his necktie, her fingers working the knot loose with ease. She knew how to undress a man. Her kisses moved down his throat as she opened the top buttons of his shirt. His skin was warm and slightly salty, with a clean, musky scent. Memories of touching him and tasting him floated through the back of her mind, just out of reach. Once, she had known all of him, and she wanted to know him again.

"Anna, you drive me wild," he gasped. His hands traced her body from hips to breasts, molding to her curves, making her long to remove the layers that separated them.

She lifted her head to capture his lips again, snatching brief, hungry kisses. "Quinn, I lo—"

She froze. *I love you.* A memory, with no sense of time or place. If she had said that to him, their affair must have been more than a casual fling. Would she ever know what had happened between them?

"Anna, we should…" He pulled back enough that she could see the glistening of his moist lips and the flush of desire in his cheeks. His eyes were a dark gray, his pupils wide. "We should stop."

"Y-yes." Her fingers loosened their grip on his half-unbuttoned shirt. Muddled memories danced through her lust-fogged mind. Images of Quinn naked, lying beside her in

bed. The two of them on the floor of a library, where he was…
"Bloody hell."

"Aye." He lifted her off his lap, setting her on the bunk beside him. "Memories are crashing in on me, and I can't even begin to sort through them."

"For me as well. Most are vague. Images, feelings. All about you. One or two, though, are very vivid." Were her cheeks red? Her skin burned just thinking about that library tryst.

"Like the closet."

Anna shook her head. "I still don't remember the closet. Do you remember the library?"

"No."

"We must have been lovers for quite some time."

"Or briefly but very… thoroughly." Quinn inched away from her. She made the mistake of glancing down. He still had a cockstand, and the sight of it tenting his trousers caused a quiver in her belly.

"Do you remember anything useful?" *Say yes. Give me a reason to kiss you again.*

"I don't think so."

"Damn." That kiss had been like throwing a combustible potion into a bonfire. Her desire raged out of control and she had no idea how to quench it. Giving in was a tantalizing prospect. "Do you think if we made love, it would trigger more memories?"

"Undoubtedly." He moved further away. "But I'm wary of what we might discover. I don't want to start something that either of us might regret later."

"You don't want to finish something, you mean. It started the moment we met. Met again, that is. I still don't remember meeting you for the first time."

"Nor do I." He brushed a hand through his hair. "Sometimes it feels like the more I remember, the less I know.

Perhaps we ought to go up on deck. Walk about, clear our heads with some fresh air before dinner."

She looked down at his groin again, this time letting her gaze linger. "You might want to take care of that first." Was it strange that she wanted to watch him? Probably another indicator of her promiscuous profession.

"I'll, uh, clean up in here." He set about picking up all the pieces of the games, carefully counting and stowing them, while pointedly avoiding looking Anna in the eye.

No. She wouldn't allow their relationship to become awkward again. She was tired of awkward.

"I had fun this evening," she said.

He paused and looked up at her.

"I'd like to do it again sometime. Even if we never have anything more for our wagers than hairpins and kisses, I will always be willing to join you for a game. You are a worthy competitor and a fine companion."

The smile started as just a tiny twitch of his lips, before spreading to encompass his entire face, lighting up his blue-gray eyes.

"I concur. I would be happy to play again in the future. Shall we head up top?" He tucked the board games underneath one arm and offered her the other.

"Yes, let's." She took hold of his arm, feigning imperviousness to his touch. If he felt the little shiver that ran through her, he didn't comment on it. "We should review the new memories that we've had. Not the intimate details," she added hastily, "but anything at all that might be helpful. Places, other people, furniture, rooms, and so on."

"Good idea." One blond eyebrow twitched. "Why don't you begin with that library you mentioned?"

Anna shook her head. "You're impossible, you know that? One minute you're all but hiding from me, and the next you're back to flirting."

"My apologies. I want to be flirting all the time, but I'm

striving to control myself. I like you too much to destroy your life."

"You seriously need to revise that section of your notes that says you're a scoundrel."

"You may be right. Perhaps I was only a man in love with a woman I couldn't have."

Anna shivered. There was that word again.

I will find out, she vowed. *Someday I will know what we once were to one another.*

Her hand drifted across her belly. If only she had a better sense of time. She wanted to know what the chances were that Quinn was the father of her baby.

"Something wrong?"

Her head snapped up. "Hmm?"

"You're frowning. Do I need to flirt more?"

"No, it's nothing. Let's have dinner."

As she expected, they learned nothing new from sharing their memories, but they talked and made notes and had a pleasant meal. By the time they returned to their cabin, she was yawning.

"I'll leave you to prepare for bed," Quinn said. He took hold of her hand and lifted it to his lips, but instead of kissing her glove, he flipped her hand over and kissed the inside of her wrist again. "A very good night to you, Mrs. Harper."

A very good night to you, Miss...

The memory eluded her. Who had she been when he had said those same words in that same reverent voice? She pressed a gentle kiss to his lips, lingering as long as she dared.

"Goodnight, Mr. Smith."

The moment he closed the door, she plopped onto her bunk, more remembered words ringing in her mind. No context. No images. Simply the warm tones of her own voice.

Goodnight, Mr. Harper.

"Damnation."

She *did* have a husband. The question was, who was he?

XVI

Man and Wife

"ISEE YOU EYEING my meat, Mrs. Harper."

Quinn gave her that little eyebrow waggle he couldn't seem to stop. She was right. He was a shameless flirt. It was such blasted fun, flirting and teasing with her. Their night of board games was the highlight of his remembered life. And that damned kiss...

It put the closet memory to shame, that kiss. Exciting, exhilarating, and erotic, he'd wanted it to go on forever. He'd wanted to strip her bare and kiss every inch of her skin, in the hope she'd do the same to him. He wished he'd given in, taken her to bed, and relived the awesome reality his memories could only hint at.

But, again, Anna was right. He was no scoundrel. He had to restrain himself. *He had to.* Because if she had a loving husband back home who would make her happy and be a good father to their child, Quinn couldn't take that from her. And, really, all they had was a strong physical attraction and mutual enjoyment of one another's company. It wasn't as if she loved him. She hardly knew him. How could she, when he hardly knew himself?

But you know her, he reminded himself. *You love her.*

Anna reached across the breakfast table and speared his ham with her fork. "You're not eating it and the baby is hungry." She bit a chunk off, chewing slowly as Quinn stared at her lips. "Delicious."

"You enjoy tormenting me, don't you?"

"Yes. Because I'm a scandalous, dissolute woman." She delivered the jest with a smile, but her tone lacked its usual brightness, and her eyes didn't sparkle. Something was bothering her.

"What's wrong?"

Her eyes widened and then narrowed as she frowned. "Nothing's wrong. Why would you think that?"

"Not 'wrong,' perhaps, but 'off.' You're a tiny bit distant, or distracted. Is something weighing on your mind? I'm happy to listen, if you need to talk."

"Thank you, but I'm quite well. I don't even have any morning sickness today." She ate another bite of ham, as if to prove her point.

"Hmm."

"You don't believe me?"

No, I don't. He'd memorized her during these days together, and the fragments of memories he'd recovered only reinforced what he knew. He could lose all five of his senses and he would still never forget the sight of her face, the sound of her laugh, the scent of her perfumed soap, the taste of her lips, and the touch of her soft leather gloves against his skin. If this intimate knowledge of her could slice through the cloud around his memories, was it any surprise he could read her moods? She was holding back from him, and he knew because it was different. In the past she hadn't done that. She'd once trusted him with everything.

He was certain her idea was right—if they made love, they would remember even more. But they would arrive in Newcastle within the hour. Better to wait. Better to spark his memory another way, at least until he knew more. All he wanted was for her to be happy.

"I think *you* are off this morning," Anna said, gesturing with a bite of the stolen ham. "You've hardly touched your breakfast. Are you nervous about Newcastle?"

"Yes."

"Don't be. I'm sure anything you learn about yourself will be perfectly non-scoundrel-y. My only worry is that we have no money for food or lodging."

"Once I exchange the Dutch coins for English ones, I should have a few shillings. That can buy us food. I'll have to sell something else to pay for a room. But I hope I will find some clues to myself and follow them to my bank account. Then I can cover our expenses until we find your life and your bank account and you can pay me those two pounds you owe me. Although that fails to take into account the Mansion of Happiness pot. I'm not entirely certain who won that game."

"I did, obviously. But I'm willing to forgive your debt."

He expected her to add, "in return for another kiss," or a similar flirtatious demand, but she didn't. Something was definitely wrong.

The mystery gnawed away at him as they packed up their things and prepared to make landfall. He couldn't do anything to help her, no matter how much he wanted to. Not unless she asked. And why would she? He was nothing more than an ex-lover thrown back into her life through some nefarious scheme. She would handle her troubles her own way, find her own path.

Ironically, he admired her all the more for it. He adored her unconventional habits, her analytical mind, and her feisty spirit. Even without his memories, he was wildly, madly, head-over-heels in love with her. And he couldn't do a damned thing about it.

Brooding didn't suit Quinn. Instead of sinking into a bad mood, he typically looked for ways to escape it. Today, he had to physically restrain himself from taking up Anna's hand and kissing it to lift his spirits. He swallowed back several inappropriate puns about docks and putting in to port, even knowing they would make her laugh.

By the time they disembarked, he was so preoccupied trying to think of a joke that couldn't possibly be interpreted in a sexual manner, that her elbow to the ribs caught him entirely by surprise. He gasped and stumbled, his legs unaccustomed to dry land.

"Did you hear that?" Anna demanded.

"Hear what?"

She pointed. "I think that woman just asked if there was a Mr. Quinn Smith on this ship."

He followed the direction of her finger, to where a woman stood talking with a crewman. Nothing about her sparked any sort of memory. Her brown hair was piled into an enormous mass on top of her head, and her bright red dress looked to have been made over from a style several years out-of-date. Ropes of pearls hung around the woman's neck, and long, gold earrings dangled from her earlobes.

"Smith," the woman repeated. "I'm looking for a Mr. Quinn Smith."

Quinn strode toward her, studying her face. A pointy chin. Plump cheeks. Large, pretty eyes that were pale green or blue. None of it remotely familiar. Did she know him, or only know of him? He had to ask. Any clue to his identity must be explored.

"I'm Mr. Smith."

The woman turned. Her eyes widened, and her jaw dropped open. "Quinnie!" she squealed.

Quinn recoiled. No one called him Quinnie. Ever. Not even Anna could make him respond to such a ridiculous nickname.

"Quinnie, darling!" the woman shouted, launching herself at him.

He dodged just quickly enough that her sloppy kiss caught him on the side of his chin. Anna grabbed the woman from behind and hauled her away.

"Get your hands off my…" She broke off, her nose crinkling in confusion, as if unsure what she had meant to say.

The strange woman put her hands on her hips, staring Anna down. "Your what? Who are you? Some fancy woman he's picked up?" She rounded on Quinn. "How could you?"

"How could I what? Who are you?"

She smacked the side of his head. "I'm your wife, you cad! Where in blazes have you been?"

Quinn gaped at her. Impossible. He hadn't even the slightest inkling of memory about her, even when she touched him, and he was quite certain he had never lived with anyone who screamed at him and struck him the way she had. Even if he wrote off that behavior as shock and anger at his supposed infidelity, the entire situation left him with a sense of wrongness.

Anna again pushed the woman away from Quinn, interposing herself between them. "You are *not* his wife."

The woman smirked. "You don't think so? Then prove it." She pulled a wrinkled piece of paper out of a purse and waved it about. "Oh, wait. You can't. But I can."

Anna snatched for the paper, but the woman stuffed it down her bodice. There was no way in hell Quinn was going fishing for it there. Anna, however, flexed her fingers inside her emerald-green gloves, looking right down the woman's décolletage.

"I'm willing to dig that forgery out from anywhere you might shove it. I don't know who you're working for, or what your goal is, but you do not get to do this to him."

"As if the words of some harlot are any threat to me?" the

so-called Mrs. Smith scoffed. "What do you know of him? I bet you can't even tell me his birthday."

"You're right, I can't," Anna replied. "When is it?"

"September seventeenth."

"A lie."

Was it? Quinn had no idea when his birthday was. Anna's was in early spring, he remembered suddenly. He had been walking through the park, picking brand-new flowers and sticking them into her hair, teasing her by not showing her the real present he had bought.

Spring. Late March, or early April. That meant they could have been a couple as recently as six months ago. Or it could have been a year prior, or even two.

"I don't think you know a thing about Mr. Smith," Anna said, her voice calm but no less determined. She had pulled out her notebook, and her pencil was poised above it. "What is his favorite drink?"

"Whisky," Mrs. Smith retorted.

"Mmm. Good. Probable connection there. What is his favorite color?"

"Red." She smoothed down the front of her bright skirt.

"Wrong. It's green."

Another memory sparked. Anna's hands, covered in the same bright-green gloves she wore today, holding a cue stick as she bent over a billiard table, lining up her shot. Her mouth was twisted in a frown of concentration. An evening dress in a paler shade of green hugged her curves.

"Definitely green," he agreed.

"What would you cook for him if he asked you to make his favorite meal?"

"Mutton stew." Mrs. Smith sounded less certain of herself with every answer.

"Trick question. If he wanted a favorite meal, he'd cook it himself."

"I have had enough of this nonsense!" His supposed wife

gestured at the porter who stood by Quinn's luggage. "You, there. Load Mr. Smith's trunk onto that carriage there. He is coming home with me."

"Load both trunks," Quinn ordered, pointing at Anna's.

The porter nodded. "Yes, sir."

"What?" the woman grabbed his arm. "You can't bring *her* along!"

Quinn shook himself free. "Madam, if you are indeed my wife, then you are sworn to obey me, and I say she comes along. We are taking both trunks and traveling to your house, where we will continue this discussion in a rational manner, and I will not hear a word against it. Is that understood?"

She gaped at him.

"Well, that was appalling," Anna muttered. She gave Quinn a disapproving glare.

Mrs. Smith looked at her for the first time without hostility. "Yes. Men are so tyrannical, aren't they?"

"He's not usually like that."

"They're all like that, dearie. Don't you ever go binding yourself to a man. Better to be a whore and be able to leave them behind when you've had your fill of them."

"Um…"

"Come along, then, dearie. Let's go talk this over."

Quinn stared after the two women as they climbed into the carriage. "What the devil just happened?" he wondered aloud.

The porter shrugged. "Damned if I know."

XVII

Sleuthing

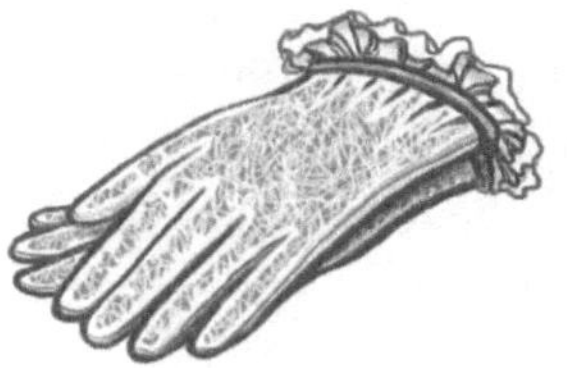

THE CARRIAGE STOPPED in front of a squat brick building, old and worn, but clean. Anna gave it a brief study as she stepped from the cab. Quinn certainly didn't live here. Judging by the quality of his clothing, he ought to have a flat or a row house in a nicer part of town. Assuming he lived in Newcastle at all, which she wasn't convinced of.

"This is where you live, Mrs. Smith?" she asked.

"Call me Polly, dear," the woman replied. "Got a nice flat on the first floor for myself and Mr. Smith." She cast a glance at Quinn, who was helping the driver unload their trunks. "Though I'd rather have it to myself, to be honest. Men are trouble, aren't they?"

"They certainly like to tell us what to do," Anna agreed. "As if we can't think for ourselves."

"Insecure, they are," Polly whispered. "Need someone to look up to them." She raised her voice and said, "Mr. Smith, could you be a darling and carry those things up the stairs for us?"

Quinn started up the stairs with Anna's trunk. "As if I would let an expectant mother carry her own trunk," he muttered.

"A gentleman." Polly beamed.

"Usually," Anna replied. "Not what you'd expected in your fake husband?"

Mrs. Smith sighed. "Is it really so obvious?"

"Yes."

She shrugged. "Well, let's go up and I'll tell you all about it."

The flat upstairs had two rooms, both sparsely furnished. Anna's stomach had begun to rumble, so Quinn poked around in the cabinets until he found a few basic food items.

"I'll make us some lunch," he declared. His gaze settled on Polly. "Since this is my food if I'm your husband."

"Perhaps we might inspect that marriage license now?" Anna inquired.

Polly hesitated.

"I promise we won't make any complaints or tell anyone," Anna added. "All we want is to discover what's going on. And we ladies need to stick together, don't we?"

"Very well." Polly plucked the paper from beneath her clothes and handed it over. "See for yourself."

Anna smoothed out the wrinkled document against the peeling wallpaper. "It's not even a *good* forgery. Someone just rubbed out the name of the real Mr. Smith and wrote 'Quinn' on top of it. They didn't even try to match the handwriting."

"His real name's Hubert, and he's in prison for the next fifteen years, the cad," their hostess complained. "I only married him for his money, then come to find out it was all stolen. Never get married, dearie. Men aren't to be trusted, and whorin's more honest anyhow."

Too late.

"Uh-huh," Anna managed to say.

"How'd you know I wasn't his wife?" Polly jerked her head in Quinn's direction. He'd taken the food to a battered table, where he now stood slicing bread, cheese, and vegetables to make sandwiches.

"You called him 'Quinnie.' Does he look like a 'Quinnie' to you?"

"Sure does. Such a cute thing, with that strawberry hair and those big, pretty eyes. Don't you just want to cuddle him?"

Yes.

"Then there's the matter of your clothing," Anna continued.

Polly smoothed her hands over her skirts. "What of it? This is my best dress!"

"Exactly. Mr. Smith is wearing a bespoke suit. Your dress, I imagine, came from a second-hand shop. Why would a man who can afford his own tailor not purchase similarly custom-made products for his wife?"

"Well, he said he was rich, so I wore all my favorite jewels," Polly said, twisting her pearls around a finger. "Where's all your jewels? Don't your lovers treat you right?"

"I don't wear jewelry."

"Why not?"

Anna didn't need to ponder her answer. She simply knew. "I don't like it."

"Don't like jewelry? Strangest thing I ever heard. What do they give you, then?" Her gaze settled on Anna's belly. "Besides little bastards. You know, you could pull your corset a bit tighter and hide that bump for at least a few more weeks if you want."

"No!" Anna had loosened the side panels only that morning, and she thought her bump was adorable.

"Suit yourself. Guess your Quinnie doesn't mind looking at another man's get. Or is it his?"

Before Anna could admit that she didn't know, Quinn cut in with his own reply. "Her Quinn doesn't think it's any of his business to tell her how she should or shouldn't dress, especially as it concerns her body and her child. Also, luncheon is ready."

Anna gave him a smile, her heart doing a little happy flip-flop at the fervor in his voice. She and Polly joined him at the table, sitting in the only two chairs. Quinn placed a generous-sized sandwich in front of each of them, then dragged his trunk up to the table and sat on it to join them. The trunk makers were definitely missing out if they weren't advertising the suitability of their products to double as furniture.

"I really can't believe anyone thought this altered marriage contract would fool us," Anna said, handing it to Quinn for perusal. She opened her notebook and picked up her pencil, eating her sandwich left-handed in case she needed to make notes.

Polly shrugged. "He said it would pass from a distance. Didn't figure I'd let anyone see it up close."

"Who is 'he?'" Quinn asked. "You were hired for this, I assume?"

"Don't know his name, but he paid me five quid. He could've picked my friend Betsy, but she's a Rathbone, and he liked that I was already a Smith. All I had to do was ask for Quinn Smith at all the ships coming in until I found him, then pretend to be his wife and bring him here, and I did all that. I've earned my pay."

Anna nearly dropped her sandwich. "Bring him here, specifically?"

"Yes. He rented it for a whole week. I like it. My place only has one room."

Anna hopped out of her seat. "We need to leave. As soon as possible."

"Well, I'm not leaving," Polly replied. "I have four more days here, rent-free."

"We'll have to leave our things for the moment," Quinn said. "I need to either earn enough money to pay for a hotel or find out who I am and access funds of my own. And, unfortunately, Mrs. Smith doesn't appear to know anything useful about me."

Polly spread her hands apologetically. "Only your name and that you'd have a lady with you and might be asking about whisky."

"We can't leave the trunks," Anna argued. "If he means to come here—which seems likely—he could put poison or some other harmful potion into our things while we're out. We must leave and take everything with us."

"You could stay at my place," Polly offered. "Only the one room, but it's less than half a mile off and no one's using it while I'm here."

Quinn gave her a skeptical look. "And you won't give us away to the man who hired you?"

She sniffed. "I don't owe him a thing. I earned my five quid. And I like your lady. She's like an investigator, with her notebook and her questions. You don't tell on me for the fake license, I won't tell on you."

"Thank you," Anna said. "That is an entirely sensible agreement. If your employer demands to know what happened, you can say we became suspicious because this apartment was too small and too old for a man of Quinn's apparent wealth, so we ran off."

Polly grinned. "I like that. Puts the blame right on him."

"Where it belongs. Let's hail a cab and leave this place. Polly, could you describe the man who hired you on the way to your home?"

"Sure can. Let me see, he wasn't the handsomest sort, but not bad looking either, if you know what I mean. A bit ordinary. But pleasant enough. His hair wasn't anything special, either, but tidy enough, and he wasn't losing it yet that I could see under the hat, and..."

Anna nodded, touched pencil to paper, and listened.

The cluttered one-room apartment would do for now. Anna could understand why Polly preferred the other flat. After trudging up a narrow, uneven staircase, she and Quinn had been greeted with a small, dark space, into which was crammed a bed, a rickety table, a single chest, and several shelves of questionable integrity.

Anna surveyed the clean sheet she had spread across the bed. At least she hoped the sheet was clean. She'd found it in the chest along with other linens. It looked clean enough. She didn't think it was supposed to dangle down the sides of the bed, though.

"You've never made up a bed before, have you?" Quinn asked.

"Apparently not."

"Allow me." He stepped up beside her and began tucking and spreading layers of bedding in a quietly efficient manner. "I told you you were born and bred a proper lady. You have always had servants to attend to your needs."

"At least I can dress myself," she huffed, smothering the feeling of uselessness with annoyance.

"You are extremely independent," he agreed. "I'm certain you're capable of doing all these sorts of tasks, you simply have had no need to learn. But no matter. You have skills aplenty. Why don't you tell me what information you gleaned from Mrs. Smith's description."

"Not much, I'm afraid. You picked up on the basics, I'm sure. Our villain is about your height, and thin. Brown hair. Dresses nicely. All I can gather is that he's a man from a gentlemanly profession, not a manual laborer. Polly didn't have much to say about particular facial features. Ordinary. Unremarkable. Nose maybe a bit crooked. If I were an artist, I could perhaps have sketched something to help her remember more, but my drawing skills are poor. Well, there's something new I've remembered about myself. Can't draw."

"I don't think I can, either." Quinn straightened up and scrutinized his handiwork. "That will do. I'm afraid we'll have to share the bed, because the floor here is filthy. Those sheets might be well-used, but at least they've been cleaned now and again." He shook his head. "I should go out. I still want to make an attempt to learn about myself. Who knows, perhaps I'll have a stroke of luck and we'll be able to spend the night in a posh hotel."

"Be careful. Our villain might be lurking. If he guesses that Polly has helped us, he could track us here."

"All the more reason to move to new quarters as soon as possible." Quinn strode for the door, pausing with his hand on the knob. "Will you be all right here? I know you think you may have been a lady of ill-repute, but an upper class courtesan is very different from the ladies who live in this area. I would hate for you to be accosted by some man hammering on the door, thinking you're selling."

Anna grinned at him. "What makes you think I intended to stay here? I'm going out investigating too. We can cover twice as much ground that way. You start with banks and clerk's offices and the like. I'll go shopping. I could use another pair of gloves."

Quinn frowned at her. "You haven't any money."

Anna sniffed. "Of course not. Ladies buy on credit. Rest assured, Mr. Smith, if you are a businessman here in Newcastle upon Tyne, I will discover you."

Several silent seconds ticked by, during which Anna was certain Quinn was cataloging reasons she couldn't possibly go wandering about town on her own. But when he spoke, it was only to say, "Meet here for dinner at seven?"

There went her chance to use all the feminist arguments she'd picked up at University. She would have to save them for when she berated him for those comments about obedient wives. "Uh, yes. Fine. Did you know I went to University?"

"I can't say it surprises me."

"Cambridge. Girton College. Not that they recognize us as full members of the university yet, of course, but our schooling was equally rigorous, I assure you."

"I don't doubt it. Good luck with your investigations, Mrs. Harper." He tipped his hat and departed.

With a few pointers from locals, Anna made her way to the shopping district. The first shop she tried had no interest in extending credit to an unknown woman, but in the next store she introduced herself as, "Mrs. Anna Harper of the Harper-Douglass Whisky Company."

The shopkeeper dove immediately for his account book. "Welcome, welcome, Mrs. Harper! I hope you are enjoying your stay in Newcastle upon Tyne. How can I be of assistance to you?"

And so it went. The Harper-Douglass fortune was known and coveted. Shops showered her with impeccable service, and when she peppered the employees with questions, they were only too happy to respond.

"Do you do business with a Mr. Quinn Smith, by any chance?" Anna asked the flirtatious man who had offered her a tempting discount on a lovely pair of purple gloves. "My husband is considering a deal with him, but we never rush into anything, of course."

"Smith, hmm? Can't say that I've heard of him."

"Pity. I'll take the gloves, thank you."

Anna tucked the gloves into one of her bags and started back toward Polly's apartment. Her number of packages had grown so burdensome that her insistence modern women didn't need footmen to carry things now verged on ludicrous. Walking all the way with her awkward armload was probably asking for trouble, but she hadn't even a single coin for cab fare. If anyone threatened her, she would drop everything but the hatbox and use it as a combination shield and cudgel.

She had gone no more than a single block, when a voice shouted, "Mrs. Smith!"

Anna whirled to see a woman running straight at her. She dropped her packages and clenched her fingers around the handle of the hatbox, prepared to swing it.

"Oh, Mrs. Smith, I'm so sorry!" the woman exclaimed. "I didn't mean to startle you. I was so surprised to see you here."

She skidded to a halt beside Anna and began gathering up the spilled packages. "But that always seems to happen when one travels, does it not? You go out, and all of a sudden you've bumped into someone from home!"

"Yes." Anna bent to help pick up her things, studying the strange woman who seemed to know her under another name. Middle-aged, Anna guessed. Her blond hair showed little signs of gray, and her clothing was well-made and fashionable. Her accessories included a modest necklace, diamond earrings, and a jaunty, feathered hat. A maid stood off to one side, carrying two bags of purchases.

"It's so good to see you, Mrs. Smith," the woman gushed, once they were both on their feet again and Anna had somewhat of a grip on her purchases.

A little shiver ran through her. *What is going on here? Who am I to this woman?*

"I never did properly thank you for what you did for Mirabelle. I was shocked—so shocked—when your investigations proved that suitor of hers to be such a rogue, but we are all overjoyed she was saved from a disastrous match. She has now formed an attachment with one of the men you deemed suitable, and I'm certain he will be waiting with a proposal when we return to London next week."

"How delightful," Anna replied, feigning a smile. She was a Mrs. Smith who conducted investigations? Was it a false name? Smiths were terribly common.

"But, how are you, dear?" the woman went on. "You are looking well, all rosy cheeked. How is your darling husband?"

"My husband?"

"Yes, dear, don't you remember I met him the once? Not a man one forgets easily, with those penetrating eyes and that ginger hair. And so well-dressed and well-mannered. I always tell people, 'Never you mind that working man's accent. Here's a man who's made an honest living.' Of course, I'm a merchant's daughter and a merchant's wife, myself. And you know firsthand that no Lord So-and-So can compare to a dependable Mr. Smith."

Anna could only stare in shock. Was she talking about *Quinn?*

"I'm surprised he's not here with you, helping to carry all those things. The way he looked at you, I thought he'd never leave your side."

Anna's heart threatened to pound out of her chest. Beneath her gloves, her hands had begun to sweat.

"I, uh, have been buying things for him. He has a birthday soon."

"Ah, surprises! How sweet you are. I'll let you be going, then. Give him a kiss for me. It was so lovely to see you, my dear."

"Yes, and you as well. Please excuse me." Anna began to turn, then paused, some portion of her brain still working, thankfully. "Before I go, could you remind me when it was that I conducted the investigation on behalf of your family?"

"I believe it was February. Yes, indeed, because it was just before St. Valentine's Day when I saw you with your sweetheart, and it seemed so fitting. Little winter lovebirds. Goodbye, dear!"

"Goodbye."

Anna stumbled home in a daze, trying and failing to fit these new pieces into the puzzle of her life. One man along the way did saunter in her direction, eyeing her packages, but a harsh, "Fuck off," startled him enough to make him back away. She let herself into Polly's room, locked the door, and dumped all her purchases on the bed, sinking down beside them.

"Maybe I'm a courtesan after all," she sighed. "And I simply use the name of my current lover. But a courtesan *and* an investigator? That's so peculiar, even for me. It seems I would risk alienating the respectable women who would be my clients."

Which might explain why she would pretend to be married

to Quinn when they encountered Mrs. Whoever-She-Was. And then there was Mr. Harper. Anna knew he existed, remembered saying his name. She simply couldn't put it with a face or a voice or anything, really. Two fake husbands? Two real husbands? One of each?

A key turned in the lock, and Quinn entered, his hands full with steaming pies. "Evening. I brought dinner. How was your day?"

His words, so pleasant and domestic, hit her like a lead weight to the chest. A half gasp, half sob left her throat as the memory assaulted her, and a lone tear trickled down her cheek.

"Anna? What's wrong?"

"Quinn, I…" She composed herself. "I am ninety-nine percent certain we were once married."

The pies crashed to the floor.

XVIII

Mr. and Mrs. Smith

"I'M SO SORRY." Quinn swiped at the remains of their dinner with a square of cloth he hoped wasn't one of Polly Smith's shawls.

"So you said. Twice. It's only pie. You needn't worry."

Quinn glanced up, then returned to his cleaning. He didn't know what to say. Married? To Anna? The idea was too appealing. He couldn't consider it in any rational manner. He couldn't fathom marrying her and then somehow losing her. What could possibly have happened to bring them to where they were today?

"I'm sorry," he muttered again. He was referring to his inability to communicate, not to the destruction of their dinner, but she couldn't know and she sighed.

"Quinn, that spot is cleaner than it's been in years. You can stop. Please. I don't care about the food. I need us to talk about this."

He tossed the cloth aside and rose, pulling up the stool

from the cluttered dressing table and seating himself near the bed where Anna sat.

"I don't know what to say." Admitting it out loud eased something inside him. He didn't have to make any profound statements. He only had to listen. "What happened? Why do you think we were married?"

"I ran into a woman who recognized me from London. Where I did investigations for genteel ladies."

Of course she did investigations. Her courage, her analytical mind, her pockets, her notes—so much more thorough than his own—all testified to the truth of it. Quinn couldn't suppress a grin.

"I wager you're good at that."

"She seemed pleased with the results of my sleuthing," Anna replied. "But what is relevant to us is that she addressed me as Mrs. Smith. She spoke of meeting my husband and described a man just like you. It made no sense to me. It still seems so strange. But when you walked in the door, I knew it was true. We lived together, once, as man and wife." She pulled the glove off her left hand and reached for him. The simple gold band on her finger glittered in the lamplight. "I remember our wedding."

Quinn gripped her hand, giving her fingers a squeeze. They were cold, and he wanted to press her hand to his chest to warm her. "Tell me."

"We stood in a church, holding hands like this. I had white lace gloves and I had to tuck them into a pocket."

She'd had pockets in her wedding gown. Was anyone else, anywhere, so utterly adorable?

"I don't remember much else. Touching you. Looking into your eyes."

Quinn bit his bottom lip as he considered the matter. "We were married, then. I don't doubt your memory. But why are you now married to Mr. Harper? I can't imagine why I would have divorced you."

Unless she asked for it. If she'd wanted out of the marriage, for whatever reason, he would have let her go.

"It's baffling to me as well," Anna replied. "According to the woman I met, we were together in February of this year."

"February? We haven't even yet reached October. Are you telling me that in the past seven months you have, in some unknown order, divorced me, conceived a child, and remarried?"

"So it seems."

Quinn released her hand and rocked the stool onto its back legs. "I don't know, Anna. Something truly drastic must have occurred."

The corners of her mouth ticked upward. "As drastic as losing our memories?"

"Yes. We get along so well that I can't understand why you would leave me for another man, and I wouldn't have left you for another woman."

"That's not sufficient grounds for divorce in any case," she said, her mouth pulling into a tight line. "Only the woman's adultery matters." She shrugged. "Maybe it's not so farfetched. I rather feel like divorcing Mr. Harper, and I don't even remember him."

The shriek of a high-pitched horn made them both jump. The rattle of a carriage coming down the street drifted through the drafty window. Anna rose and walked to the window to look.

"That's a steam car!"

"In this neighborhood?" Quinn came to stand beside her, peering over her shoulder at the road below. Wisps of steam rose from the narrow chimney at the back of the two-seater, open-topped vehicle. A man in a felt bowler and a charcoal suit stepped out. "Peculiar."

"It's more than peculiar. It's suspicious."

Anna tugged on the window until it slid open a few inches. She put a finger to her lips.

Down at road level, the man rapped on a window until it opened and a woman's head popped out.

"What do you want?" she growled.

"Has a well-dressed man recently taken up residence here?"

Quinn jerked backwards. Was this their villain, come to track him down?

"Well-dressed men come here all the time, dearie," the woman replied. "This building is full of lovely ladies and men always want to pay their respects."

"He may have had a woman with him. A lady of some means. Do you know of any such couple?"

"Can't say I do."

"Do you mind if I go inside and look around?"

"Why would I mind? Go bang on anyone's door you want. You just stay out of my apartment."

Anna pushed the window closed and yanked the dusty curtain over it. "He'll be here any minute, and if we don't answer, I expect he'll break in."

Quinn looked around the room. Nowhere to hide. No way out but the door. "What if I lower you out the window and then climb out myself? Once he's inside, he'll never know."

"No good. Our trunks are here. They will give us away and he might poison some item of ours or lay a trap."

"Then what do we do?"

Anna's brow crinkled in thought, then her eyes widened. "Ravish me."

"What?"

She began to yank at the buttons of her bodice. "Ravish me, Quinn. Now, before it's too late." He stared in stupefied wonder as she wriggled out of the bodice and tossed it aside. "Don't just stand there. Either help me undress or start undressing yourself."

"Right." Quinn tugged his necktie loose, beginning to understand her reasoning. If they looked like nothing more than a man come to visit a lady for an evening of pleasure, they could hide in plain sight.

He tossed the necktie and his jacket onto the bed and grasped the top button of his waistcoat. His fingers moved slowly, his mind distracted by her peacock-blue satin corset. It had special ties up both sides so as not to compress her belly as the baby grew. A bit of her lacy chemise and the rounded swells of her generous breasts peeped from the top. Anna stepped out of her skirts and tossed those aside as well.

"Goddamn," Quinn breathed.

The chance that she had chosen these underthings for him was slim, but he couldn't have picked better himself. Her drawers and her stockings—both matching the corset—displayed gorgeous, long legs well-shaped by her active lifestyle. His eyes ran over her body, feasting on the curves of her hips, the creamy color of her exposed skin, and the swell of her belly. He didn't think he was responsible for the latter, but he would have liked to be. Maybe someday.

"I'm glad you like it." Her smile was delicious temptation with a hint of shyness. Not the practiced lure of a professional. More like a woman undressing for a new lover for the first time.

The second first time? If only he could remember the real first.

"Did you deliberately match your favorite gloves?"

Her grin broadened. "Would you like me to put them on?"

"Yes." Quinn took three steps, closing most of the space between them. "And then I will ravish you as slowly and completely as you desire."

The thud of a fist against the door shook Quinn from his erotic imaginings.

"Too late." Anna backed him into the wall beside the door and kissed him.

The kiss was entirely unlike their eager, spontaneous kiss on the ship. It was hard, deliberate, and full of premeditation. But no less thrilling. Quinn tugged bits of Anna's hair loose from the tidy knot, while his other hand settled on her deliciously rounded bum to pull her closer. She yanked his shirt free from his waistband. A button popped off, spinning away into a long-untouched corner of the room.

The heavy knock sounded again.

"Go away!" Quinn shouted. Had any actor ever had an easier part? Playing Anna's irritated, interrupted lover was as natural as breathing.

Thud. Thud. Thud.

Quinn jerked the door open a few inches and glared at the man in the hall. "What the hell do you want?" he snarled.

Anna's fingers delved inside his shirt, cold against his warm skin. He inhaled sharply.

"Tell him we're busy," she murmured, just loud enough for their unwelcome visitor to catch.

"I'm searching for a man who meets your description," the stranger said. "Seems he's been causing trouble. Mind if I step in for a moment?"

"Yes, I do mind," Quinn replied. "I am…" He reluctantly tugged Anna's hand out of his clothing. "Otherwise occupied." He pressed a kiss to her palm. "I'll be right with you, darling."

The man clamped a hand on the door to prevent Quinn from closing it. "One man. Wealthy. Light-haired. Traveling with a dark-haired woman. That's not you?"

"Afraid not. I'm a local. Good luck with your search."

Quinn attempted to close the door, but the man responded with a powerful kick, flinging it inward and nearly knocking Quinn onto his backside.

"How dare you, sir?" Anna shouted. "This is a private residence."

The man smirked. His eyes drifted over her unclothed body, and Quinn had to clench his fists to avoid grabbing the scoundrel and flinging him into the hall. The last thing they needed were accusations of assault.

"I don't recall ever seeing you before," the man said to Anna. "New to town?"

She met his lascivious gaze with an icy stare. "Not particularly."

"Well, then." In the blink of an eye, the man whipped out a pair of handcuffs, seized Anna's wrist, and manacled her to himself. "I hereby place you under arrest under the Contagious Diseases Act."

"Release me, you bastard!" Anna's free arm flew, landing a solid punch to the side of her captor's head, but he recovered quickly.

"I am no bastard, young lady. I am Inspector Fitzhubert of the Newcastle police, and I am entirely within my authority to arrest suspected prostitutes and see that they are submitted to the proper medical exams."

Quinn's world went red. No one, anywhere, would subject a woman to an unwanted intimate examination if he could do anything to stop it. He grabbed the inspector by the lapels and slammed him against the half-open door, ready to pound him into submission or unconsciousness. Anna, still shackled, stumbled along with him.

"You're in over your head, boy," Fitzhubert scoffed. He pulled something from his pocket.

Quinn's fist flew, but before flesh met flesh, a fine mist sprayed across his arm and half his face. He fell backward, gagging, his throat burning and eyes watering.

"I'll be back for you soon enough," the inspector said. "Come along, miss."

Anna strained against the chains, forcing him to drag her. "Mrs. Smith. I'm not a prostitute. I'm his wife."

"That's what they all say."

"Stop," Quinn gasped. The room had begun to swirl around him, and he could hardly even discern which way was up. He tried to move, but his limbs had grown heavy. "Don't harm her. For God's sake, man, she's not even dressed."

"They never are." Fitzhubert's voice had taken on an icy calm. "Have a nice nap, Mr. Smith. I will see you in a few hours. Not that you'll remember me." He opened the door and pulled Anna along with him.

"Quinn!" she shrieked.

"Anna." She was no more than a blur of blue. He couldn't even lift a hand to reach for her. The door banged closed and the room around him faded into oblivion.

XIX
House of Correction

ANNA HAD NO CHOICE but to walk down the stairs alongside her captor, but the moment her feet touched the ground, she began to struggle again. Escape might be a long shot, but she wasn't going to make this easy on him.

He slapped her across the face. "Enough, you stupid bitch."

Anna responded with a kick to the shins. He winced, but didn't falter. Tough, this Inspector Fitzhubert.

He dragged her to his steam car and pushed her into the passenger seat. With one fluid motion, he unsnapped the cuff from his wrist and closed it around an iron ring welded between the two seats. He did this sort of thing often, apparently.

"I am an innocent woman!" Anna shouted. "I have had my privacy invaded, been forcibly removed from my home under spurious charges, and been thrown into the street in dishabille! You'll be sorry you ever touched me!"

He ignored her shouting, walking silently around to the back of the car, and rummaging through the trunk strapped there. A moment later, he threw a ragged heap of cloth that may once have been a dressing gown at her. He climbed into the driver's seat and the vehicle lurched into motion.

126

For a few seconds, Anna considered grabbing at his hands or pummeling his head with her free hand.

No, her logical side warned. *You can't fight without risking a crash. Save your strength and plan for later.*

Anna gripped the tattered robe, shielding herself from view without letting it touch her body. Who knew what sorts of germs and vermin might infest it? A chill wind stung her skin as the car zipped down the street. Her undergarments offered little protection from the brisk autumn air. She shivered. The inspector glanced at her, smirking.

A renewed sense of rage rushed through her. Yes, she was cold. Yes, she was embarrassed to be undressed in public—her courtesan theory was crumbling—but she wouldn't be cowed by this man and his reprehensible behavior. She wadded up the dressing gown and flung it into the street. A scrawny little boy snatched it up and ran.

"Are you mad, woman?"

Anna gave the inspector a triumphant smile and sat up straighter, resting her free hand in her lap, like a lady at tea. This was how Lady Godiva must have felt. Proud. Defiant. Unashamed.

"You kidnapped me and put me in this position. It is only fitting that the world see just what sort of man you are."

He snarled a curse and drove faster. Anna shook the rest of her hair free to blow in the breeze. The cold bite of the wind on her exposed flesh felt like victory.

The reckless drive through town ended abruptly when the inspector slammed the steam car to a halt beside a massive brick wall. Anna's muscles clenched, fighting the shiver of dread the sight of the gaol produced. There would be no easy escape from such a fortress, and Quinn lay on the floor of that run-down apartment, unconscious and in danger. They might never see one another again.

Unacceptable.

Anna walked through the gate with her spine straight,

wasting no energy fighting a battle she couldn't win, forming plans in her mind. She would get herself out of this mess and then go save Quinn. No low-life whisky thief would lay a hand on her kind, adorable ex-husband and get away with it.

Inspector Fitzhubert escorted her through the gate and into the House of Correction. The other prisoners, most of whom had probably been arrested for drunk and disorderly conduct, jeered and cheered at the sight of a woman in her underthings. Anna took an odd sort of comfort from the taunts. A noisy, unruly atmosphere would provide a good distraction during an escape. Most importantly, Fitzhubert hadn't taken her to the much sturdier and better-guarded prison area. The prisoners here weren't dangerous and would be treated as more of a nuisance than anything else.

The inspector unfastened the handcuffs and pushed Anna into a cell where another woman lay snoring on the single bench. "I will be back to check on you and bring you something to wear. I expect cooperation this time. Our guards will not hesitate to punish prisoners who misbehave." He reached into his pocket and withdrew the small spray bottle that he had used on Quinn, handing it to the nearby guard who lounged against a wall, an expression of ennui on his craggy face. "If she acts up, use this on her."

The guard tucked the bottle into his front left pocket. "Yes, sir."

Anna paced the small cell, rubbing her hands together to warm them. She wished she had her gloves. She hoped whatever Inspector Fitzhubert brought her to wear would be at least moderately acceptable. She would need it eventually.

For now, however, she had more important concerns than what to wear.

Step one: get that potion bottle
Step two: get the keys
Step three: get the hell out of here

A good plan. Pity she didn't have much of an idea yet how

to achieve all of those goals. But she had time yet to spare. She would wait. Watch the guards. Consider her options.

The other inmates shouted lewd things at her, and after ignoring them for a few minutes, she walked up to the bars and stated in a calm, ladylike tone, "I beg your pardon, gentlemen, but you can all kindly go fuck yourselves."

The hoots and leers turned to uproarious laughter, and even the apathetic guard chuckled. Perfect. She had them all relaxed and liking her. She would continue to banter. Be calm. Non-threatening. Funny.

To everyone except Fitzhubert.

The moment the inspector returned, the general hubbub changed from jovial to angry. No one shouted at him directly, but they took out their aggression on one another instead, pushing, shoving, and hurling insults. Anna had no need for such an outlet. She didn't fear Fitzhubert.

No, that wasn't entirely true. She did fear him. Her cheek was still tender where he'd slapped her, and she suspected he could become far more violent if provoked. But that was nothing next to the fear that she might not escape and the fear of what might befall Quinn during her imprisonment.

Fitzhubert reached between the bars, dangling a black dress in front of her. "Put this on."

Anna remained where she was, giving the dress a brief inspection. Lacy. Likely too short. A horrid, probably choking, high neckline. Odd little ribbons on the sleeves. Not at all the simple, practical style she preferred.

"No, thank you," she said.

Fitzhubert dropped the dress on the floor. "Put it on, bitch. It's not a choice."

Anna didn't move. "You don't think so? Because I appear to be choosing not to wear it."

Someone laughed. The inspector whirled around too late to determine who. With a snarl, he turned back to Anna. "You will wear that dress, and I will not tell you again."

"I really don't think either half of that statement is true." She prodded the dress with her toe. "It's probably covered with lice. If you'd had the decency to allow me to dress, we wouldn't have this problem, now would we? But, of course, if you had that sort of decency you wouldn't have arrested me in the first place."

She would argue with him all night, if she could. The longer he remained here, the longer Quinn had to wake up and get to safety. Assuming he even realized he was in danger. Fitzhubert had said Quinn wouldn't remember him. Anna had no idea what was in that mist. The thought of Quinn suffering a double dose of memory loss potion made her shudder.

Fitzhubert stared her down, eyes ablaze with fury, but his posture was relaxed, unhurried. "I know you think you're clever, Mrs. Smith, but you won't best me. If you won't wear the dress now, the physicians who come to examine you will dress you once they have finished their inspections. Have a good evening."

"You have no right to do this," Anna retorted, refusing to let him see how sick it made her to think an unscrupulous doctor might assault her at any moment. "I am a respectable, married woman, dragged from her home and subjected to the grossest indignities!" He ignored her, but she pressed on, desperate to keep his attention as long as possible. "You drove me here in the cold, in view of everyone, with nothing to cover me!"

He paused. "That was your own doing."

"I've been provided nothing to eat or drink, and I don't have my daily medicine drops for the morning." She stepped up to the door, grasping the bars with both hands. "If anything happens to my baby because of you, I will rip out your throat with my bare hands!"

Fitzhubert stalked away, neither replying nor glancing back.

Damn. There was nothing more she could do for Quinn.

Time to focus on escape. She picked up the ugly dress and stuffed it through the bars.

"And I wouldn't wear this if it were the last dress on earth!" She hurled it as far as she could. It landed a few feet in front of the craggy-faced guard.

Anna allowed herself a moment to sink to the ground and cry. Quinn was in danger, she was worried about her baby, and horrible doctors could arrive without warning. She had thrown away the dress she needed to escape, and all she could do was wait to see if that aided her plans or ruined them.

"Miss?"

Anna wiped away tears with the back of her hand and looked up. The guard held the dress in his hand and frowned down at her with an expression of concern that softened the harsh lines of his face.

"We all have mothers, miss, and no one wants to harm your baby. Please put this on. I'll see about getting you some water and a bit of bread."

Anna shook her head. "I don't want to get lice."

"Please, miss. I think it's clean." He pushed the dress back through the bars. He was a large man, and well-trained, standing with his right hip turned away from the door so no one inside could grab at his keyring. The stance also put his left pocket in easy reach.

Anna rose slowly, stepped right up to the door, and let her left hand trail across the gauzy, black fabric. "Perhaps I could try it."

"I'd really appreciate it. You shouldn't be left like this. It's not right."

Shielded by the dress, the tip of her forefinger probed into his pocket, brushing the smooth metal of the spray bottle. She carefully pinched it between her finger and thumb, pulling it out at the same time she took hold of the dress. She took one step backward, her heart pounding. The bottle was slippery against her fingers, and she wished once again for her sturdy leather gloves.

"Thank you," she said.

"You're welcome, miss. I'll send someone to fetch you a bite to eat."

As he turned to shout for assistance, Anna tucked the small potion bottle down between her breasts.

Step one: check.

. . . ❧ . . .

The bread was moldy.

Anna picked out what good bits she could find and dumped the rest into the rusty bucket that passed for a chamber pot. Then she plopped down on the threadbare woolen blanket that had been brought with the food and pretended to inspect the dress for lice.

Hours ticked by. The noise faded to a murmur, as many of the prisoners succumbed to the late hour and drifted to sleep. Anna's cellmate continued to snore.

Sometime before dawn, a new group of guards arrived to relieve those who had been patrolling throughout the night. Anna's head snapped up, jerking her fully awake. Her guard was leaving. Taking his place was a slimmer, younger man, fresh-faced with eager, wide eyes, even in the early morning hours. Just right for her plans.

She let her head droop again, slumping against the wall, the way she had dozed for half the night. Her muscles, however, wouldn't cooperate. They had tensed up, her heart pounding in anticipation of the next big obstacle to her escape.

"Not too much trouble here tonight," her guard said. "Typical drunks, mostly sleeping off their overindulging, so should be quiet a few more hours. This one here's a lady."

Anna squeezed her eyes closed. *Relax. Relax. Sleep. Peaceful. Pretend you're in a big, soft bed.*

"She won't dress herself because she's afraid of vermin in

the cloth. Maybe she'll come around when she wakes. Doesn't like rough, angry men, so talk gentle to her and maybe she'll listen."

"How'd she get here?"

"Fitzy claims she's a whore and needs a medical exam. She says she's innocent. Maybe a fancy courtesan? Don't know. Too costly for this place, that's for sure."

"I'll try to talk to her. She shouldn't be… like that."

Anna cracked one eyelid open. The young guard was blushing at her state of undress. Excellent.

Keys jingled as the ring passed one guard to the other. Anna held her breath. Would the original guard remember the mist potion? If he tried to pass it on and discovered its absence, all her plans would crumble.

The big man clapped the smaller man on the shoulder. "'Til next time." He turned and walked away. Anna didn't exhale until he had disappeared from sight.

Thank God. Now for step two.

She gave the new guard a few minutes to settle himself, then sat up slowly, yawning and stretching, rubbing her sore neck. He noticed, but said nothing. She inspected the dress again, not that any bugs would be visible in the low light. It didn't matter. She was reasonably certain the dress was clean, and right now she was only putting on a show.

She stood up, losing the warmth of her huddled position to the cool air of the poorly insulated gaol. She shivered and her teeth chattered. It was time to dress before she took a chill and hurt herself or the baby. "Maybe I can wear this. I don't see anything crawling on it."

The young guard glanced at her, then quickly looked elsewhere. "I've been assured that it's clean, ma'am. You should put it on. Keep warm."

"Yes. I… I'll try it."

Anna stepped into the dress. As she had suspected, it was

too short, and would also be tight across her chest and belly. But it would do until she could get back to her own clothing.

If her trunk was still at Polly's. A shiver entirely unrelated to the cold shook her. Inspector Fitzhubert had not returned. What had he done during the night? Was Quinn safe, or had he been thrown into prison as she had? Or worse?

She had to pause and take several slow breaths to calm herself. She refused to be anything but hopeful. She would get out of here, find him, and save him.

She tugged the dress up, buttoning the cuffs and what she could reach of the buttons that ran up the back. This was the one part of the dress she loved. The part that played into her plans.

"Um, excuse me?"

The guard turned at her hesitant question. His nervous expression relaxed when he saw that she was covered.

"Yes, ma'am?"

"I'm so sorry. This is so awkward, but I, er, I need some help." She presented her back to him, looking over her shoulder. "I can't reach the buttons. Do you think you could? I'm so sorry to ask, but I'm cold, and…"

"Oh, yes! Of course. I, uh, let me, uh…"

"Thank you so much. You're so kind."

He turned red. Anna gave him her best smile. He really was kind. Most of the guards here probably wouldn't bother. She was lucky. Not only because of who her guards had been, but lucky to have the looks, accent, and manners of an upper-class woman. She had advantages many others never could.

The young man walked up to her cell, and she pressed her back to the door so he could reach the buttons. His fingers fumbled, and something felt slightly misaligned, but Anna repeated her thanks as he finished. She palmed the mist potion. He didn't deserve what she was about to do to him.

Before he could step away, she spun around and sprayed the potion directly into his face, grabbing a fistful of his shirt to prevent him from falling out of her reach. He coughed and gagged, then sank to the ground.

"I'm so, so sorry," Anna said.

"Wh-why?" he gasped.

"I need to escape. I have someone I need to save. I'm sorry."

The boy didn't respond. Anna tugged the keychain from his still body and quickly found the key to her cell. She slipped out and knelt briefly beside the unconscious guard to make certain he was in no distress.

"Thank you for your help."

She rose to her feet, readied the potion for its next victim, and started for the exit.

Step two: check. Step three: in progress.

XX
Forgotten and Remembered

"Ow."

Quinn rolled onto his side, trying to blink away the grogginess. A steady throbbing pounded inside his head. Had he drunk too much? And was he lying on the floor?

"Fuck."

He couldn't come up with a reason he would have drunk until he'd passed out. He'd never done that. And if he'd been ill, Anna would have made certain to get him into a proper bed.

The room came slowly into focus. Dirty floors. Peeling wallpaper. Clothing scattered about.

"Where the hell am I?"

He sat up and spent several seconds looking around. The tiny apartment reminded him of the building in Covent Garden where he'd grown up. Except that his mother would never have stood for the cobwebs in the corners, the stains on the curtains, and the lack of anything bright and cheerful.

He pushed himself to his feet and began picking up clothes

off the floor. His jacket and tie. Anna's dress and petticoat. Why was everything such a mess? This usually only happened when they were in the throes of passion. Which ought to have ended with him in bed.

"Anna?" he called out.

Unless she had actually crawled underneath the bed, he didn't think she was here. Which made the entire situation even more confusing. She wouldn't have left the room in disorder if she were going out. She wouldn't have left him alone, lying on the floor.

Or had he collapsed? Perhaps she'd run to fetch a doctor.

Quinn stretched out his arms and legs, flexing muscles and testing joints. Everything seemed in order. His breathing was normal, he felt no weakness or dizziness, and all his senses were operating as expected. No pain except for the headache. Nothing that suggested a medical emergency.

He sat down at the small table to think. His memory did seem to be off. He couldn't remember anything about how he'd gotten here. Or even where he was. The last thing he remembered was Copenhagen. Examining the adulterated shipment that had come through the new Esbjerg warehouse. Preparing to take the ferry and train to Esbjerg to meet Anna and learn what she'd discovered in her investigations.

He had no answers, so he tried to approach the situation the way she would have done. Make observations. Look for clues.

He stashed their clothes in their trunks and went to examine the pile of parcels sitting on the bed. Two new pairs of gloves, of course. Her only real indulgence. The other packages were more unusual. Handkerchiefs. A folding fan. Several items for him: 2 neckties, a pair of cufflinks, and a pocket watch.

Quinn patted the pocket in his waistcoat. Where was his watch? Had he lost or broken it? It wasn't especially valuable— this new watch was nicer—but he always kept it with him.

His business often relied upon punctuality. He tucked the new watch into his pocket, then stowed the remaining items in the trunks.

"I had more suits than this," he muttered, poking through his possessions. "And we have no money." Had they been robbed? That could explain the mess. Maybe he'd caught the thief in the act, then been clobbered on the head as the villain tried to escape. Quinn ran a hand over his temple. "No. No lumps, no pain. Wrong sort of headache."

Still, a thief made the most sense. It explained the mess, the missing items, and the reason the door didn't appear fully closed. He hurried to the window and pulled it open, leaning out in hopes of spying a thief dashing down the street, Anna hot on his tail.

Nothing. Surely he'd been unconscious too long for them to be anywhere near.

He examined the nearby buildings, searching for clues to his whereabouts. A long row of squashed tenements on either side of a narrow, cobbled street. The scarcity of lamps made it difficult to determine more. Not Esbjerg, certainly. From what he knew, it was a small town, newly built up around the harbor. This building was decades old, if not more.

A steam car turned onto the road and trundled toward him, and a sudden sense that he'd seen all this before flickered through his mind. He pulled back slightly, watching.

The car rolled to a stop in front of the building, and a man in a gray suit stepped out. Fear tingled across Quinn's skin. Could this man be his thief? And where was Anna?

Heavy footsteps pounded up the stairs. Damn. Quinn didn't want to be caught here. He was alone, unarmed, and missing a substantial chunk of his memory. He had one way out. He climbed through the window, dropped to the ground below, and dashed across the street to conceal himself in the shadows of a recessed entryway. He leaned back against the door, trying to slow his pounding heart, and watched the window.

The light coming from the apartment wavered a bit. Someone passing in front of the lamp? A moment later, a figure appeared at the window, a dark shape blocking out most of the light. Quinn stood frozen, praying that his hiding place was as dark as he'd thought.

The figure vanished from sight, and a short time later the man exited the building. He hammered on a ground-floor window with his fist until it opened.

"The man upstairs, where is he?" he demanded.

"How should I know?" the woman inside replied.

"When did he leave? Where did he go? You must have seen or heard something."

"I've heard nothing since you left here with that whore earlier. No man, no woman, no nothing. Now go away and leave us all be."

"Goddammit. At least I have the girl. He'll come after her, if he remembers anything."

The man climbed into his vehicle, slamming the door before tearing off down the road.

Quinn stared after it for some time after it had vanished from sight. He had the girl? Did he mean Anna? His fingers clenched. If that son of a bitch had kidnapped her, Quinn would strangle him. Assuming Anna didn't do it first. Most men had no idea how resourceful she was.

He cursed and ran a hand through his hair. If only he could remember what had happened. As things stood, he had no idea where to even begin a search. He couldn't remain here, though, that was certain. He walked to the nearest intersection and waited for a cab to roll by. Flagging it down, he showed the driver the gleaming new pocket watch.

"I will pay you this if you can help me carry a pair of trunks down from an apartment and then drive me to a nice hotel."

The driver's greedy grin showed crooked teeth. "Certainly, I can, sir. Show me the way."

Quinn saw his and Anna's things loaded into the carriage, and checked the room over quickly for anything of theirs he may have missed. All that remained was a chamber pot filled with what appeared to be some ruined meat pies and a wardrobe of frilly dresses that must have belonged to the room's proper resident.

He scribbled a note on the back of a receipt from one of Anna's purchases, leaving it on the table in case she came back

Not safe here. Find me at a hotel.

He had no idea how many hotels this town had, but Anna knew how to figure things out. If she were free, she'd find him. And if she weren't, he'd track her down and free her. Or die trying.

"So pleased to do business with you, Mr. Harper."

Quinn shook the banker's hand. "Thank you. I look forward to engaging your services whenever we are in Newcastle."

Newcastle. He was still baffled over that. He'd never been in Newcastle before in his life, didn't know anyone who lived in the area, and had no business associates here. Some people here bought his whisky, shipped from his warehouses in London or Edinburgh. That was the entire extent of his dealings with and knowledge of Newcastle upon Tyne. Until now.

What on earth had Anna discovered that would have led them here? And where the hell was she? He'd hardly slept last night, worrying over what might have happened to her. This was one time when he cursed his active imagination, and he'd spent all morning vowing not to let it run wild.

He stashed most of the money in his coat, in the small pocket deep inside that Anna had suggested he have tailored there. Not every suit of his had one, but he wore the ones that did whenever traveling.

That was one problem settled. Quinn walked back to the hotel and paid his bill, leaving a large tip for the concierge who had let him stay the night on credit. He then took their trunks to another hotel several blocks away, where he arranged for a room under the name of Smith. Hopefully the ruse would throw off anyone following them. Anna would have no such trouble. She often conducted her investigations under a pseudonym. Quinn not-so-secretly loved being known in certain circles as the tag-along husband to the mastermind behind Mrs. Smith's Discreet Inquiries for Genteel Ladies.

On to the next problem. Finding his wife. With luck she'd seen the note he'd left and was busy searching hotels for him.

Or she's held captive somewhere by the man with the steam car.

Quinn pushed the thought away. He had to remain optimistic. He knew nothing of that man, not even what he looked like. No way to track him down. The only choice was to investigate the one clue he had—Anna's peculiar shopping spree. He checked her receipts and headed for the first of the shops.

"Ah, Mr. Harper! So good of you to visit us. Your wife has very fine taste. Please, allow me to show you some of our merchandise and help you select a gift for her."

Quinn allowed the man to drag him in front of the wall of fans. He couldn't remember the last time he'd seen Anna use one. She wasn't the sort of woman to suffer from the vapors, nor to pretend such. And she avoided parties and crowded gatherings where she might overheat.

"My wife was here yesterday?" he asked.

"Yes, indeed. She purchased one of our finest fans. She has exquisite taste."

"Naturally." Quinn knew the lingo of business. Finest meant most expensive. Anna didn't choose expensive unless it meant sturdy and practical. And the fan he'd seen among her purchases was dainty and frilly. Which meant she'd been investigating. But what? "She only chooses the very best. I'm sure she peppered you with questions."

"Indeed, indeed. She was most selective."

"Did she inquire after other customers, or..." Or what? How did Anna do this? Quinn was used to straightforward talk. He liked organization and numbers.

Here's my product. Try it. You like it? Good. Here's the price.

Flattering customers? Awkward. Dropping vague hints? Difficult. Prying information out of a stranger? Impossible.

"No, no." The fan seller laughed. "She doesn't care for trends. She sets trends. Now let me show you what I recommend for her."

A quarter hour later, Quinn considered himself lucky to escape with only a single new fan—a sturdy, pale green one that reminded him of the dress Anna had been wearing on the day they met. He left the shopkeeper with the name of his new local banker to settle the account and reluctantly headed for the next store on the list.

Quinn visited three more shops—barely managing to keep from purchasing unnecessary things while learning absolutely nothing—before giving up and heading back toward his hotel.

Please, God, let Anna have left me a message.

If much more time passed with no sign of her, he would have nowhere to turn but the police. *Kidnapped by a man with a steam car. Maybe.* But at least he could describe her and give some idea of her whereabouts the previous day. For now, he would check back at the flat where he'd woken yesterday. He could see if she'd found his note or left one behind for him.

"Mr. Smith! I'd been wondering what had become of you."

Quinn whirled around at the sound of the familiar voice, thinking he must be mistaken. His eyes tracked over several men in similar suits, then snagged on a crooked nose. Memory flashed of his friend and employee, battered and bleeding. Quinn blinked, then looked again. Wilhelm Petersen. It *was* him. What was he doing here, where Harper-Douglass had no warehouses, and did it have anything to do with the ruined shipments?

"The police have been searching for you, Mr. Smith," Petersen said, striding toward Quinn.

Quinn frowned at his friend and employee. "Why are you calling me that, Peterson, and what the hell are you doing in Newcastle? Who's overseeing the shipments? What the devil is going on? Where's Anna?"

Petersen stumbled to a halt, his mouth opening in surprise. He snapped it quickly closed and composed himself. "Mr. Harper. I see you have remembered yourself."

Quinn stalked toward him, not wanting to shout on a public street. "I don't remember a goddamn thing. I woke up in bloody Newcastle, robbed of all my money. My wife is missing and one of my chief distributors is wandering town calling me by a false name instead of in Edinburgh doing his job. Care to explain?"

"Ah." A smile spread across Petersen's face. "I would be delighted to explain. Let's go have a drink and I'll fill in all those pesky missing details for you."

"No."

"Come now, Harper, you're obviously in distress. A glass of your best Scotch will do you good."

"What will do me good is finding my wife. Where is she? I don't even know where to begin to look. I'm terrified she could be lost, or even imprisoned."

Petersen's smile dissolved. "No, she's certainly not imprisoned." Was that anger in his voice? Why? Petersen had always liked Anna. "Let's go for that drink. You'll want to be sitting down for this."

Quinn grabbed his friend by the lapels. "Tell me where she is, goddammit."

Petersen pried Quinn's fingers off of him and stepped back. "She's left you, Harper. Gone. Run off."

"What?"

"I think there's another man."

Impossible. Anna loved him. He could recall with perfect clarity the way she looked up at him with rapt adoration. He remembered the unshed tears shimmering in her eyes when they had parted weeks ago. Her echo of his own sadness that day: *I'll miss you.* The passion in her kiss. Quinn had never, not once, doubted her affection and loyalty.

"Don't be daft," he said.

"I swear it's true. She's deceived you, old chap."

Quinn shook his head. "You don't know her the way I do. If she's run off, it's for some other reason."

"I'm afraid not. I'm sorry to bring you such terrible news. Are you certain you don't want that Scotch?"

"Fine, fine," Quinn relented. "Let's go have a drink. You can tell me everything you know, and I'll explain why you're entirely wrong." *As much as I can without revealing that she's been secretly investigating everyone in the whole damned company.*

"Excellent." Petersen's cheerful grin returned at last. "I've got a bottle waiting with your name on it."

XXI

Search and Rescue

ANNA PEEKED OUT the carriage window. Across the wide street, chaos still swirled around the gaol's main gate. She was taking a risk, remaining so close, but when she'd seen the parked cab with its sleeping driver it had seemed the perfect place to rest and regroup. She was tired, hungry, and still a bit cold. Too easy to catch if she ran. Men had been dispatched in all directions, however, assuming she had done exactly that.

At the moment, her perilous hiding place was ideal. She had a prime view of Inspector Fitzhubert, who stood scowling outside the gate, receiving a thorough dressing-down.

"I question your reasons for incarcerating the woman in the first place," Fitzy's superior was saying, "but that was, perhaps, the least irresponsible thing you have done in the past twenty-four hours. You made unauthorized use of a memory potion, allowed said potion out of your control, and did it all within sight and reach of a woman whose intellect is obviously far superior to your own. We have ten men in there who can't even remember what day of the week it is, much less how they came to be sprayed. Ten! Do you think we can afford such a lapse in security? I had to pull a dozen extra men away from their wives and children to take care of this mess. And now men are dashing all about town, merely to track down a single prostitute. I think I'll have you stand in for some of the guards for a time. You seem to have forgotten where you came from. Come with me. I don't want you out of my sight until I've written up my report and reprimand."

The two men disappeared through the gate, and Anna pulled back from the window. Blast. As enjoyable as it was to watch Fitzhubert receive a scolding, she would have preferred some hint as to who had hired him. He'd come for her and Quinn specifically, and that meant someone must have sent him.

The driver of the cab snorted and stirred. Her cue to leave. Anna slipped from the vehicle and hurried down the street, keeping her head down and shoulders hunched, as if in distress over whomever she was mourning. A dead husband would be best. The straight, slim styling of her skirt made her belly more obvious than usual. People would be likely to help a bereaved, young mother-to-be.

The brisk walk to Polly's neighborhood relieved Anna of much of the lingering chill from the night in the gaol. Her hands, though, remained cold, and her stomach had gone a bit queasy from lack of food. Soon, fortunately, she would be reconnected with her possessions. She could don her gloves and take her pregnancy potion. She would have to pawn some of the items she had bought yesterday, but then she would spoil herself with a hearty breakfast. She'd be no help to Quinn if she were weak from hunger.

Anna still held out hope that he might have escaped. Certainly he hadn't been brought into the drunk tank last night as she had. And it was too terrible to think of him elsewhere in the prison, with the hardened criminals. She'd never be able to rescue him. Everyone at the gaol was now on high alert, and the mist potion was all but empty.

Anna slowed her steps as she turned onto Polly's street,

bowing her head again and playing her best mournful widow. She had to assume that men would be watching the apartment. It was a logical place for her to return to. But what choice did she have? She had to know what had happened to Quinn.

She approached from the opposite side of the street, looking for any men who looked out-of-place. Directly across from the apartment, a man sat slumped against a wall, a half-empty bottle in his hand. Several people stepped right over his outstretched legs as they walked down the street. Anna followed right along with them. The man reeked of spirits and his clothes were soiled, but he had suspiciously nice boots. A fake drunk. She continued on until she could duck around the next corner.

A plan of attack formed quickly in her mind, but she stood fidgeting on the street corner for several minutes before appropriate assistance came along.

"Excuse me, sir," Anna said to the white-haired man who thunked along the road too quickly to truly need the cane he was using. "I'm so sorry to trouble you, but I need help. M-my things are just around the corner, on the upper floor of number thirteen, b-but I'm afraid to go there. This drunk man, he was y-yelling and l-leering at me and I'm so scared. My brother is supposed to be waiting for me, but I don't know if he's h-home and I can't get to the apartment to find out. Could you look and see if he's there? Tell him Anna is waiting around the corner. And if he's out could you fetch me a few things? P-please? I'm so alone."

She buried her face in her hands to disguise the fact that she couldn't actually cry on cue.

The man withdrew a handkerchief and held it out to her. "You poor dear. The nerve of some men, preying on a sweet, grieving lady. What do you need me to fetch for you?"

Anna dabbed at her eyes. "The medicine for my baby." She placed a hand on her belly to emphasize the bump. "It should be at the bottom of my trunk. And a gold pocket watch. Still in its box. It was to be a present for my husband."

She covered her face again, turning away.

"I will be right back. Number thirteen, you said?"

"Yes. First floor. The apartment on the left. Thank you so, so much."

The man rushed off, eager to play white knight to her damsel in distress. Anna toyed with the ugly ribbons on her sleeves, contemplating picking the stitches out while she waited. Several minutes later she again heard the thunk of the cane on the pavement, and her gallant older gentleman reappeared.

"I'm terribly sorry, my dear, but there were no trunks in the apartment, nor any young man. Only this note. You did say number thirteen, didn't you?"

"Yes." She accepted the slip of paper and looked it over. One of her receipts, with a brief message written in Quinn's handwriting. He hadn't been captured. She let out a long, slow breath. "He's gone to a hotel."

"Er, yes. So it appears. I think he would have done better to wait for you and escort you there himself, rather than all this cryptic note writing. These young boys…"

"Oh, he's older than I am. Almost thirty."

His birthday is November the second. What a useless time to remember such a thing.

Her helpful gentleman huffed. "All the more reason to behave sensibly. When I was a youngster, we were expected to be working like a man at sixteen and married at twenty. Why, by thirty I had a whole heap of little ones."

Quinn wouldn't have any little ones by thirty. Her little one would belong to Mr. Harper. Mr. Harper whom she couldn't remember at all and who didn't appear to have made any effort to come after her. The bastard. For a woman who did inquiries, she apparently didn't do proper research when choosing her own husbands.

"You've been so kind, thank you." Anna returned the handkerchief, made a little curtsy, and turned down the road. She would loop around and head back the way she had come. Yesterday's explorations around town remained fresh in her mind, thankfully. The area near the train station housed a number of hotels, and she knew her way there.

Anna tucked Quinn's note into her sleeve, because the awful dress had zero pockets. Ridiculous. She didn't know what he had sold to pay for the hotel, but as long as she had a dress of her own and her gloves and her medicine, she wouldn't mind. She only hoped she wouldn't need to search too many hotels to find him. She would vastly prefer to have her breakfast before lunchtime.

Partway down Neville Street, she stopped, frozen with the sudden certainty that she knew where he was. She read the sign again and laughed aloud. Several people cast puzzled glances at the jovial widow, but Anna couldn't have suppressed her amusement if she'd tried. There, splashed across the side of a five-story stone edifice with pretty, round-topped windows were the words, "The Douglas Hotel."

"Harper-Douglass," she chuckled softly. If Quinn had selected any hotel, it would be this one. She gave herself a moment for her laughter to pass, then headed inside.

"Excuse me," she said to the man at the desk. "Is a Mr. Quinn Smith registered here? I'm supposed to meet him. I am his sister, Mrs. Harper."

Her widow-with-a-baby appearance worked its magic again, and the concierge jumped to help her. The deception gnawed at her conscience. This world held too many real widows and fatherless babes who needed far more help than she did. Anna was a practiced gameswoman, however, and she wasn't one to let an advantage go to waste. Her opponent certainly wouldn't hesitate to grab any opportunity.

"Mr. Smith checked in this morning, but he is out at the moment. Would you like to wait for him to return? I can seat you in the lounge. Or you are welcome to take breakfast in the dining room."

Her stomach growled audibly.

"The dining room it is. Please follow me, Mrs. Harper."

Anna filled her belly with the best breakfast in all the days she could remember, all the while wondering how many things Quinn had sold off to afford such quality accommodations. The gold pocket watch, certainly. Maybe his cufflinks. Her amber-colored evening gown. She hadn't given it much thought before, but it would fetch an excellent price, even sold second-hand.

Sudden, surprising tears filled her eyes. She'd never worn that dress, and it had been special. If it was gone, she could never show it off for him.

Him. Him who? Her husband? Quinn? Someone else entirely? She wiped away her tears with her napkin. No sense crying over something that might not even be gone. Especially when she couldn't entirely remember her reasons for having it.

If it wasn't gone, she would try it on at the first opportunity. Perhaps wearing something that had sentimental significance to Past Anna would help Present Anna remember more of herself.

Much revived by the late-morning repast, Anna left a note at the desk in case Quinn returned and she started out to look for him. He would almost certainly be out looking for her, which unfortunately pointed her right back at the gaol. She hated to go back, but it was a risk she had to take. She needed to catch him up before he did anything foolish. From here, she could walk up Grainger Street toward the markets, then take a right and head toward the gaol. It probably wasn't the most efficient route, but it was the one she knew, and she certainly didn't have "getting lost" on her to-do list.

The streets were bustling this morning, with steam cars and horse-drawn carriages jockeying for position while pedestrians dashed here and there in pursuit of business or leisure, many wielding umbrellas in deference to the grayish clouds that blocked out most of the sun. Anna had no umbrella, no cloak, no hat. If it rained, she'd persevere.

In the midst of all the commotion, she caught a flash of red-blond hair. She spun around for a better look. Was that Quinn across the street? The crush of traffic obscured her view. She darted around an ox-cart and dodged an elegant coach-and-four in time to see the ginger headed man disappear into a public house. It looked like Quinn, but from behind at this distance she couldn't be certain. And why would he be visiting a pub at this time of day? Was he so discouraged in his search for her that he needed a drink? She raced down the street and reached for the door. She had to see if it was him.

"Hey, now, you can't go in there!" A rough hand clamped down on her wrist. "No women allowed."

Anna pulled away from his grasp. "What? Don't be absurd. Surely there are women inside, serving the food and drink."

"Women work here. They're not customers. You can't go in. We can't have ladies smoking cigars and drinking whisky. Next they'll be wanting to sit in Parliament."

"I think that's an excellent idea, and I happen to be very fond of whisky. Excuse me." She reached for the door handle again, but he stopped her once more.

Anna sighed and fished the mist potion out from beneath her bodice. "You have a choice. Either you allow me to enter, or I spray you in the face with a memory loss potion."

"Are you off your head, woman? Go away."

"Very well." Anna took a step backward to keep from inhaling any of the mist and sprayed the man fully in the face. Moments later, he lay on the ground, unconscious. "Sadly, you are not likely to recall our conversation, but just in case some of this gets through to you, I suggest you reconsider your opinion on women in Parliament." She stepped over his prone body and opened the door.

It took a few moments for Anna's eyes to adjust to the dim lighting inside the pub. The chatter of voices echoed off the low ceiling, and serving girls bustled from table to table with drinks and sandwiches. Anna scanned the customers, ignoring their curious stares.

There! She rushed deeper into the room. It *was* Quinn! He sat at a table near the rear of the pub, talking to a man whose back was to Anna. Quinn held a glass in his hand, and a partly empty bottle sat on the table in front of him. A familiar, square, glass Harper-Douglass Whisky bottle.

"No! Quinn!"

He looked up at her cry. "Anna!" He sprang from his seat. "Anna, you're here! You're safe!"

"Quinn, don't drink that whisky!"

The man sitting with Quinn swore as he, too, leapt to his feet. He grabbed the glass of whisky, tossed the contents in Quinn's face, and ran off, shielding himself from view.

For a second, Anna considered running after the villain, but then Quinn wobbled and grabbed for the back of his chair. Anna rushed to his side.

"Anna? What's going on?" He plopped into the chair. "I'm sorry. I don't feel well. My head is... I'm all dizzy."

"Who was that? Who were you drinking with?"

"What?"

She grabbed the nearest chair and sat beside him, grasping his hand. "Quinn, look at me. Do you remember me?"

"Anna. What's happening?"

"Think, Quinn. Think very hard. Who was that man? Who gave you that drink?"

"I... I don't know. I'm sorry." He closed his eyes and massaged his temple. "I think I'm ill. Maybe if I rest a moment..."

"Quinn."

He neither opened his eyes nor responded.

"Quinn. Look at me. Remember. Please, try to remember."

He shook his head. "I'm sorry, did someone say something?" He took a deep breath and opened his eyes again. "Strange headache. I think it's fading, though." He blinked several times. "Where am I?" His gaze settled on Anna and he stared at her in perplexed silence.

"Quinn?" His name came out in a trembling whisper.

"I'm sorry, do… do I know you?"

XXII

Love at Third-First Sight

BEAUTIFUL YOUNG WIDOW sitting in a pub, weeping her heart out. That was something you didn't see everyday.

Or at least Quinn thought it wasn't something one saw everyday. It was hard to be certain when he couldn't seem to remember much of anything. He knew his name was Quinn, because someone—the weeping woman, he thought—had called him by name several times during this strange wave of illness that had left his head all muddled. He looked down at the empty glass and the bottle sitting on the table. It didn't appear that he'd drunk much. So why was his head pounding? And why did he feel sick to his stomach?

The sensible thing would be to lie down until he recovered, but at the moment his own woes paled beside the broken-hearted tears of the woman sitting next to him. He wanted nothing more in the world than to pull her into his arms and soothe her. Which was ridiculous. He didn't even know who she was.

"Please don't cry," he said.

Quinn wanted to smack himself. Of all the inane things to say. She had every right to cry if she needed. He could have said, "What can I do to help?" or, "Here's a handkerchief," or even better, he could have simply let her be.

Everything in him recoiled at the "let her be" idea. *Hold her,* his brain screamed. *Kiss her. Tell her you will never let her go.*

Apparently he was some kind of obsessive madman. He patted down his pockets, looking for a handkerchief. He didn't find one, but he did discover an enormous wad of banknotes tucked into a secret pocket. Apparently he was a very wealthy obsessive madman.

"Oh, Quinn," the woman sighed, dabbing at her astounding amber eyes with her sleeve. She wasn't wearing any gloves. Why did that strike him as peculiar? "Do you remember anything at all?"

"I'm quite certain my name is Quinn. And you look so…" *Beautiful. Desirable. Like my every erotic fantasy come to life.* Goddamn, but he was a scoundrel. "Familiar." His stomach churned again, and he closed his eyes against the nausea. "Please pardon me. I'm not feeling well."

Tears were still leaking from her eyes, but the dazzling woman rose from her seat and held out a hand to him. "We need to talk, but it shouldn't be here. Will you come with me?"

I'll come with you anywhere, love.

Quinn took her hand, the feel of her cold fingers against his sending a new jolt of protectiveness through him. He wanted to warm her with his own body, skin-to-skin. Which meant he ought to stay right where he was. To keep her safe from his lecherous thoughts and unseemly desires. For God's sake, she was a grieving widow. A grieving widow who was in a family way, from the looks of things.

He rose from his seat. "Where are we going?"

"The hotel. Do you remember taking a room at a hotel?"

"No."

"Do you remember where you are? Or how you came to be in this pub? Any details at all?"

"No. Sorry." The room spun, and he stumbled.

The woman gripped his arm. "Let's get you out of here. We can pretend you're drunk, I suppose."

His head pounded. He didn't think he was drunk. Was he drunk? He felt ill. How had he gotten here? Who was clutching his arm?

He blinked at her to clear his vision. God, she was beautiful. Inky black hair that he wanted to wrap around his fingers. Luminous eyes that were neither brown, nor gold, nor orange, but some color that mingled all three. Her clothing suggested she was a widow, which was perfect, because he wanted to marry her.

"I think maybe I've lost my mind," he said, unsure if he was talking to himself or to her.

"You'll be all right." Her voice carried a little tremor, but she spoke firmly. "I will make certain you'll be all right."

She guided him out of the… the what? Pub? Was that the word? Had he been inside? And where was he now? Walking down a… street?

Words were slow to form in his mind. The world swayed around him, and his vision blurred. His stomach clenched and heaved.

"Ex-excuse me. I think I'm—"

He staggered, fell to his knees, and lost the entire contents of his stomach over the curb and into the road.

"I'm here." Gentle hands came to rest on his shoulders, rubbing slow, comforting circles. "I'm here, Quinn. You'll be fine. I promise."

He gagged and retched until his throat burned and his eyes watered. He gasped big, heaving breaths as his stomach at last began to settle.

"God. I feel like I've been poisoned."

"Yes."

Quinn looked up at the woman as she continued to rub his back. She had the softest touch and the sweetest voice.

"I think I love you," he said.

"You may have, once. We used to be married."

"We did?" His brows knit in confusion. "But we no longer are?" He made a thorough examination of her person, taking in her sad, red-rimmed eyes and the ill-fitting mourning dress. "Fuck. Am I dead? Is that what this is? Are you my widow?"

Her eyes grew round for several seconds and then she laughed. A long, hard, belly-shaking laugh that brought tears of mirth to her eyes. "Oh, Lord, Quinn. I'm so sorry. I shouldn't be laughing, because you've lost your memory again and it's so awful, but the look on your face, and you were so serious, and…" She dissolved into laughter again.

"Not dead, then."

"No." She blew out a long, sharp breath, composing herself. "Have you recovered, Ghost of Mr. Quinn Smith? Do you think you can walk now? We have many things to discuss. I'm going to do all I can to help you regain those memories."

Quinn pushed himself to his feet. He wobbled a bit, and a bad taste remained in his mouth, but the nausea had passed and the headache was fading. "I think I can walk."

"Good. Let's go to the hotel and get you a glass of cool water and a bed to lie down on." She gripped his arm and helped him to his feet.

"Hotel?"

"Yes. The Douglas Hotel. You have a good, but slightly twisted, sense of humor when you remember yourself."

"I seem to have forgotten it, because I can't understand what would be funny about the name of a hotel."

"We have something of a history with the Harper-Douglass Whisky Company."

"We do? You and I? We have some sort of connection then?"

"We used to be married. I just told you that."

"I'm sorry. I'm having a hard time remembering anything." He put a hand to his stomach. "And I'm beginning to feel ill."

The lovely woman tugged him down the road. "This might be a very long walk."

Quinn looked around the hotel room, trying to recall if he'd been here before. A sense of familiarity nagged at him, but he honestly wasn't certain if it was the room, the table, or the woman seated across from him. He lifted a steaming cup of tea to his lips and took a sip. He grimaced at the peculiar floral taste.

"What *is* this?"

Anna's cheeks paled. "Have you forgotten everything again?"

"I haven't forgotten. But this is *not* tea."

"Oh. Yes. My apologies. It's chamomile. It should help you relax and recover."

Quinn attempted another sip. The flavor did not improve with time. "It's disgusting. It might make me vomit again."

"Please don't. Four times was quite enough, thank you."

"I only remember twice."

Anna rubbed her temple with a gloved hand. "It was four times, believe me. You were frighteningly ill and you couldn't remember a thing for more than a few minutes at a time. You scared me, Quinn."

She was still scared. The little worried crinkles at the corners of her eyes betrayed her. Quinn hated that he'd done this to her and wished he could remember anything at all about the events that had led him to drink the poisoned whisky.

He took another sip of the chamomile tisane. It tasted like flowers steeped in sewage, but if it would bring Anna some peace, he'd drink it anyway. He was rapidly falling in love with her. A habitual problem of his, apparently.

He scanned the notes and various items that covered the table. The bits and pieces of his recovered life.

"Would you like me to review again?" he asked.

"If it helps you remember." She poured herself a cup of the not-tea and sipped it. Strangely enough, she looked to take pleasure from it.

"My name is Quinn Smith. You are Anna Harper, formerly Anna Smith, nee some maiden name that we don't know. We were married once and I must have been the world's biggest fool to let you get away."

She smiled at that. "Maybe I discovered something about you that made me leave. I'm an investigator, you know. But maybe we are different people now. Better people."

Quinn glanced at his notes. "I used to think I was a scoundrel, but you have disproved that theory in multiple ways. I, likewise, have disproved your theory that you are a courtesan. We met in Esbjerg, both having lost our memories." His recollection of that time had begun to return after reading through their notes, though it all remained fuzzier than he would have liked. "I have since had some other memory difficulties." He reached across the table and laid his hand atop hers. "Thank you for helping me through that."

"You're welcome. It must have been a particularly large dose of potion. You were far worse than either of us were the first time. I think you are fortunate to have expelled as much of it from your body as you have."

His fingers curled around hers, giving her a little squeeze. "These blue gloves are your favorite. I remember that. And more. You dislike jewelry, but you love pockets."

Another small smile touched her lips. "Which brings us to the contents of your own pockets." She withdrew her hand and gestured at the stack of banknotes. "Sometime after Fitzhubert sprayed you with one memory potion and before you drank another, you acquired a large sum of money."

"Fifty pounds, apparently. I can still read and count. Both positive signs."

"But how did you come by this money? Did you rob a bank? Did you win an enormous wager? Do you have a banker in town? I could find no evidence that a Mr. Quinn Smith was known here, but perhaps I was asking the wrong people."

Quinn rubbed his own brow. "I remember nothing of that time, I'm afraid. I barely remember the tussle with the police inspector, and then only because…"

"Because what?"

His eyes locked on her gloves. If he concentrated, he could pull up the image of Anna clad only in a corset and drawers of the same color. "Because of what you were wearing."

"Ah."

"The bright colors help me remember."

She smirked at him. "Of course. And my state of undress is merely a coincidence."

"No, that is memorable as well. But I'm serious about the bright colors. Your gloves are the same. I look at them and it triggers memories."

Anna nodded. "Yes, stimulating the senses has helped in the past. Sounds. Scents. Tastes."

She was looking at his mouth. Was she thinking about kissing him? God, did he hope so. He wanted to kiss her more than just about anything. He'd drink the whole revolting pot of chamomile tea, if it meant she'd kiss him.

She popped up out of her chair. "I have an idea!"

"Does it involve kissing?"

Quinn cursed his loose tongue as he rose from his seat. He remembered enough to know that manners dictated he stand when a lady did, but apparently he couldn't remember how to carry on an appropriate conversation.

Anna seized his hand. "Not just yet. Let's concentrate on getting you back to your old self first. The self you were yesterday, that is. Before all this madness. Follow me."

She led him from the room, down the stairs, and through the hotel dining room. She didn't stop at the swinging doors to the kitchens, but rather walked right in, as if she owned the place, saying no more than, "Pardon me."

A maelstrom of smells engulfed him, infiltrating his nose, penetrating his brain, triggering a deluge of memories of food, kitchens, and meals cooked and eaten.

Anna gestured at a massive stove, where multiple dishes sat simmering in their pots. "You like to cook. Make us some dinner. See what you remember."

Quinn's hands acted of their own volition. Under the stares of the dumbfounded chefs, he began to gather ingredients, chopping and mixing with practiced efficiency. Anna fended off questions and protests with the explanation that, "Mr. Smith is an extremely important guest."

Code for, "he's rich." Carries-fifty-pounds-on-his-person rich. Who even did that? Who the hell was he? Rich men didn't cook for themselves.

Unless he'd become rich by opening a restaurant? No, this stew he was making—new memory, he had a fondness for stew—could serve a small family and no more. He didn't know how well it would scale up. Not a professional chef, then.

"Is there bread we could serve with this?" he asked the crowd. "Small rounds that I could hollow out would be best. I won't need it immediately. This should simmer for at least a half hour before we eat it."

His heart lightened. He knew this. He enjoyed this. The memories were unclear, but he hadn't lost himself. He was stumbling in the dark, perhaps, but he was there, making his way. He glanced at Anna. Her smile was radiant, the worry gone from her face. She'd done this. She'd given him this connection to himself. Such a brilliant, astounding woman.

If there's one good thing about this brain rot, it's that I get to enjoy relearning all the reasons that I love her.

And he was going to make her a dinner to remember.

While the stew simmered, he began snatching up other ingredients. The chefs had mostly returned to their duties, but they seemed to respect that he knew his way around a kitchen, and tolerated his presence.

"The stew will be simmering longer than half an hour," he said to Anna. "And I'll be adding a special surprise. Why don't you head back to the room, do your investigating, take a bath, read a book, or whatever you'd like. I'll be ready around seven with dinner."

A bit of the worry returned to her eyes. "I don't want to leave you. Last time we were apart, bad things happened."

"Could you perhaps peek into the kitchen every half hour to check on me?"

Her mouth twisted slightly as she considered his suggestion. "A fair compromise. And I would love a nice hot bath. I will see you again shortly."

Promptly at seven, Quinn entered his hotel room carrying two bread bowls filled with meaty stew. He set them down at the table and shared a quiet, happy meal with the woman he loved.

"Thank you for that, Anna. It helped more than you can possibly know. I remember so many things now. My childhood home. My mother. Holidays we shared. Cooking for you in Esbjerg. Making sandwiches for you and Polly just the other day. But more importantly, I feel like Quinn again, not a Quinn-shaped shell."

Her face glowed with happiness. "I'm so glad."

They said little else as they ate, but Quinn was content to watch Anna. Every smile was precious. He treasured each tiny memory sparked by the way she turned her head or drummed her fingers.

They had just finished up when a knock sounded at the door. Perfect timing. Quinn rose and accepted the tray containing half-a-dozen lemon tartlets he had made just for her.

"Ooh!" Anna licked her lips and eyed the dessert with a greedy gleam in her eye. "I love lemon tarts."

"I know. The moment I smelled lemon I remembered that. Here. Try one." He held one up to her lips and she took a bite, closing her eyes and sighing with pleasure.

"It's so good. You made these?"

"Yes. Just for you. To thank you. For everything. For caring." He popped the rest of the tartlet into her mouth, shivering as her tongue brushed his fingertips. Standing this close to her, he could smell the soap she had used to wash her hair. A hint of rose.

She sighed again and a memory flashed through his mind. One she had told him of, but that he hadn't been able to recall until this very second. No space between them. The same scent. But a different sort of sigh.

"Anna."

She opened her eyes. "Yes?"

"Anna, I remember the closet again."

She took the tray from his hands and set it down on the table, then wrapped her arms around his neck. "Show me."

XXIII
No Regrets

QUINN DIDN'T KISS HER. Anna's heart sank as he grasped her wrists and freed himself from her embrace. Perhaps he didn't want her after all. Maybe this crazed attraction was more one-sided than she had realized. Had he recovered enough of himself to have some sense of why he'd divorced her?

"No, no," he murmured, spinning her around. He pressed up against her and put his lips to her ear. "It was like this."

Anna relaxed in his arms. Not one-sided after all. He sucked gently on her earlobe, triggering a delicious tickling sensation that raced clear down to her toes. Her brain swept her away to another time and place, where he had kissed her and whispered this way.

"Your earlobes have no holes. Do you not wear earrings?"

"Never. I don't like jewelry."

"Interesting." He kissed along her neck, tugging the sleeve of her gown down to expose her shoulder. "What do you like?"

"This."

Yes, she certainly liked this. She liked the softness of his lips and the gentle brush of his fingers. She liked the memories of Past Quinn his touch triggered. She liked the way Present

Quinn popped the buttons of her bodice one-at-a-time, whenever he ran out of skin to caress.

"In the closet you were wearing an evening gown," he said. "It showed a great deal more skin. One button and a few little tugs and it was practically falling off."

"That sounds very naughty of me." Quinn's hand dipped inside of her bodice and she gave a little squeak. "Was I trying to seduce you?"

"I doubt you needed to try."

His hand covered her breast, massaging it through the fabric of her corset. She pressed into his touch. Part of her wanted to fling all her clothing aside and have him now. The other part wanted him to take all night. She wiggled her hips, pushing her bottom more firmly against him, wanting to feel the hardness of his erection.

Quinn ground against her in response. "Yes, love, you drive me as wild as I drive you." His tongue dragged across her shoulder where he had pulled away her clothing. "Maybe more so."

"Quinn," she gasped. "Why do I feel we've been apart too long? How long? I can't remember."

"Weeks?" He tugged her bodice off and began to unlace her corset, his mouth still feasting on her bared neck and shoulders. "Months?"

Anna's whole body was afire. She needed more of his touch. More of herself exposed to him. She unfastened her skirts and let them pool at her feet. "I don't understand."

He unhooked the busks of her loosened corset and tossed the garment aside. "Don't understand what, love?"

"Why I would ever leave you."

He stilled. "We shouldn't be doing this, should we?"

"I don't know." Nothing made sense. Her body longed for him and her brain couldn't seem to process anything else. Perhaps she had potion-brain as well. Had she inhaled some of the mist potion while escaping the jail? Because she couldn't reconcile the rightness of his embrace with the wrongness of having a different husband. Shouldn't it have been the other way around?

Quinn stepped around to face her and pressed a kiss to her forehead. "I won't do anything you don't want. As much as I want to make love to you, I don't ever want it to be something you regret."

Anna brushed her lips across his, her fingers loosening his tie. "I want to make love too. I won't regret it."

He kissed her reverently, easing her lips apart to begin a full, leisurely exploration. "You taste like lemon tart," he murmured when at last they paused for air.

Anna grinned and slipped from his arms. "I think you should as well."

She selected a tartlet from the tray and held it to his lips. He downed it in one bite, slowly licking his lips to capture any stray drops of filling. Their eyes locked.

"Delicious," they said in unison.

They both burst out laughing. Quinn held his arms open, and Anna tumbled against him, kissing him between giggles. He scooped her off the floor and carried her to the bed. He threw off his waistcoat and shirt and lay beside her.

"I adore you, Anna Harper." He teased her nipples through the sheer fabric of her chemise. "Every moment that passes, every memory I regain, increases my desire for you."

Anna snaked a finger down Quinn's chest. "This is what I can't understand. We fit so well together. We make such a good team." She paused just above his waistband, then lifted her finger to his mouth, tracing his upper lip. He nipped playfully at her fingertip. "This passion between us is magnificent. Why ruin something so fine?"

"We were penniless and feared our child would starve. You divorced me and married a wealthy man to keep us all safe."

"That's ridiculous. You clearly have a great deal of money."

His mouth scrunched up as he thought. "Perhaps I'm a

gambler. I ruined us. You made an advantageous match. I happen to be on a run of good luck of late." He lifted her chemise, and she allowed him to pull it up and over her head. "Extremely good luck."

"I don't believe it. You're not reckless enough."

"No?" He pressed a kiss between her breasts, then beneath them, working his way down over her round belly.

"Perhaps I discovered you couldn't have children and I desperately wanted a family of my own."

Quinn found the ties of her drawers and undid the bow. "You wouldn't need to marry the man to get a child. And you're a good-hearted woman. You would have suggested we adopt a child in need." He whisked the drawers away and kissed her inner thigh. Anna trembled. "No, it must have been for money. A marriage of convenience to a boring old man. Hopefully impotent as well."

"I don't find it very convenient to be… ooh… married to someone I… oh… don't love. Oh, Quinn."

His tongue stroked across her sex, teasing the taut nub where her pleasure centered. Anna clutched the bedsheets and arched into him.

"Oh, yes," she sighed. *Just like in the library.*

As his mouth continued working magic, he slipped a finger inside her, nudging her bit by bit toward climax. A second finger followed, hitting just the right spot. Anna gasped.

Yes, yes.

How long had her body been craving this? Craving him. Them. Together, soaring to new heights of pleasure. Anna contorted as Quinn's skillful mouth sent her spiraling into bliss. She cried out his name, trembling as waves of ecstasy washed over her.

When the tremors subsided, Quinn slowly crawled up beside her, nuzzling her neck. "More?"

"Yes, please."

He shucked his trousers and lifted her atop him, letting

her position herself for maximum comfort. Anna took control, taking him inside her, riding him slowly at first, watching him close his eyes and lick his lips in pleasure. His eager moans spurred her on.

Mine. My Quinn. My own.

Anna rocked faster and harder, loving his desperate groans and rapturous expression. His eyes had glazed over. His fingers tangled in the sheets, crushing them the way she had only moments ago.

Passion built inside her again, her body thrilling to the erotic sight of Quinn finding his release. When he let out a strangled cry, it took her over the edge. Together, they collapsed into a tangled heap.

"Did I say before that you were amazing?" Quinn asked. "Because I was wrong. You're super, extra, marvelously amazing."

Anna snuggled him. He was warm and cozy and exactly where she wanted to curl up and sleep. This was where she belonged. Distant memories fluttered just out of reach. Time spent in his arms. Happy times. She was too sleepy to grasp them.

She kissed him, then burrowed beneath the bedclothes. "Your tarts are sweet and your kisses are sweeter." The drowsy, happy words tumbled out of her. "It was so lovely. Thank you."

He crawled beneath the blanket as well, curling up beside her. "It was my extreme pleasure, love."

"Goodnight, Quinn."

"Goodnight, my Anna." He dropped one final, brief kiss on her lips. "And I remember the library now."

Anna giggled softly and fell asleep with a smile on her face.

XXIV
Time of Departure

THERE HAD BEEN A TIME when Quinn had hopped eagerly out of bed every morning, ready to get to work and be productive. In the Before Anna era. She preferred to linger in bed when she woke, and it hadn't taken long for these early morning minutes cuddling with her to become a special time.

Quinn nuzzled her cheek. Her hair was a tangled mess this morning, which meant he had acquitted himself well last night. She typically braided it before bed, and it only ended up this way if she dozed off after sex.

He shifted slightly, stretching his sleep-heavy limbs. Something was strange. The bed felt harder than it should have been, and the sheets oddly scratchy. He rubbed his eyes and sat up. Where was he?

Whatever he had been thinking about evaporated, the way dreams often did. He surveyed the room, his mind taking its time waking up.

The hotel. His remaining lemon tarts sat on the table.

My tarts?

Quinn cocked his head, frowning at the tray of desserts. He knew he'd made them, but he didn't remember doing it.

"Quinn?" Anna sat up and touched his shoulder. "Is something wrong?"

He turned to look at her. She was supremely lovely, with her hair tumbling about and the sheets falling away to display beautiful, full breasts. They had made love last night. He knew that with utter certainty, but the act itself was no more than a blur. Why? He could remember their closet tryst in detail. He could almost feel the warmth of the fire beside them as he'd burrowed underneath her skirts that night in the library. But last night? A haze.

"You're not regretting our lovemaking, are you?"

He shook his head. "No. Trying to remember it."

Anna's arms wound around his waist. Her head dropped onto his shoulder. "Oh, darling. I'm so sorry."

Quinn pulled her into his lap and gifted her with a soft, tender kiss, telling her without words how he felt about her. A sliver of memory flashed in his mind. The taste of lemon on her lips. But no more.

"We ate tarts," she said, as if reliving the same memory. "We laughed. You kissed me all over."

"I would love to remember it, but my mind is fuzzy. I can't remember making the tarts, either, though I know I did."

"We'll get you help," Anna promised. "In a city of this size, we should be able to find a fine potion shop. We'll buy something to clear your mind. Maybe even cure us both entirely."

His brow furrowed. "Do we have the money for that?"

She stiffened in his arms. "You don't remember that, either? Quinn, you have fifty pounds in banknotes and some coins besides."

He whistled. "Damn. I'm a bloody top-shelfer. Or a highly accomplished thief."

Anna's mouth opened in an O shape. "Maybe that's the solution!"

"To what?"

"To why I left you, of course. You must have been stealing money from the company. Mr. Harper caught you, and I struck a bargain with him to keep you from being thrown in Newgate for what would be a short, miserable rest of your life. But I couldn't stand being with him, so we arranged to run away together. Unfortunately, we were discovered and our minds were wiped, probably in the hopes that we would never remember one another. It all makes perfect sense."

"Maybe it's my mushy mind, but I can't tell if you're serious or not."

Anna gave him a flirtatious grin. "Would I ever be anything but serious? I never tease you, Quinn."

"Aye. And you have no competitive spirit and play games in a quiet, refined manner. If you play them at all."

"Precisely."

"So. Thief, Newgate, Harper, running away, poisoned." Quinn ticked off each word on his fingers. "Perfect sense."

"Well, perfect sense except for the part where you are a master thief," she admitted. "It doesn't seem to fit with your general goodness. But it would explain the fifty pounds."

He laughed and kissed her. "I have an idea."

"Yes?"

"I make love to you again, this time so entirely that I cannot forget it. Then we eat the remaining tarts for breakfast, then go out visiting banks to see if someone remembers me and can explain my sudden wealth."

"I wholeheartedly approve of this plan." She pushed him down onto the bed, straddled his hips, and kissed him as thoroughly as he could have hoped.

Quite a bit later, Quinn slipped from the room and made his way down to the lobby to speak with the concierge. He didn't think he would learn much here, but it was something to do while Anna finished with her hair and clothing. He also thought he might grab a bite to eat, since he'd let her eat all the remaining lemon tartlets.

"…Harper?"

Quinn ducked behind a decorative potted fern, shielding himself from whomever had spoken that too-familiar name. He parted the greenery just enough to peek at the front desk. He could make out a black suit and a wide felt hat, but no other defining characteristics of the man standing there. Quinn also couldn't hear more than a few mumbled words of the concierge's reply.

"What about Smith?" the suspicious man asked.

The concierge mumbled again, but Quinn thought he made out the words "multiple Smiths."

He cursed under his breath. Harper and Smith. Anna and Quinn. This man, whoever he was, was searching for them. No good could come of that. Quinn's memory wasn't what it should have been, but with the help of Anna's notes he knew they'd stumbled into danger. Anyone lawless enough to run a large-scale whisky-thieving operation wouldn't hesitate to do them harm.

Quinn leaned further into the fern, trying to give himself a clearer view through the fronds. A tap on the shoulder startled him so badly he nearly cried out and gave himself away. He spun around, knocked into the pot, and set it swaying. He steadied it just in time to avert a disaster, but lost his balance in the process and fell hard on his rear.

A porter standing at least six feet tall and built like an ox scowled down at him. "Can I help you, sir?"

"Simply, er, admiring the specimens," Quinn babbled. "Ferns are all the rage, you know."

The porter's scowl deepened. Quinn cast a glance back over his shoulder toward the desk, but could neither see nor hear whether the man hunting him was still there.

"Uh, excuse me. I should be going."

Quinn scrambled to his feet and hurried for the lift. The potion-powered contraption rose slowly from floor to floor, and he paced the tiny passenger box, cursing himself for not taking the stairs.

When the blasted thing at last reached the third floor, he stumbled out and raced to his room, nearly colliding with Anna as she stepped into the hall, looking ready for the out-of-doors in her brown dress and bright green gloves.

"We need to leave," he gasped.

"What?" She grasped his arm and pulled him into the room. "Quinn, what's wrong?"

"A man was at the front desk looking for someone by the name of Harper or Smith. That can't be anyone but us. We're in danger. We need to leave at once."

"Did you recognize the man? Can you tell me anything about him?"

"No. I couldn't get a good look. I hid myself the moment I heard him speaking."

She nodded. "It could be Inspector Fitzhubert, or it could be the man who drugged you with the whisky. Or someone else working with them, I suppose. Regardless, you're right. We ought to leave before they locate us. The question now is, where should we go? We can't hop from hotel to hotel. They will continue searching, and eventually find us among the Smiths."

"Aye. We'll have to leave town."

"Edinburgh? It's where I planned to go and our best hope for learning more about the whisky thefts."

"I leave the choice entirely up to you. My memory isn't what it used to be." He grinned at her, but her shoulders sagged.

"I'm so sorry, Quinn. I very much wanted to go potion shopping for you. I promise to try in Edinburgh."

He took hold of her hand, lifted it to his lips, and kissed the inside of her wrist. "You are good to me, Anna. I can wait. I know I'll have you by my side."

She grasped the lapel of his coat, pulled him close and

pressed a fierce kiss to his lips. "Yes. You will. Because I'm not leaving you again."

"I'll call a porter and arrange to have our things taken straight to the train station. We can take the first available train."

"Good. I dislike leaving our things, but perhaps we ought to travel separately from the luggage?" Anna suggested. "It will be easier for us to move about unobserved without large trunks and the people necessary to move them."

"Spoken like an investigator."

She was so remarkable, this woman. So smart and competent and strong. Quinn thought back to their morning lovemaking, trying to fix the memory in his mind so it wouldn't slip away like so many others had done. He was a damned lucky man, despite his potion problems.

They saw their luggage off, took a quick breakfast—or second breakfast in Anna's case—in the dining room, and then followed on foot. Quinn didn't notice anyone following them, but with no professional experience he couldn't be certain.

They arrived at the station to an unpleasant discovery. The earliest train to Edinburgh was long gone, and the next wouldn't depart until the afternoon. They had hours to kill. Hours during which someone could discover their plans.

"We will have to make do," Anna said. She pulled a stack of penny dreadfuls from her trunk before closing it and leaving it to the porter who would see it onto the train. "We can move from place to place within the station, but I don't think we ought to leave."

"I agree. And we should stay together."

"Absolutely! You're not leaving my sight. I won't let anyone else scramble your brains. Let's start by stopping at that newsstand over there and buying a pair of newspapers."

He frowned at her. "You're not going to read your naughty novels?"

"Of course I am. But it's difficult to hide behind a small book."

"An excellent point. We can sit anywhere and read the paper without drawing attention. Would you mind lending me one of your novels, however? I can't imagine the news will hold my attention terribly long."

"I would be happy to." She handed him a book from her stack. "I think you'll like this one. The heroine is in dire danger of seduction when a thief breaks into her room in the night."

Quinn examined the lurid cover, where a horror-stricken maiden in her nightgown clutched a quilt that only half-concealed her.

"Is she ravished?"

"Read it and find out. It's one of my favorites."

Five pages in, Quinn was hooked. He crouched behind his newspaper, devouring the wild tale. He adored the intrepid heroine who bashed the thief over the head with a chamberpot to avoid ravishment, not knowing he was, in fact, the hero in search of a family heirloom that would prove his identity and restore his title and inheritance. When the dastardly villain kidnapped her at gunpoint and cast her adrift at sea, Quinn cursed aloud.

When the train arrived at last, he boarded with his nose still buried in the book.

"Thank goodness you have this all collected in one volume," he said to Anna as they found their seats. "If I'd had to read this issue-by-issue, waiting to see how it ends, I would have gone mad! Though I must say, as much as I like Miss Sally Ryder, here, I think you would have put up a better fight against the villain than she did."

"Well, she's a young thing fresh out of the schoolroom. I'm a woman of the world." She lowered herself into the seat and patted her belly. "Obviously."

Quinn took the place across from her. "Something tells

me you have always been a force to be reckoned with, Anna Harper."

The smile she bestowed on him was proud, with just a touch of mischief. "I try."

"I think you succeed wonderfully. Here's to a relaxing journey to Edinburgh." He arranged himself comfortably in his seat and returned to the last few chapters of his book. "And may you finish your book soon so we can swap."

Anna laughed. "I'll do what I can."

XXV
Trouble on the North Eastern Railway

Anna couldn't shake the feeling that something wasn't right. It had all been too easy, the way they'd left Newcastle. No one had bothered them. They'd seen no signs of Fitzhubert or anyone else Anna recognized from the gaol. They'd heard no talk of Harpers or Smiths.

Merely lingering nerves, she told herself. The sudden flight followed by too long waiting would do that to anyone. She would calm down soon enough.

And yet, an hour into the journey, her agitation hadn't diminished. Not even *Seduction by Steam Car*, the raciest of her novels, could hold her attention. She squirmed on the finely upholstered seat, crossing and uncrossing her legs and repeatedly adjusting her skirts.

It didn't help that the woman across the aisle kept eyeing her in disapproval. The woman had said to her companion—quite louder than necessary—that the trend of novel reading was a certain path to dissipation and ruin. She was probably one of those people who took Mansion of Happiness seriously.

Quinn ignored everything, engrossed in a second book. He had paused in his reading only twice, both times to complain that the heroine didn't even attempt to get herself out of a predicament but instead sat around having the vapors and waiting for help. Anna liked that particular book mostly because the hero was especially dashing, carried a sword, and ended up with his shirt ripped open in almost every episode.

Quinn turned another page, shaking his head. "I swear, if she gets clonked over the head one more time…"

"That can't be good for her health."

"No." He looked up suddenly. "Do you have any books where a character suffers from amnesia?"

"Um…" Anna concentrated for a moment, but could recall no specifics about her library or any particular books. "I don't remember. When I look at these books I remember them, but I couldn't tell you what others I own."

"Whether you own it or not, I'd like to find one. I'd like to see how well the author relates the situation and whether I particularly sympathize with the character."

"Mmm-hmm," Anna replied, her attention caught by a man passing down the aisle. He'd walked by before, and something about him struck her as not quite right.

She studied him as he walked away. Medium height, and a bit more muscular than average. He wore an ordinary black suit with pant legs hemmed a touch too short. His tailor had done a poor job.

Her head cocked to the side. Or else he'd bought the suit pre-made or second-hand. That was the oddity about him. He didn't look first class. As tidy as he was, he didn't have the extra polish a staff of servants and a great deal of money could create.

"Quinn."

"Hmm?"

"Don't turn around now, but there's a man down at the far end of the car who seems out of place."

Quinn set down the book. "'Out of place' meaning you think he's up to no good?"

"I'm not certain. I could be overreacting because of what you overheard this morning. I don't recognize him, but maybe you would. *Don't* turn around. We can't let him know we're interested. Why don't you get up and walk to the dining car. It's late enough that we can have dinner. Fetch something to eat and while you go in and out, look at the man in the very last seat on the left side, facing toward me. Report back with anything you recognize or whether he looks suspicious to you."

"And what if he's a threat and he attacks you while I'm gone?"

"I'll stab him with my bookmark."

"Fiercely."

"Oh, you remembered!" She gave him a wide smile. "That's wonderful."

"Except that now I also remember I have competition for your affections from someone named Nick." He sighed and pushed himself up out of the seat. "I'd better go fetch you some dinner before another man does and I lose you to him."

Anna pretended to think about it. "Hmm. Well, perhaps if he made lemon tarts just for me…"

She watched Quinn depart, then returned to her book, determined not to let anyone suspect she was watching the man at the other end of the train car. She read the same paragraph three times over before closing the book and admitting defeat.

The man hadn't moved. He sat with his head back against the seat cushion, eyes closed. Resting, supposedly, like many of the passengers were doing. He wasn't asleep, though. He remained too upright, showing no signs of slumping or of his head tilting to one side or the other.

Anna drummed her fingers on her thigh. Where was Quinn? Waiting for food to be prepared, perhaps? Or had some trouble befallen him? If anything happened because she'd sent him off on his own, she'd never forgive herself. She tried once again to return to the book, but had no better luck than before.

She'd finally determined that she needed to get up and go after Quinn when the door at the far end of the carriage opened and he stepped through. He walked calmly to his seat, giving her suspicious man no more than a passing glance.

"Here you are." He handed her a small parcel, wrapped in white paper. "There is fancier food for those who eat in the dining car, but I thought a sandwich would do."

"Thank you." Anna unwrapped her sandwich and took a bite.

"There are two of them."

She swallowed hard so she could answer. "Two sandwiches?"

"Two men. Another man is seated across from the one you mentioned. He's dressed in a similar fashion. They don't look terribly suspicious from what I saw, but they don't look especially wealthy, the way most of these passengers do. I didn't recognize either of them, but that doesn't surprise me."

The train began to slow, approaching another station.

"I don't know. Perhaps I'm only overreacting."

"No, you're wise to be cautious. Better safe than sorry, aye?"

Anna shrugged. She nibbled on her sandwich as the train pulled into the station, and a handful of passengers departed, soon replaced by new faces. Her out-of-place man remained in his seat, fake napping.

Perhaps a quarter of an hour past the station, he opened his eyes and rose. Anna nudged Quinn, who closed his book and set it aside. The strange man walked down the aisle, his companion rising and following several paces behind. Halfway down the aisle, he stopped and reached into his jacket.

Gun!

Anna clutched her dagger bookmark, her eyes darting to and fro, searching for anything else that might possibly serve as a weapon. No villain would ever find *her* a swooning damsel.

"Ladies and gentlemen," the man announced in a calm, but authoritative manner, "there is no need to panic. Kindly remove all jewels from your person and money from your wallets and purses. My companion and I will be coming by to collect them. Do as you're told and keep quiet and we will be on our way shortly."

Murmurs of shock and outrage spread across the car. One woman began to openly weep. A man one seat down from Anna clutched his pocket watch in both hands, all color drained from his face.

The gunman took off his hat and held it out to the couple nearest him, angling the gun in their direction. "Right in here, if you please."

Anna turned to the woman across the aisle. "Make a fuss when he reaches us," she whispered.

The woman frowned at her. "I beg your pardon?"

"Cry or plead. Anything at all. As long as you hold his attention."

"I don't think…"

Anna stared her down. "Do it."

Seat-by-seat the man moved closer, collecting valuables from men and women who complied with few protestations. In this first class carriage they could all easily afford replacements.

"Your jewels, ladies," the man said, pausing beside Anna's seat.

Anna caught the eye of the woman across the aisle and gave her her very best determined look.

"Please, sir," the woman said. "These were from my mother. Surely you have enough. Can you not pass a poor woman by?"

"You're anything but poor," he laughed. "Hand them over."

The woman clutched at the pearls around her neck. "Please, no."

The robber reached for her, and Anna took her opportunity. She leapt from her seat and raced down the aisle, launching herself at the unprotected back of the other criminal. Taken unaware, he went sprawling, and Anna rammed her knee into his kidneys. Another woman sitting nearby jumped atop him as well, grabbing for the hat full of loot while Anna snatched up the gun.

A commotion behind her made Anna spin around. A gun fired, passengers screamed, and Quinn landed in a heap atop the robber.

"Quinn!" Anna scrambled toward him.

"I'm not hurt!" He rammed his elbow into the back of the criminal's head. "Get the gun!"

The stunned robber struggled to lift the weapon, but Anna was too fast. She stomped on his hand and he squealed and dropped the gun. Anna scooped it up and stashed both revolvers in her pockets.

"Hold him down. I'm going for the authorities."

She turned back toward the man she had brought down, to find that two other women were now sitting atop him, pinning him to the floor. The first woman who had helped had taken up the hat and was returning valuables to their rightful owners. Anna squeezed past on her way to the door.

"Thank you, ladies. I'll be back short—"

The door swung open and another man with a gun barreled into the carriage.

Anna didn't even think. She launched herself at the man's legs, sending him flying over the top of her to sprawl on the floor of the carriage. She spun around, yanked both guns from her pockets, and jammed them into the man's ribs.

"Drop your weapon!" she ordered.

"For God's sake, woman! I'm here to rescue you!"

She jabbed him harder. "Drop it!" He tossed the gun away. Anna looked down the car at Quinn. Emboldened by Anna and her helpers, other women had joined him in holding down the criminal. "Quinn, can you grab that gun?"

"Quinn?" the new intruder echoed. "Anna? Is that you?"

Anna flinched, and the man used the opportunity to

scurry away from her. He sat up and she stared at him, vague memories tickling the back of her mind. She knew this man.

"Anna! Darling! Oh, thank the Lord!"

He lunged at her, and Anna sprang back, raising the pistols. "Don't touch me! Who are you?"

"Darling, don't you recognize me?"

Behind him, Quinn aimed the other gun. "Back away from her."

The man looked over his shoulder at Quinn. "Smith," he snarled. "What have you done to her?" He turned back to Anna. "Anna, it's me. It's Wilhelm. I've been searching everywhere for you. Don't you recognize me?"

"You look familiar," she admitted. "Who are you?"

He cast a smug glance at Quinn and then favored her with a winning smile. "I'm Wilhelm Harper. I'm your husband."

XXVI
Rivalry Games

Q UINN KEPT THE PISTOL trained on the man's back. If he made even the smallest attempt to hurt Anna, Quinn wouldn't hesitate to pull the trigger.

"Don't you remember me, my love?" the so-called Mr. Harper asked.

She is not *your love!*

Quinn tried to tamp down the raw, primal jealousy boiling inside, but the possessive thoughts filled his mind, urging him to fight this sudden rival with everything he had.

Anna is mine! he wanted to scream. *I held her all night. I gave her every pleasure. I was inside her. Part of her.*

Good God, what had he done?

Anna sat motionless, the pair of pistols still clutched in her hands, a stupefied expression on her face. Her usually glowing cheeks had taken on a grayish pallor.

"I am *not* your love." Her echo of Quinn's thoughts came out as a horrified whisper.

Harper shot Quinn a furious glare again. "What has he done to you, Anna? What lies has he told you? Who did he tell you he is?" Harper's voice had a natural calm that made him sound reasonable, even when he was angry.

"Why are you asking her?" Quinn retorted, trying and failing to keep his own voice even. "When you seem to know us so well."

"You stay out of this."

Anna struggled to her feet. "That's quite enough!" Her cheeks were still pale, her eyes wide and worried, but the weapons were steady in her hands. "This is neither the time nor the place. You, Mr. Harper, if you were truthful in your claim that you were here to rescue us, ought to be apprehending these villains."

"I did come to rescue you. I heard gunfire and screaming and rushed to help."

"Excellent. Then I'm sure you will be happy to escort them out of this car and see they are locked up and watched over until they can be turned over to the police."

She waved one of the guns at him and he stood up, shuddering a little. "If you would kindly not point that at me?"

"What? You don't trust a woman with a gun?"

"Anna, please. This isn't like you."

"I think it's exactly like me. Ladies, please bring our would-be robbers to the door. Mr. Harper will be escorting them away from us."

Several smiling women yanked the dazed criminals to their feet and dragged them down the aisle. Anna gestured at Harper to follow.

"Might I at least have my pistol returned to me?"

"No. Get rid of them. We can continue our discussion in a private location once we have reached Edinburgh."

"Yes. You and I should talk alone."

"Over my dead body," Quinn snapped. No way in hell was he leaving Anna alone with anyone. Not when there were enemies about with mind-altering potions. He wouldn't let her end up with a mind as muddled as his own.

"I'm happy to arrange that," Harper said.

"Might be difficult, since I'm the one holding the gun. Now, move."

Harper pushed the two failed robbers toward the door. "It's time you gentlemen had a talk with the authorities." He caught Anna's eye and held her gaze for several seconds. "I will return shortly, Anna. We will have that talk."

"What about the loot?" one robber whined. "I was promised loot!"

Harper smacked him in the head. "Out the door, you oaf!"

Quinn kept his gun trained on the three men until the door closed behind them. He heaved a sigh and lowered the weapon. Every eye in the entire car was on him and Anna. They needed to return to their seats and make some effort toward regaining normalcy.

He wouldn't be relinquishing the pistol, however. There would be no arguments about Harper and Anna or marriages and memories on this train, even if Quinn had to hold Harper at gunpoint to keep him silent. They had drawn too much attention already. The last thing they needed was for the rest of the passengers to start thinking this entire incident was some sort of staged melodrama.

Hell, this could have come right off the pages of one of Anna's penny dreadfuls. Maybe I'll write it all down. I could become Quinn Smith, Author of Sensation and Smut.

"*The Railway to Ruin*," he mused aloud. "*Scandal on the Edinburgh Express.*"

"This isn't an express," Anna replied.

"Everyone will be clamoring for the second installment, because they won't know who is the villain and who is the hero."

Anna pushed him into his seat. "Quinn, are you all right? Is your memory faltering again? You're talking nonsense."

She sank down onto the seat across from him, her face still a mask of worry. He couldn't even imagine how she felt at a time like this, what she must be thinking.

"Shit, Anna," he muttered. "I'm so sorry. I should never have…"

"No," she interrupted. "Stop, right there. I know what you're thinking, and I won't have any of it."

"But…"

She held up a single finger to silence him. "No. Regrets. Full stop."

Her passionate words brought a smile to his lips. "No regrets."

Anna reached out and grasped his hand, the smooth leather of her gloves cool against his bare skin. She edged forward in her seat, bringing them close enough together that they could talk privately.

"I will unravel this mystery," she vowed. "In another hour we'll be in Edinburgh. We'll find a hotel, perhaps someplace less well known, then review our notes and make a plan. In the morning I'll investigate, find some people who know me, sort everything out. Once I have all the details straight, you and I can sit down and decide what comes next."

"What about Harper?"

"He's just one more thing to be sorted out. Did you recognize him? Do you remember anything about him?"

Quinn shook his head forlornly. "He's familiar to me, but any tangible memories are out of reach. I know that I knew him."

"Yes. It's the same for me."

"When I looked at him, and now when I think of him, my brain screams, 'Enemy!' But I don't know if that's because he truly is a danger or merely because I'm jealous."

Her fingers moved in soft whorls over his hand. "Don't be."

"Anna, if the man is really married to you…"

"If he is, I must have been forced into it somehow, because

I can tell you for certain that I'm not in love with him. I would remember that."

Quinn wasn't so certain she would, but with the way his own memories seemed to fade in and out arbitrarily, he'd give her the benefit of the doubt. She had a better sense of the past than he did, certainly.

"I have this sense that he was a friend," she said.

Quinn almost pulled his hand away. Friendship was not a word he wanted to hear her associate with his rival. Friendship meant affection, and that could easily lead to something more.

"Perhaps it was an amiable marriage, even if it wasn't a passionate one," he forced himself to reply.

"No. That doesn't seem right. I had a feeling of anger and betrayal when he said he was my husband. I can't quite put it together, but my best guess is that he was once a friend but no longer is."

"That fits with the idea that he somehow forced you into marriage."

"Blackmail, perhaps. He must have threatened you. Or my family. I have a mother and a brother, if you remember."

"I don't, I'm afraid."

"Well, I remember them. What they look like, at least. My brother is extremely tall. When I hug him, I have to wrap my arms around his waist, and he can rest his chin on my head."

"I don't think I approve of this little tête-à-tête," Harper's icy voice interrupted.

Anna straightened up and sat back in her seat, but didn't relinquish Quinn's hand. "I don't think your approval or disapproval has any relevance whatsoever."

"You are my wife. You are sworn to obey me."

"No, that can't be right. That doesn't sound like me at all. Unless you also swore to obey me."

"What utter nonsense."

"Quinn did it."

Quinn stared at Harper, wondering if his own face mirrored his rival's dumbfounded expression. "I did?"

"I can picture it clear as day. You were grinning, almost laughing. I thought you would give us away because we wanted to see if you could add it in without anyone realizing during the ceremony."

"And did I?"

"I don't remember that part."

"This is insane." Harper gripped Anna's arm. "Anna, come with me. I want you away from this madman before he drugs you again. These false memories of yours could do permanent damage if we let them continue to fester."

Anna let go of Quinn's hand and drew one of the pistols from a pocket. "Release me."

"Anna…"

Quinn raised his own weapon. "You heard the lady."

Harper relaxed his grip and took a step back.

"Go away, Mr. Harper," Anna commanded. "Do not try to contact me again until we reach Edinburgh. When we arrive, I will make arrangements to discuss this matter further. In a time and place of my choosing."

"Anna, please. Be reasonable."

"Reasonable? You come barging into our train car, pretending to be some kind of hero, when we clearly don't need you, and then you claim to be my husband. I don't remember you. You have no proof. Aside from a passing familiarity, you are in all ways a complete stranger to me. I think it is perfectly reasonable not to go with you or do what you say until I have investigated the situation further."

Harper's jaw was clenched, but he nodded. "Very well. I will meet you on the platform in Edinburgh. But we *will* discuss this further. You will see, Anna. I will show you the truth." He pivoted on one foot and stalked away down the corridor.

Quinn exhaled slowly. "Well. I suppose we have a decision to make now."

Anna's brow furrowed. "Oh?"

"Do we go to Edinburgh as planned, or do we hop off at one of the stops along the way to get away from him?"

The woman across the aisle leaned toward them, her pearls swaying as she moved. "Are those horrid novels of yours as interesting as this? Perhaps they would not be so terrible to read after all."

Quinn tried not to cringe as the train pulled away from the last station before Edinburgh. He wanted to flee. He had those fifty pounds tucked safely away, deep inside his coat. They could live quite nicely for some time on that amount of money. They could find a remote village where no one would think to look for them. Or head to London and lose themselves in the crowd. He could find them a flat and get a job as a clerk or doing some other sort of organizational work. Maybe he could find his family and restore some memories. Maybe he could open a restaurant and sell stew and lemon tarts.

He stared out the window, watching the town disappear, taking his fantasies with it. Fleeing had never been an option. Anna needed this. She needed to return to Edinburgh and finish her investigations. If she found nothing, then they could consider a new path, but until then she would not stray from her intended course. The detective in her wouldn't rest until all leads had been followed.

Quinn would trust in her skills, trust in the process. She would unravel the mystery, discover the poisoner and the whisky thieves, turn them into the authorities, and then be free to… what? Let Harper drag her away against her will?

They sat in silence, books in hand, but neither reading, together in their uncertainty. Quinn passed the time trying to remember things. He played recent memories over in his head to keep them from fading and recited childhood rhymes and bawdy bar songs. What he wouldn't give to trade some of those lyrics for a few more memories of Anna.

She took his arm as they disembarked and handed him all the books. Her fingers brushed her skirt where a pistol lay concealed in her pocket.

"I intend to arrange a meeting with Mr. Harper for tomorrow. I want a location that is public, but where we can converse privately. And no restaurants or pubs. I don't want to run the risk of either of us ingesting another memory potion."

"You'll get no arguments from me. I can't speak for Mr. Harper." He paused, his brows narrowing. "Do you think he could be our poisoner?"

"I'm still considering that. I wonder what he would stand to gain by it? If he truly is the Harper of Harper-Douglass, is he stealing his own whisky? To what end? The tainted products will lose customers and hurt business. The illegally-gained profits from selling the stolen merchandise couldn't begin to make up for that. Unless he means to run the business into the ground, which seems a ridiculous thing to do to a company that by all indications is flourishing."

"Could the memory potions and the theft be two entirely unrelated problems?"

"I don't believe in coincidences of that magnitude. I was poisoned on the way to Esbjerg, which is an important stop in the theft operation. I'm an investigator. Clearly I was investigating and someone wanted to stop me."

"But why was I there? Not to run away with you, then."

"But perhaps to reunite with me." Her eyebrows twitched suggestively.

"I couldn't have waited for you to return home? Denmark's a long way to go for a bit of wick-dipping."

"True, but you love me."

Madly.

She stared him down, waiting for him to reply, but Quinn

remained stubbornly silent. He'd already used lemon tarts to lure her into an affair. He wouldn't further complicate the matter by declaring his feelings. Not until he was certain that whatever was between her and Harper was truly against her wishes.

He met her piercing gaze head-on, proving himself a worthy competitor, just as when they played games.

Games!

Flashes of board games on the ship from Denmark passed through his mind. Mansion of Happiness? They'd played that before, longer ago. Played it with a lot of laughs and a bottle of whisky. Wisps of other memories warred for attention. They played games often. Board games, card games, billiards.

"Oh, fine," Anna sighed. Her words snapped him back to the present, and the flood of memories vanished as quickly as it had begun. "Don't admit it. But we both know it's true."

Quinn couldn't deny that. He only wished he knew whether she loved him in return.

He was spared further contemplation on the matter when Anna's fingers tightened on his arm.

"There's Harper. He's headed this way. I won't go anywhere alone with him. Not until I'm certain he can be trusted."

"I won't let him put a hand on you."

"Thank you. I had a thought, about if he were the poisoner."

"Oh?"

"What if he's not my husband? What if he erased our memories in order to steal me for himself? If he planted the tainted whisky, he could have changed the name on my luggage. Maybe I'm not Anna Harper." She twisted to look up into his eyes. "Quinn, what if you and I are still married?"

Yes, yes, a thousand times yes.

Quinn quashed the excitement roaring through his veins. He couldn't let his own desires keep them from the truth. As much as he wanted Anna to be his, he first and foremost wanted her happiness and her safety.

Her grip on his arm tightened more as Harper came within earshot. She squared her shoulders and faced him with poise and determination, despite her anxiety.

Their shared anxiety. Quinn's heart pounded a steady rhythm. His muscles tensed, preparing to flee or fight.

Protect your lady. Protect your child.

Quinn had no idea whether he had fathered her baby, but he found he no longer cared. When at last they ran away together, he would welcome any child of Anna's as his own, even if the father was Harper or some random man who had taken her fancy one day. The child would be a girl, he predicted. She'd be fierce like her mother and he would dote on her. He'd teach her to read and do sums. He'd teach her to make lemon tarts. He'd teach her unladylike things such as billiards and…

"Goddamn." He staggered and nearly fainted from the force of the memories. "Anna."

Her other hand came up to support him. "Quinn, what's wrong? What happened?"

"Anna. I… I remember the day we met. I remember…"

"What? Can you tell me?"

"I remember who you are."

XXVII
Who I Am

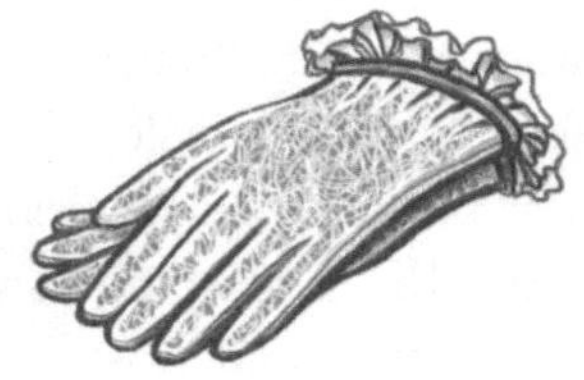

WHO I AM.

The very idea terrified her. If Quinn told her she was Anna Harper, true, legal, uncoerced wife of Mr. Wilhelm Harper, it would break her heart. She wouldn't let herself hope that she was Anna Smith. Either way, things would be different. Whether for better or worse, she didn't know.

Harper hurried toward them. "Don't listen to him, Anna."

Anna ignored him, focusing on Quinn and peering up into his eyes. "Quinn? What can you tell me?"

"I remember a billiard room. I walked in to see you bent over the table, lining up a shot. You wore a pale green dress and the same green gloves you are wearing now. You were teaching yourself to play. We talked. You wanted to learn all sorts of things ladies weren't allowed to do, like drinking and swearing. I offered to teach you whatever I knew. You were smart and determined. Admirable. And adorable. I fell in love with you that very night. When we parted, you gave me your card."

"This is absurd," Harper snarled. "Anna, he's a madman. He makes up wild tales like this on a regular basis."

"It sounds true to me. Please continue, Quinn. I'd like to hear the rest."

"That's it. That's all I remember. It's hazy, and the details are already fading."

Harper sniffed.

"But I can still picture the card," Quinn continued. "Clean, elegant typeface. 'Lady Anna Masterson,' it said."

Masterson. The name sank into her brain, excavating memories buried beneath the mud the potion had deposited.

"Masterson," she said aloud. "Anna Masterson. Nicholas Masterson. Nick is my brother. He gave me that dagger-shaped bookmark as a birthday present."

Quinn grinned at her. "We've done it, then! We've uncovered you. All we have to do is find him and he can tell us everything."

"He lives in London," Anna said, picturing the townhouse in her now less-befuddled mind. "He's the Earl of Sharpe."

Quinn's grin vanished, replaced by a slack jaw. "The Earl of Sharpe is your brother? Who the devil am I then, to have married you?"

"You *were* my employee," Harper replied. "I terminated your employment when your madness came to light. Just like Lady Anna terminated your marriage. But you know all that, I'm sure. You are merely trying to endear yourself to my wife to drive a wedge between us and steal her for yourself. Anna, my dear, let us go find a quiet place to sit where I can tell you the rest. I will treat you to dinner."

"Oh, no. Not a chance. I will handle my own food choices, thank you. And the only place I'm going now is to the telegraph office to write a message to my brother. After that I will be going to a hotel for the night. I won't tell you which I will choose. Tomorrow, at nine a.m., promptly, we will meet outside the Palm House at the Royal Botanic Gardens for further discussion."

"You want to wander all the way up to Inverleith, when there are perfectly good places to meet here in town?"

"Oh, for heaven's sake, it's hardly more than a mile from

here. And it's near the Harper-Douglass distillery, which is my second stop on tomorrow's itinerary. Now, if you will excuse us, we have a telegram to write and luggage to send on to a hotel."

She tugged on Quinn's arm and started off toward the cluster of porters waiting to transport passenger trunks to their next destinations. Harper jogged after.

"You can't wander off with him!"

Anna didn't even look in Mr. Harper's direction. She didn't trust him in the slightest, though she did still want to hear his side of the tale. Any new information was good, even if she had to sort through it to pick out the bits of truth.

Things were coming together. She had a connection to her family. More Harper-Douglass questions would be answered at the distillery tomorrow. She was in a city she knew well. Who knew what a simple walk around town might drag out of her memories? She shivered, half with excitement, half with dread.

"Anna, please," Harper begged. "I am your husband. You cannot go away with another man."

"I can do whatever I want." *If* they were married, which she wasn't convinced they were, it hadn't been her own free choice. Or if it had, she'd since changed her mind. Every time she looked at him, that same stab of betrayal shot through her.

Another potential item for tomorrow: find solicitors Messrs. Lachlan and Stewart. Arrange a divorce.

"I will not stand for you staying in a hotel with him. He is unstable. He could do any number of depraved things to you."

"Ah. There's our luggage. Excuse me while I make arrangements."

Harper followed right behind, like a trained lapdog. "You, there," he called to the porter, "please have these things taken to the Waverley hotel."

Anna rounded on him. "How dare you give orders on my behalf?" She spun back to face the porter. "Don't take those trunks anywhere yet."

The porter's eyes darted nervously between Anna and Harper. Quinn handed the man a coin.

"That's my trunk. Take it wherever the lady asks to have her trunk taken."

Harper cut in with a coin of his own. Anna caught a glint of gold as the money changed hands. The porter pocketed the bribe with a greedy gleam in his eye.

"The Waverley," Harper repeated.

"Are you daft?" Anna asked, suppressing the urge to slap the obnoxious man. "The Waverley is a temperance hotel."

"What of it?"

"Aren't you the Harper who owns a whisky manufactory?"

"I fail to see how that matters."

"Temperance is bad for business. Obviously." She rolled her eyes. "I guess Douglass is the brains behind the operation," she muttered. There was no way in all the nine circles of hell she would have happily married someone of as little intelligence as Wilhelm Harper had thus far exhibited. "But no matter, the Waverley will do, I suppose." She nodded at Quinn. "Come, Mr. Smith, let's go send that telegram. Then we can continue on to the hotel, where we will prevent Mr. Harper from doing anything rash, like trying to put me up in a room with him."

Harper gave her the smirk she was rapidly coming to despise. "I will give us side-by-side rooms until you are ready to come to me, darling."

"Fine. As long as Mr. Smith is on my other side and there are no connecting doors."

"You and I could stay at the Balmoral," Quinn suggested. "It's closer and not a temperance hotel. And I could use a drink about now."

Anna glanced at the porter as he rushed away, pushing the cart loaded with their trunks. "Our luggage is headed for the Waverley, I'm afraid." She stepped closer to Quinn and lowered her voice. "I think Harper slipped the man a half-sovereign. No sense wasting our own money trying for a larger bribe. And it occurs to me that a temperance hotel might be a good idea. No chance of poisoned whisky."

"Good thinking." Quinn crooked his arm and Anna took hold of it.

"The telegraph office is this way." They started off, through a train station Anna knew as well as any place she'd been since Esbjerg. Mr. Harper prowled along behind them, but even his presence couldn't suppress an upwelling of happiness. Her memories were returning. She'd found more of herself. She *would* triumph in this.

"I'm glad you remember these things," Quinn replied. "My head is still a bit of a muddle, I'm afraid. It's aching, and I can barely remember what happened this morning. Yet I keep having flashbacks to various episodes that I think are from early in our history. I believe I once gave you a scholarly dissertation on the many various grammatical forms and usages of the word 'fuck.'"

Anna grinned, her heart swelling with the knowledge that Past Quinn had appreciated Past Anna for who she was. Present Anna loved him all the more for it. "Verb, noun, adjective, adverb, interjection. Am I missing any?"

"Not that I can think of, but, you know…" Quinn pointed at his head. "Brain rot. Tell me more about your brother the earl. What will you write to him?"

"I don't know." She glanced behind her at Harper. As long as he remained in earshot, she would have to take care what she said. "I want to write, 'Tell me everything,' but that's impractical via telegram. One or two questions, perhaps. I think it will be most valuable if he can come here to talk with me. I'm certain he will rush to help. We are close, I remember that." She blinked back a tear. Her memories of Nick still had holes—mostly notably their more recent adult life—but she had regained the emotions and the love of close family ties. She missed her brother dreadfully, and would have given almost anything for one of his big, awkward hugs just now.

"And what if he's not in town? With Parliament not in session, many people will be at their country homes. Do you know where Sharpe's country estate is?"

Anna tried to picture Nick in the country, but all that conjured up was childhood images of running through gardens. Nothing useful.

"I'm afraid not."

"And do you know his address in London?"

"No. But if we say, 'Send this telegram to Lord Sharpe,' it ought to reach him eventually, don't you think?"

Quinn pursed his lips and made a noise of uncertainty. "Yes, but it won't get the rapid response we would receive if we had his direction."

"No matter. I'm certain I will learn much more tomorrow when we visit the Harper-Douglass distillery." She could wait a few days to hear from Nick. He had his own life, including a wife, she was relatively certain. Knowing she hadn't lost him for good was the most important thing at the moment.

"Which is where?"

"North of here. Nor far from the botanic gardens. Don't you remember town? You knew about the Balmoral hotel only moments ago."

"I remember better when I'm not thinking about it." Quinn glanced down at the books he still carried. "I think I've entirely forgotten what I read today."

"Another item for the list. Visit a chemist and get you a potion. We'll fix this, Quinn, I promise."

He smiled at her. "Thank you, love."

"She's not your love," Harper growled. "She is *my* wife."

Quinn turned around and scowled at him. "Are you still here? Don't you have a company to run? The company you supposedly fired me from? Don't you have your own home where you can stay, instead of following us to a hotel?"

Anna bit her lip to avoid groaning out loud. She didn't know how much more of this she could stand. Harper made her furious. The thought of being married to him made her sick. Quinn's presence made the man all the more antagonistic.

Tomorrow. Tomorrow I will learn more. And soon Nick will contact me and tell me everything not just about who I was, but about who I am now.

· · · ❧ · · ·

Anna ducked into the telegraph office on her own, leaving Quinn standing outside to make sure Mr. Harper didn't attempt to interfere. She kept her message straightforward.

Nick

Dnt panic. Was drugged w potion & lost memory. Remembrng now bt cld use help. Send reply 2 Edinb Sta.

Anna

Nick would likely panic anyway, but his wife—whose name Anna still couldn't remember—would prevent him from doing anything rash. Anna thanked the man who took her message, then rejoined Quinn and Harper, who stood several feet apart, glaring at one another.

Men.

The Waverley Hotel was near to the train station, but much to Anna's chagrin, Harper refused to let her be upon arrival. He walked up to the front desk and said, "A room for myself and my w—"

"Three side-by-side rooms, please," Anna interrupted. It seemed the only practical solution. "Under the name Anna Harper."

"Of course, Mrs. Harper. Happy to help," the concierge replied. "My Pa loves your whisky."

Harper placed a coin on the table. "I'll be paying for my room and the lady's. But not for his." He jerked his head in Quinn's direction.

The concierge only shrugged, and accepted another coin from Quinn.

Anna didn't bother to protest. This saved Quinn money. His fifty pounds were their security. If everything went wrong, they could flee to America. Surely someone in New York would have need of a lady investigator.

After an awkward, silent dinner in the dining room—where Anna could see her food brought out directly from the kitchen and feel relatively certain it hadn't been tampered with—the trio at last retired to their respective rooms for the night. Anna waited in her doorway until both men had gone into their rooms and closed their doors before locking herself in. Even then, she remained silent, listening for the sounds of opening doors. Her one comfort was that she and Quinn still had the guns. She wouldn't hesitate to use them. She would defend herself and her baby. And no one would ever harm Quinn again on her watch, even if she had to run to his rescue half-dressed in the dead of night.

Anna changed into her nightgown and braided her hair, though she suspected sleep would elude her. The bed was cozy, the blankets soft and warm against her skin. She closed her eyes, breathing slowly, trying to leach some of the tension from her muscles. All day she'd been sitting, but the stress of their flight and the events on the train had left her exhausted nevertheless.

Her ears betrayed her. Each footstep in the hall or creak of the floorboards made her jerk, her hand reaching for the pistols that lay nearby. One anxiety-filled hour later, she rose from the bed, gathered a few things, and strode to the door. She eased it open, peered out into the empty hall. Not a sound. Anna slipped from her room and closed the door, releasing a sigh of relief when the latch fell into place with no more than a soft click. She inserted her key, turned the lock, and double-checked that the door was secure before tiptoeing to Quinn's room.

He answered her quiet taps almost immediately, ushering her inside and shutting the door with considerably less care than she had taken with her own. She didn't bother to scold him for it. They were together. That was what mattered.

"I expected you might come by tonight," he said.

Anna nodded. "Defendit numerus."

"I don't know Latin, love."

"Safety in numbers. It comes from *The Satires of Juvenal*."

"Well, there's that fancy Cambridge education for you."

"I detect a bit of snobbery in your tone, Mr. Smith. Allow me to demonstrate the usefulness of my Latin knowledge. I think the Harper-Douglass company could use a motto. Something to write on the label. Latin will appeal to the aristocracy with their 'fancy Cambridge educations.'"

He folded his arms across his chest and regarded her with a fond smile. "And?"

"Ex aqua vitae felicitas. Happiness from whisky."

"How do you say, 'Memory loss from whisky?'"

"Ex aqua vitae amissus memoriae."

"Excellent. I'll make it the new Smith family motto."

Anna laughed. "This is why I love you, Quinn."

"Anna." He reached for her, then abruptly pulled back, refolding his arms. "No, we shouldn't. Not until we know. What if there's more to the situation with Harper? What if I really am mad, as he says?"

"You're not."

"We don't know that. We should try to maintain some distance. I don't want you to become committed only to find out that I'm a danger to you and your child."

"You never will be, and I'm already committed. Didn't you hear me say that I love you?"

"I'd rather you live with Harper or find a new man than be with me if there is any chance I will harm you." He gestured at the bed. "Please, get some rest. I'll sleep on the floor tonight."

Anna raised her eyes to the heavens, begging for patience.

"Quinn, I've had a very stressful and confusing day today. I'm anxious about tomorrow. I'm exhausted. This is not what I need right now." She reached into her pocket and pulled out the folded slip of paper with his IOU scrawled across it. The paper was worn, the words faded, but still readable. "And you owe me. 'One unconditional surrender.'"

Most men, she suspected, would have been angered at being outmaneuvered, but not her Quinn. He smiled and chuckled. "Well played, Anna. You win. What can I do for you?"

She could have asked anything, made a demand of any sort, knowing he would honor his promise, but she wanted only one thing tonight.

"Hold me." Quinn opened his arms and Anna burrowed against his chest, taking comfort in his strong arms and solid body. "Just hold me."

XXVIII
Fern Fever

A QUIET MORNING walking hand-in-hand with Anna through the botanic gardens gave Quinn plenty of time to think and reflect. They'd woken early and left immediately, picking up breakfast from a bakery along the way. Anna said little. He couldn't pretend to know what she was thinking, but he could tell much of her anxiety from the night before still lingered.

It had to be difficult for her, this hovering on the edge of knowing and not knowing. Her desire to learn and discover drove her on, despite well-founded fears of what she might find. Her dislike of Wilhelm Harper was evident, and if they were truly married, she would be in his power. He would hold legal rights over her and her child. Quinn was terrified for her. He couldn't imagine the depth of her own fear.

He'd held her all last night, stroking her hair and nuzzling her cheek until she'd fallen asleep in his arms. For hours thereafter, he'd lain awake, watching her sleep and jotting notes about the things that had happened that day. The writing had helped. His memories of yesterday were clearer and more numerous than those of the day before.

He knew what he had to do. The moment the meeting with Harper was over, Quinn would be heading back into the heart of town, seeking the best potion shop he could find. He was no use to Anna in his current state. Until he could unravel the mess of his mind, until he could be certain of who he was, he couldn't be what she needed. He couldn't commit to being a husband and a father. He had to be certain whatever had torn them apart in the past would never repeat itself.

"It's nearly nine," Anna said. She slipped her watch back into its pocket. "It's time I was going outside to meet with Mr. Harper. I intend to lure him into this greenhouse. I will tell him I asked you not to come because you and he argue too much, and I can't get my questions answered."

"But clearly I'm here."

"Yes. You'll be hidden, listening."

Quinn nodded. "An excellent idea. Where am I to hide?"

Anna gestured at the six-foot tall, multi-tiered plant stand that ran along the entire wall of the hothouse. "Underneath this. You'll have to sit or kneel, but I believe there should be enough room. The plants are packed so densely no one will be able to see you."

"True, but how am I to get back there?"

Anna dragged a large potted fern aside, opening a narrow gap beneath the bottom tier. "This is where we are both glad you are not an excessively large man."

"We?" He dropped to the floor and wriggled into the small opening. "I think you mean you."

"Nonsense. You love getting to be a part of my intrigue."

"I love... oof... *you*. Don't think I'd do this for anyone else."

The space beneath the plant stand was narrower than Quinn had anticipated. He had to twist sideways to pull himself all the way in, and once he was in place he could only sit cross legged, with his back against the glass. A tall row of hedges on the opposite side of the windows shielded him from the view of anyone outside the building.

The potted fern scraped across the floor as Anna pushed it back into place. "Perfect," she said. "I can't see you at all. You wait there quietly, and have your notebook ready. I'll be back in a few minutes with Mr. Harper."

"Anna, I can't get out of here if you need me. Are you certain you'll be safe?"

"I have guns in both pockets. If he tries anything, he'll find himself full of holes. And in the event of a true emergency, just stand up and shove. You'll spill many plants, but I don't think it's strong enough to hold up if you push hard enough."

"I'll pray it doesn't come to that."

"Good. But do it silently, because there are more visitors headed this way. I'll be right back."

Her footsteps faded as she hurried from the room, replaced soon thereafter by a booming Scottish brogue that could have belonged to either a man or a woman.

"Ferns everywhere," the unknown person ranted. "You'd think after decades of fern-fever people would have had their fill? But, nae. Here, and there! And they're nae vera bonny, if you ask me."

"I think they're elegant," trilled a second voice.

Quinn shifted slightly, as if the movement could ease some of his mental discomfort. He didn't mind spying on Harper, but eavesdropping on the conversations of random people made him squirm. And he couldn't do a damned thing about it. He was trapped here.

I have a bad habit of hiding behind ferns, he scribbled in his notebook.

The pair of visitors continued their walk about the room, discussing the merits of what seemed like every single plant and never once agreeing. Quinn did his utmost to ignore them.

He was so intent on not listening that he didn't even realize Anna had returned until he heard her raised voice saying, "…

Wanted to plead your case, and I'm giving you an opportunity. If you don't like it, leave."

"But surely there is a less… restrictive space?" Harper asked. "Anyone walking into the room can hear us. There is not even a secluded corner where we might speak privately."

"If you think I'm going into a secluded anything with you, you are extremely deluded."

Quinn nudged a plant in front of him, opening up a sliver of a gap that allowed him to see Harper and Anna. She'd stopped right at Quinn's hiding place. He might not be able to hear a whisper, but he would hear even quiet conversation.

"Outside, then? We could walk in the open, away from anyone."

"It's chilly this morning, and I will not risk my health or that of my child by spending too much time out in the cold. It is pleasant and warm in here."

"It's uncomfortably hot," Harper argued.

Quinn had to agree with the man for once, but from Anna's perspective, uncomfortable was a positive. If the man had anything to hide, he was more likely to accidentally divulge his secrets while distracted by his unpleasant surroundings.

"So, Mr. Harper," Anna said, ignoring his protests, "tell me why you believe we are married."

"Because we are. You are Anna Harper, my wife."

"And how long have we been married?"

He glanced at her belly and smirked. "Since April."

Quinn's fingers tightened on his pencil. Perhaps he cared more than he'd realized who the child's father was. Because Harper and his oh-so-superior attitude didn't deserve such an honor.

"I was married to Mr. Smith as recently as February," Anna said.

"Did he tell you that?"

Anna took her own opportunity to look smug. "No, as a matter of fact. It was a mutual acquaintance."

"What? Who?"

"Oh, you wouldn't know her. She was someone I met during the course of my investigations. You do know I'm an investigator, don't you?"

"Anna, we talked about this. You are no longer partaking in such common and dangerous work. You've given it all up. You are to be a wife and mother and oversee my household, as is the highest duty a woman can partake of."

Quinn cringed, anticipating the massive tongue-lashing Anna was certain to give.

Much to his surprise, she merely laughed. "Thank you very much, Mr. Harper. That clears things up wonderfully. Now, why don't you tell me your side of the tale. What happened between February and April?"

"Ah, well, it happens that Mr. Smith is quite mad. I know he seems very normal, and even charming."

"Quite."

Anna finds me quite charming, Quinn scribbled.

"You were not the only one to be deluded, of course. I told you he was an employee of the company. Quite a good one, in fact, until we began to notice peculiar errors in the books, random thefts, things of that sort. He would be perfectly reasonable one moment, and the next, entirely unpredictable. His condition was worsening, and the physicians I spoke with suggested it was incurable. I was forced to terminate his employment. When you discovered his madness, you arranged to dissolve your marriage, on the grounds that his madness rendered him unfit to enter into a binding contract. An annulment was, of course, granted."

"Of course." Quinn liked the trace of skepticism in Anna's tone.

Unfit, but still charming.

"And then I married you… immediately?"

"Well, er, yes. Nearly."

"I see. Then I must have been already pregnant."

Harper's eyes darted about. "Anna, really! We are in public."

"So?" She placed a hand on her belly. "I'm not ashamed of my baby."

"But to talk about such things, and with such language, where someone could overhear?"

Anna is terribly scandalous. Brava!

"It's the only logical conclusion I can make," Anna replied, ignoring Harper's discomfort. "I realized I was carrying Quinn's child and we all know how cruel people can be. A madman for a father could ruin my baby's life as well as mine. I did the only thing I could: marry another man immediately so I could pass the child off as his. Thank you, Mr. Harper, for being so kind as to leap to my rescue in such a fashion. And no one will ever know that we have never shared intimacies. I won't breathe a word."

Quinn clapped a hand over his mouth to smother his laughter. Anna was torturing the man. Which Harper richly deserved for disrespecting her and women in general. One of these days, women would get the vote and men like Harper would all suffer rage-induced apoplexies. Even now, he had turned a rather delightful crimson shade.

"Anna, what has come over you? You are not acting at all yourself."

She shook her head. "No, Mr. Harper, I'm afraid I am exactly myself. Clearly you don't know me very well. Now, tell me the truth."

"I've told you the truth. You are my wife, you are carrying my child, and we have been married since spring. Quinn Smith is unstable and dangerous."

Unfit, unstable, dangerous. No wonder she likes me.

"Whatever this is that has caused you to lose your memory is harming you, Anna. I don't know what he has told you or done to you, but he has confused and deluded you. You have become someone you are not."

Anna remained silent for a long moment, pink lips pinched

in a contemplative frown. "No, Mr. Harper," she said at last. "This is who I am, whether you like it or not. It may not have been who I was, but that is the past, and this is now, and I find I like who I am now. You are lying, but I don't know how much or about what. I will find out, eventually, and hopefully come to understand what led us here. But know this: learning my past won't change me, not in the ways you desire. If Past Anna was like you claim, I want nothing to do with her. And even if I never recover her, I'll be fine. I'll be happy. The one thing I will not be is your wife. Consider this your notice of divorce. Good day, Mr. Harper."

She spun around and vanished from Quinn's narrow field of vision. He listened to the click of her heeled boots across the floor, punctuated by Harper's futile protests. Soon enough, both faded into the distance.

Quinn scribbled a brief note to Anna and tore the page from his notebook. He wouldn't wait for her to return. She was perfectly fine on her own, and she needed him to be well far more than she needed his assistance with her investigations. A quick trip to a potion shop, a chat with a chemist, and hopefully he could restore something of himself. Just enough to prove Harper a liar. To know he wasn't mad. Once that was accomplished, he could begin the task of being a worthy partner to Anna.

He tucked his notebook away and went back down on his belly, pushing the potted fern out of his way so he could squeeze out of his hiding place. He was halfway out when a shriek pierced his ears. He scrambled to his feet as quickly as he could manage and shoved the fern back into place.

"I'm terribly sorry," he said to the terrified woman who cowered behind a large cluster of pink flowers. "Didn't mean to startle you." He laid the note for Anna atop the fern and headed for the door. With any luck, the next time he saw her he would be whole.

XXIX
Welcome Back

Well, I've definitely *been here before.*

Anna surveyed the white-washed buildings of the Harper-Douglass distillery. She knew which one housed the offices and which ones were warehouses. She knew where the whisky was aged and how the barrels would be arranged inside. She could recite the entire production process, from obtaining the barley, to making the mash, to the distillation in the proprietary stills that Quinn had designed himself.

She staggered and put a hand against the nearest wall to steady herself. Quinn had designed the stills? She shut her eyes, trying to grasp the memory. Quinn, his hand running lovingly across the copper, eyes shining almost a pure blue as he explained his improvements and the resulting quality of the whisky. She couldn't recall the words, but she knew the general sense of the conversation. She remembered the pride he took in his work.

"Damn," she breathed.

He hadn't been merely an employee. If he had designed the stills and refined the entire process, he was every bit as valuable to the company as the owners. He and Harper must have had a massive falling out. Over her? Perhaps.

Quinn certainly wasn't mad, as Harper had claimed. Though with the multiple doses of memory potion the poor man didn't trust his own mind any longer. She dug his note out from one of her small side pockets and read it over again.

Going out to recover myself. Meet me at the hotel for dinner. All my love, your ex- and hopefully-future husband.

She'd nearly ripped the note in half, she'd been so furious when she'd first discovered it. How could he wander off into potential danger on his own? By now, though, her reaction had settled into a vague annoyance. Quinn had done what he believed was right. He would never be comfortable until he had tried to restore his memories. And he didn't want to burden her with that responsibility. He'd left her to her investigations while he saw to his own needs.

Lovely man. Aggravating man. Didn't he know how worried she was about him? How brokenhearted she would be if anything happened to him?

Anna pocketed the note. She would trust him to take every precaution. He wouldn't tell her he wanted to marry her only to go do something foolish that would keep him from that goal. In return, she would take care of herself, learn all she could, and bring good news to their dinner tonight.

She started toward the offices, thinking to find someone high-up in the company to question. Men that worked directly with Harper would be more likely to know her than the average worker, she suspected.

A man pushing a trolley loaded with barrels paused and tipped his hat to her. "Mrs. Harper! Lovely to see you!"

Or perhaps everyone will know me.

A knot tightened in her gut at the knowledge that she truly was Anna Harper. Until this moment, some tiny piece of her had held out hope that she might be Anna Smith.

"Hello," she replied to the friendly employee. "I'm sorry to interrupt your work, but might you perhaps…"

"Mrs. Harper! Mrs. Harper! You're back!"

Anna turned to find the owner of the new voice. A young man raced toward her, skidding to a halt a few feet away.

"Er, yes. I'm back."

"Where have you been? Where's Mr. Harper? Did you learn anything about those strange reports of problems with some of the European shipments?"

"Ah…" She turned back to the man with the barrels. "Excuse us. It was good to see you. Have a pleasant day."

"I will, ma'am. Thank you."

She nodded and spun around. The young man bounced in place, his bright blue eyes shimmering with excitement. His blond hair was slightly mussed, his cheeks red. Never still, she guessed.

"Can you tell me anything?" he asked. "Is it all terribly secret? No one knows where Mr. Harper is. You went away, to visit family in London, I thought, but then Mr. Harper disappeared without a word. Left a note saying he'd be gone for a few weeks. No one knows why or what he's doing. It's been weeks and he isn't back."

"I saw him only this morning, unfortunately."

The young man frowned. "Unfortunately? Did you not want to see him?"

His confused smile gave her pause. Had she and Harper been on good terms as recently as weeks ago? Peculiar.

"I did want to see him, but our discussion was not an entirely pleasant one."

"Oh." Those brilliant blue eyes opened wide again. "Is it related to the shipment problems?"

"Is there somewhere we could sit and talk…? Excuse me, I don't recall your name."

His brow crinkled in confusion again. "Rabbie MacAlaster."

She nodded. "Is there somewhere we could talk, Mr. MacAlaster?"

"Oh, it's just Rabbie, Mrs. Harper. And we could sit in Mr. Harper's office, if you like." He waved a hand and began to walk toward the office building. "Since he's not here. Is he not coming back soon? Is that why you're upset with him?"

"I have no idea what he's doing or when he intends to come back. But I do have some questions for you, Rabbie. Pardon me if some of them sound peculiar. Have you known me very long?"

"Of course. Ever since you married Mr. Harper."

Her heart hammered. "And do you remember when that was?"

"Rabbie!" a gruff voice interrupted. "What are you doing away from your duties?"

Rabbie and Anna turned together. A burly, dark-haired man scowled at them, beefy arms crossed over his chest.

"Oh, Mr. Douglass," the youngster exclaimed. "Mrs. Harper is back!" He looked down at the ground. "Er… as you can see for yourself, of course."

"Aye. Back to work."

Rabbie nodded vigorously. "Yes, sir, Mr. Douglass." The boy scampered off, leaving Anna alone with the scowling Scot.

"Welcome back, Mrs. Harper. Please, come into my office."

The office he led her to was much smaller than she would have expected for a part-owner of the company. Was this Mr. Douglass not the Douglass of the company name? He could be a relative, she supposed. One step down the ladder.

She sat down on the plain wooden chair opposite his desk, spreading her skirts neatly around her. The two small pistols were heavy in her pockets, but well-concealed.

Mr. Douglass showed no inclination to begin the conversation, so Anna took the opportunity to study him. A few gray hairs among the black, a bit of dark stubble along his jaw. A familiar face, but as with Mr. Harper, not one that conjured up any specific memories.

He cleared his throat. "What brings you here, Mrs. Harper?"

"Questions."

"Questions," he repeated, his tone skeptical. "Questions about what?"

"Any number of things, but let's begin simply. Rabbie said he has known me since I married Mr. Harper. I assume the same is true for the majority of the employees?"

"Aye."

"And when did this first meeting take place, as best you can recall?"

Like Harper had done, Douglass glanced down at her belly. Apparently her condition was showing more than she had realized. "Sometime in the spring."

Anna nodded. "And what about when I was here with Mr. Smith? Surely someone here knows me from that time?"

Douglass frowned. "Smith is past history, Mrs. Harper. Why bring up such unpleasantries? Unless he's been causing trouble?"

"Actually, he's been extremely pleasant."

Douglass sniffed. "Well. That's good, I suppose."

Anna nodded. She had begun to get better a sense of Mr. Douglass, and she thought some of it stemmed from her not-quite-memories of him. He never approved of anything, rarely smiled, and always expected things to go wrong. He had a competence about him, however, that Mr. Harper lacked. He would do better at running the company.

"This might sound a bit peculiar, Mr. Douglass, but what can you tell me about Mr. Harper? How did an Englishman come to be involved with a Scottish distillery?"

Douglass' jaw clenched and he didn't reply for several seconds. "Family connections. *Distant* family connections."

"You two don't get along, then?"

"I do my job," he replied curtly.

"What do you know about the theft and adulteration of certain of our shipments that passed through the Esbjerg distribution site?"

His expression flashed from angry to shocked, then back to

angry in an instant. "I dinnae know who told you such rumors, Mrs. Harper, but they're nae for you to worry your wee bonny head about."

"Oh, really?"

He rose from his seat. "This isnae the sort of place for a woman, Mrs. Harper. Your husband will take care of everything when he returns."

"Returns from where? Esbjerg, perhaps?"

"He didnae say."

Anna rose herself and gave Mr. Douglass a nod goodbye. "You may not like it, Mr. Douglass, but you know that this is, indeed, my business. Someone hired me to investigate for this company, and someone inside the company is doing his very best to stop me. You may want to give some thought to the consequences if you are discovered to be covering for a criminal merely out of dislike for a working woman." She turned and strode to the door.

"You are not my enemy, Mrs. Harper."

Anna paused with her hand on the doorknob. "Who is?"

"I will escort you out."

"I can find my own way, thank you."

"I dinnae think that wise, Mrs. Harper. You might decide to go nosing about some of the other buildings on your investigations, and I cannae have the employees disturbed."

She smirked at him. "The employees I met earlier all seemed to like me."

"Aye. Too much. You're a distraction, lassie. This is no place for a woman."

Anna sighed and rolled her eyes skyward. So many men. The same damn thing. She was beginning to think Quinn Smith was the only man in the world who respected her. She couldn't comprehend leaving him. She couldn't shake the feeling that Harper might be lying about the entire marriage. Was it possible he could have lied to everyone here? Could she still be Anna Smith? If Quinn found himself a potion that cleaned up his memory even slightly, she would drink some of it as well. She wanted the truth.

"Quinn didn't mind having me around the distillery," she said, giving Mr. Douglass a winning smile.

"Quinn is a damned English bastard," Douglass snarled. "Now off with you."

Anna dipped into a curtsey, replying to Douglass' anger with a saccharine smile. "And a very good day to you, too, Mr. Douglass."

She walked away from the distillery without another word. If she wanted to learn more, she would have to sneak in, or find a way to meet with Rabbie or another friendly employee in another location. She could plan for that tonight, after she'd updated Quinn on all her findings.

For now, however, she had another task to complete. Find her solicitors. Find her true, legal, current name. Start the petition for a divorce, if necessary.

And then she and Quinn would celebrate.

XXX

Lost and Found

"*D*AMMIT, where am I?"

Quinn stopped on the street corner and surveyed the unfamiliar roads. This had happened how many times?

He pulled out his notebook and made another tick mark. Six. Six times, he'd paused along the way, only to realize he didn't know where he was or how to get where he was going. And this only since leaving the potion shop.

Which was the—he checked the book again—third shop he had visited. The first chemist had told him there was nothing to be done. The second that his memories would probably return eventually, and he ought to wait it out.

The third had thought about it for some time, asked him a number of questions he didn't think he'd answered particularly well, and then spent an hour testing mixtures before she was satisfied. It would help, she said, though he ought to go to London if he wanted the assistance of a true expert.

Quinn closed the notebook and returned it to his pocket.

How long had it been since he'd drunk the potion? Why didn't he have a watch? He ought to buy one if he could find a shop.

If there were any shops around here.

He chose the direction that looked the least likely to get him into trouble and started walking again, concentrating not on where he was going, but on trying to remember what had happened to his watch. He wouldn't have neglected to bring one on his travels. He was a punctual person. He disliked being late. Despised it, in fact. When he'd overslept that first morning as a dock worker in Esbjerg…

He pulled to a stop again. He remembered! He remembered working in Esbjerg and staying at the fisherman's house, where he'd slept on the hard floor to avoid disturbing Anna. How stupid had that been? He ought to have crawled into her bed the first day he'd met her. Or the second-first day, to be more precise.

He remembered that too. The hotel. Discussing their shared predicament. Sneaking into the Harper-Douglass warehouse and witnessing the men diluting the whisky. Selling his watch and his best suit to pay for their voyage home.

The memories flooded in, clear as day. He looked in all directions, recognizing nothing of the buildings surrounding him. He still couldn't remember where he was, how he had gotten there, or how to get back to where he had started.

He walked up to a man strolling casually down the sidewalk. "Excuse me, could you point me in the direction of the…" He paused to check his notebook. "Waverley hotel?"

"The Waverley? Lad, you're all turned about. Turn around, walk down this street until you reach Drummond. Turn left and walk to Bridge Street. Take a right there and go until you reach the train station. Waverley's right nearby."

Quinn scribbled the directions in his notebook. "Thank you, sir. I appreciate it."

He set off in the correct direction, glad to be done with getting lost. As he walked, he thought back again to Esbjerg and his new-old memories. The ship. Playing games. His second-first kiss with Anna. Utterly delightful. He couldn't wait to tell her he remembered it again. And then perhaps reenact it.

He'd turned onto Drummond and was nearly to Bridge when he realized he hadn't needed the notebook for the directions. His feet had carried him where he wanted to go. Somewhere in the recesses of his mind lurked the memories of this city. It was only when he consciously tried to access them that they slipped away.

And the potion didn't seem to be helping with that. It had restored a number of memories of Esbjerg, and of Newcastle as well, but nothing earlier. It hadn't improved his ability to remember recent events. If anything, his short-term memory was getting worse. Now that he thought about it, he couldn't remember the name of the street he was walking down, the name of the hotel, or who had given him the directions.

He stopped, checked his notebook, and continued on. He was bloody sick of having to look things up every few minutes. The entire population of Edinburgh now probably thought him mad as hops.

Mad as Harper claims I am.

Quinn cursed under his breath. "Why can't I have any of those memories back? Why can't I remember anything that would prove me sane?"

He caught sight of the train station in the distance. A wisp of memory tickled the back of his mind. He had something he wanted to do there. What? He wasn't going anywhere. What else would one do at a train station? Pick up packages?

Telegrams.

"Right."

Quinn walked into the station and to the telegraph office where Anna had posted her message yesterday.

The clerk smiled brightly at him. "Good afternoon, sir. What can I do for you today?"

Quinn had a sense that he'd seen the man before, but his hazy memory told him nothing more. Probably he was the same man who had been here yesterday, and Quinn simply couldn't remember.

"Has a message arrived for Mrs. Anna Harper from…" He had to check the book. "The Earl of Sharpe?"

The clerk shook his head. "No, sir. Not today. I'll keep a look out for it."

"Thank you."

The clerk nodded. "Happy to be of service, Mr. Harper."

Quinn gave the man a nod and headed down the street toward the hotel. He remembered where it was, now, but not the name.

A temperance hotel. I couldn't get a drink. Name starts with a W. West… no. Wake… Wave… Waverley. That's it!

He grinned in triumph as he walked into the lobby. He stopped at the front desk, just in case a telegram had indeed arrived and already been forwarded on to Anna at this address.

"Good afternoon, Mr. Smith," said the same smiling concierge who had made the room arrangements the night before.

"Good after… Wait. What did you call me?" Quinn blinked several times and rubbed his temple.

"Mr. Smith?" The concierge's smile vanished. "Are you unwell?"

Quinn straightened. "No, no. I'm fine. It's only… I had the oddest feeling just now that something wasn't right." He shook his head, which did nothing to clear his mind. "My apologies. Are there any messages for me?"

"No, sir."

"Any for Mrs. Harper? She's expecting a telegram."

"Nothing so far today, sir."

"Thank you." Quinn checked his notebook, knowing there was something else he wanted to do, but not what it was. "Do you know of any shops where I might obtain a quality pocket watch?"

"Ah, of course, sir. I can get you a list."

"Wonderful, and if you could arrange to summon a cab, I would appreciate it." He was done with walking. Let someone who could remember things take him from place to place.

"No need, sir. The hotel has a steam car available. The driver can take you wherever you need to go. And our rates are extremely reasonable, with the recent drop in potion prices."

"Excellent, thank you. Please add it to my bill."

A few minutes later, Quinn was trundling down the street in an enormous black steam car. He had room to stretch his legs out, and two additional full-grown men could have fit alongside him. Behind him was an additional row of seats, which could also be folded down to allow for the transportation of luggage. Another one or two passengers could even sit up beside the driver, if necessary. The car was practically an omnibus. Nothing like the zippy little two-seater that he and Anna owned.

I own a steam car. How about that.

He could picture it, and picture Anna behind the wheel, eager to learn how to drive. Yet another unladylike desire of hers. Quinn had a sense that she was still a novice, though. She hadn't had the time to practice, and the little phaeton wasn't the easiest to control. It could be fussy if you didn't give it just the right throttle, but once you had the knack, it drove like a dream. They'd been able to drive all night once, from Edinburgh to London for...

The memory died out the moment he began to concentrate on it. Damn this faulty brain of his. How was one supposed to let the thoughts flow without thinking about them?

Quinn visited a few shops, purchasing a new watch and a pair of gloves for Anna—fingerless green lace, in an organic pattern that resembled fern leaves. He couldn't resist.

Throughout his shopping, he tried thinking simple words

and phrases, in the hopes they might rekindle the memory he'd interrupted. *Steam car. Night driving. Trip to London.* He didn't let himself dwell on any one thing for more than a second or two.

His efforts were in vain. Try as he might, he couldn't access the remainder of that memory. All he knew was that the journey had happened on a warm night. Anna had been wearing a light dress and no overcoat or shawl. Had they traveled together more recently than February? Maybe he and Anna had never really been apart. Harper would hate that. What the hell could the man possibly be holding over Anna to make her marry him? Quinn couldn't think of anything.

He puzzled it over the entire drive back to the hotel, but had thought up no better ideas by the time he stepped out of the car. He entered the lobby and spied the object of his thoughts at the front desk, her cheeks red and her hair coming loose from its knot. He jogged over to her.

"Any telegrams for me?" she asked the concierge. She sounded winded. Had she been running?

"Anna."

She turned toward him and a broad smile spread across her face. "Quinn! I'm so glad you're here. Are you well?"

"Yes, I seem to be. You?"

"A bit fatigued. I was walking rather quickly. I'm about to go change for dinner. You should too."

"Change?"

"No telegrams yet, ma'am," the concierge said.

"Damn," she muttered. She took Quinn's arm and started for the stairs. "Yes, change. I know you don't have a tailcoat, but you'll want a clean shirt. Also a nice tie and a pair of white gloves. Do you have a top hat?"

He had to think about it for a moment. "No. I don't think so."

"Well, the bowler will have to do, I suppose."

"I take it we're going out, then?"

"Yes. I thought we could go to the Balmoral. So you can get your drink. Hopefully Harper won't insist upon joining us. He's been following me all day."

Quinn scowled. "If he's harassing you, I'll teach him a lesson."

"No, he's keeping his distance. He vanished when I went to visit the Harper-Douglass distillery, as if he didn't want to be seen there. No one at the distillery seems to know he's in town. He apparently disappeared about the same time that I did and hasn't been back since."

"Odd."

"Yes. I did catch him following me shortly after I left. He tailed me while I tracked down my solicitors, but again, he took himself off somewhere while I went inside. I walked particularly quickly on my way back here, hoping to lose him." She glanced over her shoulder. "We should hurry to the rooms before he arrives and spies us. I don't want him to discover my dinner plans."

"I agree with that one hundred percent. Were you able to learn anything today? Were the solicitors any help to you?"

She beamed. "Oh, absolutely. They confirmed that they booked my passage to Esbjerg, at my request, not using my name to conceal the fact that I was traveling on that ship. They also confirmed that I am Anna Harper and that I am legally married."

"Did you see the marriage papers?"

"No. I was married in London. But they gave me the name and direction of my London solicitors, who will have access to those sorts of documents."

"So he *is* your husband. Fuck."

Anna patted his arm. "Don't fret. We still have much to celebrate tonight. Messrs. Stewart and Lachlan have agreed to draw up the necessary papers to begin divorce proceedings. They were surprised by my request, but they support my wishes and they believe I will have little trouble ending the marriage.

I may have the disadvantage of being a woman, but he is a commoner. I am a Lady and sister to Lord Sharpe. Soon I will be free of the odious Mr. Harper."

Quinn grinned at her. "I can't wait."

XXXI
Dinner and a Memory

$\mathcal{A}$NNA STUDIED HER REFLECTION in the full length mirror, turning this way and that to see the dress from every angle. It was perfect. The amber silk clung to her like a second skin, curving beautifully over her round belly. Like her corset, the dress had been designed to expand, and she hoped to wear it many more times over the next several months. She wouldn't be one of those women who tried to hide her pregnancy until the last possible moment. Nor would she be the sort who hid herself until all evidence of procreation had vanished.

Maybe I will wear it as my wedding dress when Quinn and I remarry.

They could elope the moment the divorce was final. They were in Scotland, after all, and she was fairly certain she had a residence here. She would put on this dress, they would handfast over an anvil, and it would be done. Forever this time. Whatever Harper had done before, he couldn't do again. This time, Anna would let nothing tear her from the man she loved.

She tugged at the little cap sleeves on the dress, adjusting them so they sat just off her shoulders. Quinn would like that. He would have plenty of skin to kiss while he searched for the hidden hooks to remove the bodice. She wouldn't tell him where they were. It would be more fun to make him explore.

Anna picked up the matching gloves and pulled them over her hands and up her arms. A departure from the short style she usually sported, these were opera length, running all the way past her elbows. She carefully buttoned each of the dainty buttons that closed the snug gloves at her wrists. Quinn would enjoy this part too. She'd chosen a style that had buttons on the inside of the wrist rather than the more decorative buttons along the top. Now that she was wearing them, she knew she'd chosen this style just for Quinn. This dress was meant for him.

She checked herself over one final time, then picked up her possessions to stow in her pockets. The slim styling of the evening gown limited what she could take. The dagger bookmark and lockpicks went into the small pockets at her hips, and her watch into its own particular pocket. The dress had only a single large pocket, and Anna debated for some time whether to take her notebook or one of the pistols.

Satisfied that her preparations for dinner were complete, she wrapped her cloak around herself and headed for the door. As had become her habit since arriving, she waited and listened before turning the knob. Finding the corridor empty and silent, she securely locked her room and knocked on Quinn's door.

He ushered her inside quickly and locked the door behind her. His preparations ought to have taken considerably less time than hers, yet she found him with his hair untidy and his cravat undone. The worried crinkle between his brows that had become near-constant over the past few days seemed especially deep, and he shifted anxiously as he stood looking at her.

"What's wrong?"

"Everything. Nothing. It's silly." He turned to the mirror and began fussing with his hair.

Anna circled around him and took hold of both ends of his cravat. "Have you been sitting around this entire time doing nothing?"

"I've been trying to tie that. I can't get it right."

She began the pretty, twisted knot that she thought best suited him. She had done this many times, it seemed. Her fingers knew just what to do. "You can't tie your tie?"

"No. I can tie a four-in-hand without even looking, but I tried to do this whatever-you're-doing, and every time I would freeze in the middle, having entirely forgotten how to do it. Then I spent about half an hour digging through my trunk to see if I had a bow tie I could wear instead."

Anna finished the knot and patted it, pleased with the result. "You don't wear bow ties."

"I don't? They're extremely popular these days. Aren't they?"

"Yes, but you don't like them. You think they look too fastidious."

He nodded. "Bowlers and four-in-hands instead of top hats and bow ties. I prefer to look like a working man. So why a bloody cravat?"

"Because it's elegant and classic and sometimes you need to dress up without looking fastidious."

"How do you remember all this?"

Anna shrugged. "I just do. Somehow these general ideas of what you or I like and dislike or how we do things come easier than specific memories."

"Not for me. Is my hair acceptable? It's a bit wild, I think."

"It won't be any better unless you oil it down."

Quinn pulled a face.

"Yes, I agree. Don't oil it. I think you're ready. Grab your coat and we can go."

They slipped from the room and made their way to the exit, watching for Harper or anyone else who looked like he might be following them. She saw no one, but her body remained tense until they were safely inside the Balmoral hotel, depositing Quinn's hat and her cloak at the coatroom.

"Good evening, sir, madam. Here for dinner?"

"Yes, please," Anna replied, whipping off her cloak and handing it over.

Quinn's eyes widened as he took in her dress. "Anna. You look spectacular."

"Thank you." She turned in a circle for him. "I'm so pleased with it. I had it made especially for you."

Quinn offered his arm, and they walked together to the dining room. "I love it. It's elegant, yet simple. It matches your eyes. And it shows off our baby."

She paused. "*Our* baby?"

"No, I haven't remembered anything," he admitted. "But I'll be a father to your child, Anna. No matter what. Even if I can't ever fix this mess that my head has become, I promise to provide for the babe. I'll put in my will that my money goes to the both of you in the event that I'm sent to an asylum."

Anna spun to face him. "You will *not* be sent to an asylum. You are not crazy, Quinn Smith."

He grimaced. "My own name doesn't even sound right to my ears anymore. Anna, I'm losing my mind."

She took hold of his arm again and led him to a quiet corner table. "Sit. Let's talk. Tell me what happened today. Did you visit potion shops? Did you find anything?"

Quinn took out his notebook and opened it flat on the table. He pointed at a neat, numbered list. "Three potion shops. Only the last shop was able to make me a potion. The chemist gave me three small vials of it, and I drank one. I wanted to save one for you if it worked."

A waiter paused near the table and Anna nodded to him. "We'll have the cheese plate to begin, then I will have the roast chicken and my husband will have the mutton. And if you could send the sommelier with a selection of white wines, please."

The waiter stared at her for a long time, and it took her a moment to realize he had probably never in the whole of his life even considered a woman might do the ordering for her husband.

"Uh, aye. Of course," he mumbled eventually. "Anything else?" He waited for Quinn to shake his head before departing.

"Men are so frustrating," Anna sighed.

"I'm sorry, love. I wish we were better."

"You *are* better. And there are other men like you who understand and who care. It gives me hope. Now, tell me about the potion. Did it have any effect? Have you seen any improvement?"

Quinn shook his head. "I'm not sure. I had a flood of memories return. Esbjerg and Newcastle, mainly."

She grabbed his hand and squeezed it. "That's wonderful!"

"Aye. Everything else, however, is… I don't even know. My short-term memory is awful. I forget what I'm doing in the middle of doing it. I see things around town that strike me as familiar, but I can't tell if the familiarity is real or imaginary. Whenever I try to concentrate on a memory, it vanishes. Look how often I became lost." He jabbed at the notebook. "That didn't stop after drinking the potion. I'm pleased to have memories restored, particularly the ones that relate to you, but if I'd had the choice I would have preferred the potion to cure my current problems. I can live with missing memories. But I can't be a good husband to you when I can't even find my way around town or tie my own damn tie."

"Yes, you can. You're being good to me right now, simply by being here. You are good to me by not thinking anything of it when I choose the restaurant and order dinner. You are good to me by swearing to care for a child that might not even be yours."

"How can I not, Anna? The child is innocent. And I can see how much you already love him. Her? Do you think it will be a girl or a boy?"

"I have no idea."

"I hope it's a girl. She will be smart and strong like her mother."

Anna flashed him a smile. "I hope it's a boy. He will become the best of men with you for a father."

Quinn rubbed his temple. "I'm not feeling qualified, love. Not like this. I don't know what I'm going to do if I can't cure this." A man wheeled a cart laden with wine bottles up to their table. Quinn scanned the bottles and pointed to one of them. "I've been considering taking a second dose of that potion, but I'm apprehensive about making things worse." He glanced up at the sommelier who had just filled his glass. "Thank you."

"My pleasure, sir." He set the bottle on the table and departed with the cart.

Quinn cocked his head to one side. "Did I really just choose the wine?"

"Yes, and I'm very glad for it because I don't know anything about wine. Whisky, yes. Wine, no."

He picked up his glass, swirled the liquid around, and took a sniff. "Nice bouquet." He tasted it. "Excellent. See, I am competent at things when I do them automatically. But every time I put any conscious thought into it, poof! My knowledge vanishes."

Anna caught his hand and stroked it, trying to offer him some small comfort. "Do you have the other bottles of potion with you?"

"Aye."

"Try the second dose tonight with our meal. If it hasn't helped by the time we retire for the night, we will search for another alternative. But if you do see any improvement, then you can take the third dose and by morning who knows what amazing things you'll remember!"

"What about you?"

"I'll be fine. We can buy another potion for me at a later time. This is about helping you."

Quinn reached into his pocket and withdrew a small vial.

"I'll try it." He checked his notebook. "I don't have any specific instructions other than to drink it. Here goes nothing." He uncorked the bottle and downed the potion. "Ugh. Tastes terrible."

"Oh, that's an excellent sign. All medicines taste terrible. If it tastes good, it's some sort of snake oil and the seller is trying to convince you to buy more."

"Wise advice. I'll write that down." He scribbled in the notebook. "Snake oil tastes good. Preferable to medicines because those don't work either, and at least you'll die happy."

Anna's heart swelled. His self-deprecating humor slayed her every time. "Do you have any idea how much I adore you?"

"Not especially, no."

She pushed her chair back and rose, motioning at him to remain seated. "No, don't stand up. I want you to look at this dress. I had this dress made just for you, because I knew you'd love the way I looked in it. I had these gloves made just for you." She held out her hands to show off the buttons. "So you can open them up and kiss my wrists the way you do so well. This was for you. I brought it to Esbjerg to show off for you. I had no hotel room there because we had planned to room together. We weren't running away together. I'm in the middle of an investigation, and I wouldn't leave unless it was completed. But I think maybe we were arranging to come home together. To face down Harper and whatever hold he has over us. To take back the life that was stolen from us. The life where you and I are meant to be together. For better or for worse. We've been through the 'worse,' Quinn. And we're still here. We can handle anything together." She took her seat. "Here comes the cheese. Let's begin with a nice dinner."

Anna wasn't certain whether her speech had convinced him, but he did relax as the meal continued. The excellent food filled their bellies and buoyed their spirits. The wine loosened their tense muscles and their tongues. By the time they were munching on a dessert of chocolate biscuits and tea, Quinn was making suggestive comments and openly admiring her bosom.

"I have an idea."

Quinn swallowed another bite of biscuit. "Does it involve kissing? I am open to any idea of yours that involves kissing."

"I think we should get you drunk." Anna had limited her wine intake due to the baby, but he'd had several glasses, and it appeared to have done him good.

"You don't think I've had enough?" He waggled his eyebrows at her. "I'm not leering enough for you, is that it? You want a scoundrel tonight."

"I was actually thinking we might recover some memories."

He sobered immediately. "Oh?"

"You're much more relaxed now. You're smiling, laughing, not worrying or thinking too hard. I thought maybe if you were drunk you might be able to grasp those memories that are slipping away when you concentrate on them."

"An interesting theory."

"I suggest we purchase a bottle of good liquor and sneak it into the temperance hotel, where you can drink until you are silly. Then I will grill you with questions until you remember everything. And if it doesn't work, at least we will have had an enjoyable evening."

"Until I wake up in the morning feeling like a stewed monkey."

"They have potions for that."

"Given my history with potions, I'm not sure I wouldn't prefer the headache. But I like your idea. Let's try it."

A short time later, they departed the restaurant, arm-in-arm, with a small bottle of non-Harper-Douglass whisky tucked into Quinn's coat. They paused by the coatroom to collect their things. An older couple stood nearby, also waiting. The woman looked Anna up and down, frowning at her belly.

Please don't say anything. Please don't say anything.

"A word of advice, young lady," she said.

Anna stifled a groan.

"It's unseemly to be displaying your condition in such a fashion. Loose garments that do not draw attention to the belly are far more modest. You are young, so I assume your indiscretion to be the result of ignorance rather than a deliberate attempt to flaunt your… procreative situation. I must also assume you have not been briefed on healthful habits? Firstly, avoid anything that might overtax your mind, such as intellectual lectures or extensive reading. Novels, in particular, are to be discouraged."

Anna was about to open her mouth to retort, when Quinn spun her around and clasped her to his chest in an impassioned embrace.

"It's mine! The baby is mine!"

"Quinn, what—"

He danced her around in a full circle. "I'm the father!"

"Of all the indecent…" The woman flipped open her fan and waved it vigorously, not actually blowing any cool air across her face. "What an appalling display of vulgarity in a public space!"

Quinn didn't even seem to notice her. He plopped his hat down on his head with a smile of absolute delight and swung Anna's cloak around her shoulders. "I'm the father!" he exclaimed again, before kissing her on both cheeks.

"Er, yes, darling, I know. Perhaps we ought to go home to talk about this."

"Aye, home. Lovely row houses here in New Town. We were lucky to snag one."

She seized his arm. "We have a home here in town? Do you know an address? A street?"

He frowned in confusion. "I… I don't. I'm sorry. Everything's gone hazy."

"No, I'm the one who's sorry. I should never have interrupted you."

"Let's go to the hotel. I'll try out your plan and with luck

I'll spill more interesting facts." He glanced at her belly. "And we'll celebrate."

Anna beamed at the father of her child. "Yes. We will."

XXXII

Celebration

QUINN MUTTERED A CURSE the moment he stepped into the hotel lobby. Wilhelm Harper stood waiting for them, a murderous scowl on his face. He stalked toward them, but Anna pushed Quinn hurriedly toward the front desk.

"Have any telegrams arrived for me?" Anna asked.

"Anna!" Harper reached for her, but she deftly dodged his grasping hands.

"I have nothing to say to you, Mr. Harper."

"Harper?" the man behind the desk asked. "I'm glad you're here, sir. There is a small matter of your bill to settle."

Harper's eyes grew round with panic. "Er... of course. Perhaps after I have spoken with my wife."

Anna seized Quinn's arm and drew him away. "We can check for telegrams later. Mr. Harper has business we don't wish to interrupt."

Harper once again tried to chase them, but at a signal from the concierge, a porter rushed over to intercept him.

"This will only take a moment, sir."

"Anna, you are my wife," Harper insisted, his hand delving into his pocket.

Anna shoved Quinn. "Run."

They bolted for the stairs, neither looking back to see whether Harper had drawn something as innocuous as a pocket watch or a gun, poison, or other weapon. They raced all the way to their floor, where Anna pulled her room key from a tiny hip pocket.

"Your room?" Quinn asked.

"My things are already packed. Help me move my trunk into your room. I don't want to be here when Harper comes demanding entry because he paid for the room or is evicted from the hotel for overspending."

"Do you think he means you harm?" Quinn asked as he hefted the trunk and hauled it through the door.

"I think he means *you* harm. I'd put the chances of him having some kind of spray potion in his pocket at greater than fifty percent."

They maneuvered the trunk into Quinn's room and closed and locked the door. Anna shoved a chair under the handle for added security.

"You think he's our poisoner then?"

"Yes." She pulled off her cloak and hung it on a peg, then gestured at the table. "Sit. Get out that whisky and that last brain-healing potion. We're going to get this all sorted." She fetched her notebook from her trunk, plopped down across from him, and stared him down, her eyes every bit as hard as the ancient amber that lent its name to their color. "Now, what do you remember? Tell me everything."

Quinn cleared his throat. "Well, I was born in Covent Garden, and we lived in a small apartment where I used to play with this little wooden ball…" He grinned at her to show he was teasing.

She shook her head, but he caught her little smile. Some of the tension left her posture. "No, silly. About the baby."

"Oh, right, the baby." Another giddy thrill ran through him as the memory replayed in his mind. The baby was his, and more importantly, not Harper's. "We were in London. You have family there, as you know. We went for a visit with your mother, to tell her the news. She was thrilled, of course, but as we were chatting, a crowd of visitors arrived. Relatives, I believe. You have a great many aunts, uncles, and cousins?"

"Yes, I think so. I know there are many Mastersons. I wish I could remember in more detail."

"Well, what I remember is your mother gushing about the baby and a crowd of ladies bursting into the room, having overheard, and they all needed to give you advice. One of them warned you about novel reading."

"Like the woman at the Balmoral. That's what made you remember."

"You said—and this is what I remember most clearly— 'Oh, I could never stop reading novels. Then I'd never learn how *The Reluctant Rake* ends. The author has said there will be at least three more volumes. Surely spending nine months in suspense would be terrible for the health of everyone involved.'"

"*The Reluctant Rake*? I don't remember that book at all. But now I want to read it. Do you recall any other details?"

"It was well past April." Anna's mother had greeted him like a son. The other relatives had been pleased to see him. Which meant he and Anna had still been married at the time. The child was his, conceived in wedlock, with many aristocratic witnesses who could attest to his legal parentage. It thrilled him beyond belief. Harper had no right to claim the child, and could counter with nothing but unprovable lies. Anna's baby was safe from him. Quinn wanted to dance with glee.

"Harper was lying, then. Not surprising. More evidence that he is our villain. Or one of them." She sat up abruptly straighter. "Mr. Douglass at the distillery was lying too. He claimed everyone there had known me since I married Harper, which he said had been sometime in the spring. He's in on it. I'm guessing everyone knew me from when I visited the distillery with you."

"Me? I worked at the distillery?"

"You designed the stills. I remember you telling me about the adjustments you had made. You were so proud of your work."

"Damn." A feeling of rightness settled in his chest. The very same sensation as when he held Anna in his arms. *This is who I am.* He closed his eyes. "Describe the distillery."

"A large cluster of buildings, very tidy and well-maintained. White-washed walls. My memories of the interiors are vague. I know the room with the stills is large and brightly lit, showing off the gleaming copper. I know the warehouse where the whisky is aged is dimmer, with floor-to-ceiling racks to hold the barrels, arranged youngest to oldest."

Quinn nodded. The memories were there, wafting away when he tried to grasp them. So close, yet so far. "I need to pay a visit."

"That may require sneaking in. Harper is watching us, obviously, and Douglass was eager to see me off. He intercepted me when I might have learned something from a friendly employee."

Douglass. The name freed a sliver of memory in the back of Quinn's mind. "Douglass," he repeated aloud.

"Perpetually unhappy man. Dislikes women and the English. He seemed annoyed by both you and Harper, even though his lies suggest he and Harper are working together in some fashion. He did allude to some family connection..."

Quinn's eyes snapped open. "I'm a Douglass," he blurted.

"You're what?"

"The Scottish part of me. My grandmother was born and raised in Scotland. She would rock in her chair and tell stories from her childhood. Douglass family stories. That's what I called them."

"But if you're family, why would Douglass side with Harper over you? Unless he's doing it reluctantly. For the money? He didn't seem like a part-owner. Perhaps Harper has financial control over the company and therefore power over Douglass."

"But Harper looks to be having financial troubles. Could the thefts be a failed attempt to deceive customers? Stealing his own whisky so that he can sell it twice? Or if the shipments were insured, an attempt to defraud the insurance company?"

"Either is possible. I want to talk with Rabbie MacAlaster again. He was friendly and I think he'd be willing to help me. Tomorrow we can try to sneak in to learn more, perhaps leave a message for Rabbie and possibly others to meet us in secret. It might solve our mystery and trigger those memories of yours that seem so close to breaking loose. What do you think?"

"Don't move," Quinn commanded.

Anna froze. Quinn grabbed her notebook and smashed the spider that had just crawled up the edge of the table.

"Spider," he apologized. "I know you hate them." More memories were invading his unconscious thoughts, and each one made him a bit more optimistic than the last.

She shuddered. "I do. Thank you." She shifted her chair away from the dead arachnid. "I want you to drink that last potion before bed. I think they're helping."

"Drink it before I go to sleep, or before I go to bed? Because I've been looking at you in that dress all evening, and I'd honestly like to go to bed right now."

She grinned. "Whichever you prefer. I'm ready whenever you are to celebrate my impending divorce from Mr. Harper."

Quinn frowned. Why did that statement not sit well with him? Was it the lingering uncertainty? The anger that Anna had been forced into the situation in the first place? He reached for the bottle of potion.

"Tomorrow we're solving this once and for all." He popped

open the bottle and downed the contents. "Tonight I'm going to remind myself of every beautiful inch of your body."

Quinn rose and walked around the table to help Anna to her feet. In typical fashion, she didn't bother to wait for his assistance, but hopped up and threw her arms around his neck. An instant later and he was lost to her warm, inviting kiss.

Her lips moved over his, her tongue teasing and tasting while the smooth silk of her gloved fingers tickled the hairs at the back of his neck. He wrapped his arms around her and drew her tight to his chest. Her soft breasts compressed against him. *No corset. Mmmm.*

Anna dragged her tongue across his upper lip. "You taste like potion," she murmured. "Spicy."

"You don't think it tastes bad?"

She kissed him again, making a slow, deep exploration, savoring him like a finely aged whisky. Quinn groaned into the kiss, helpless in the wake of her thorough ravishment.

"Not bad," she decided. "Interesting. Just a hint of a cool bite. True, it's not lemon tarts or chocolate biscuits, but…" She dove back in and Quinn answered, eager to give her a taste of his own hunger.

His fingers were running along the seams of her bodice, searching for a way to remove it, when a distant knocking sound intruded on his pleasure. Anna stiffened in his arms.

The knock sounded again. Someone was pounding on the door that had until recently been hers.

Quinn held her close and pressed a kiss to her temple. "Ignore it," he whispered. "We're safe here."

A third knock failed to manifest, so he went back to kissing her, caressing her breasts until her nipples stood out beneath the amber silk. He dropped his head to her bosom, teasing the taut peaks with his tongue, moistening the fine fabric. A throaty sigh escaped her lips.

Wham!

The heavy knock made them both jump.

"Smith!" Harper's usually cool voice sounded strained. "Come out, damn you! You've kidnapped my wife!"

Anna slipped from Quinn's arms. She reached behind her back, slid a hand between the folds of her skirt, and withdrew one of the small pistols they'd taken from the criminals on the train. As he stared at her wide-eyed, she nudged him toward the bed, out of the path of anyone breaking through the door. She stepped in front of him, leveling the gun at where any would-be-intruder might appear.

Harper pounded again. "Smith! Anna! Are you in there? Answer me!"

Quinn and Anna remained frozen in place, saying nothing, waiting Harper out. He knocked and shouted until another voice joined the clamor, yelling at him to quiet down. The knocking ceased.

Anna waited for some time before lowering the pistol. Quinn wrapped an arm around her and kissed her bare shoulder.

"You keep a gun in your bustle?"

"It's a pocket." She flipped up the folded fabric above her bottom to show him. "The dress doesn't allow for large pockets anywhere else."

"This is going to be a plot point in… uh… whatever the name was of that penny dreadful I intended to write. Maybe I'll call it *The Daring Debutante* instead. The tagline can be: *He saved her from spiders, but she saved him from villains.*"

Anna set the gun down on the bedside table. "I'm no debutante."

Quinn embraced her again, trailing kisses down the back of her neck, his hands resuming their search for the bodice fastenings. "You could pretend to be. I'll be the unscrupulous libertine who is seducing you."

She went half-limp in his arms. "Oh, Mr. Smith, you make me feel so… so wanton. Mama says I'm not to be alone with you, but I love your kisses. That's wicked of me, isn't it?"

He trailed his tongue along her shoulder. "Very wicked. And your mama is absolutely right. I'm a terrible scoundrel who intends to ruin you this very night."

"But you're so *nice*."

Quinn pinched her nipples and she squirmed and sighed. "Yes, love. I'm going to make you feel very nice indeed."

"The hooks are down the right side, by the way," she whispered.

He found the hooks and freed her from the bodice, gently pulling the sleeves down her arms without disturbing her gloves. He spun her slowly around, taking his time admiring her round, plump breasts before cupping them in his hands and bending to taste them.

"Quinn, I'm losing my character. Am I supposed to be horrified by my nakedness or overwhelmed by the erotic power of your caresses?" Her eyes fluttered closed. "Oh, that's lovely."

"The latter." He unfastened the last few hooks, untied her underskirt and let the whole dress fall to the floor. He lifted her out of the pile of silk and set her atop the bed, crawling up beside her. "You love being naked for me. You snuck out in the hopes of meeting me alone and allowing me to have my way with you."

"Yes." She kicked off her shoes, then peeled off her stockings and drawers while Quinn freed himself from his own garments. "I am a bad, bad girl."

"Don't touch the gloves."

She ran a single silk-clad finger between her breasts and down over the rounded bump of her belly. "You like my gloves, Mr. Smith? I bought them just for you."

"I know you did, you naughty girl." He stretched out beside her, nuzzling her neck and splaying his fingers over her belly. "It appears you have been a naughty girl in the past, as well."

"You seduced me."

Quinn took hold of her left wrist and began to work the tiny buttons that closed the gloves. "Oh, I did, did I?"

"Yes. In a linen closet."

The last button popped, and he brought her wrist to his lips, feeling the little shiver that ran up her arm. "I would wager I did this."

"Yes. I was powerless to resist."

"Mmm." He sucked gently at the soft skin alongside her birthmark. "My Anna-Moon. You shine like no other. You illuminate even the darkest night."

"Quinn," she sighed.

As he continued to lavish attention on her wrist, her free hand drew languid little patterns along his bare thigh. His skin tingled everywhere the smooth silk stroked him, and he thrust against her hip in response, groaning her name.

Her wicked fingers inched closer and closer until at last they curled around his cock, the soft fabric of her gloves sliding over his rigid shaft as her hand squeezed and pumped.

"God, Anna, yes."

He eased a hand between her legs, nudging her thighs apart and stroking her as eagerly as she stroked him. She lifted her hips into his touch, a little mewl of pleasure escaping her lips.

Her fingers worked him harder, the contrast of the soft silk and her vigorous strokes the sweetest of tortures. He closed his eyes and clenched his teeth, determined not to stain her gorgeous gloves with his spend.

"Anna," he gasped. "Anna, I need to be inside you."

Her hand slowed, her fingers brushing over him in tiny caresses that were nearly as excruciating as her firm stroking.

"Yes, I'd like that," she said at last, pushing him onto his back.

She straddled his hips and he sank into her, moaning his pleasure. Her sweet, wet quim was the only thing more perfect than her gloved hand. He grasped her waist, matching her slow and steady rhythm, clinging to the last vestiges of his self-control. He wanted her to find her pleasure first. Needed her to be first.

Her back arched. "Quinn," she groaned.

"Aye, love. Let go."

He pumped faster and she jerked, gasping and shuddering as the climax rushed through her. Quinn buried himself to the hilt, gasping in relief as the force of his own release sent him tumbling into a slow freefall of ecstasy.

Anna sagged against his chest, her cheek pressed above his pounding heart, her gloved fingers moving gently up and down his arm. He wrapped his arms around her and pressed a kiss into her hair.

"You forgot to get me drunk," he said. The simple fact that he'd remembered her plan made him grin like a fool. Though he had to admit that the sight of the bottle of whisky sitting on the table might have helped jog his memory.

"I did. And I'm not sorry for it. Do you want to try it now, or would you rather cuddle and make love again?"

"Do you even need to ask?"

Anna laughed. "No, I suppose I don't." She pushed herself up to a sitting position. "I'll get the whisky."

"Teasing minx! But since you're up, you could change into the new pair of gloves I bought you."

"You bought me new gloves? Ooh. What color?"

"Honestly, I don't remember. But I can see the box sitting there on top of my trunk. Go try them on and then come back here and thank me."

Her joyful and emphatic thanks lasted well into the night, when they finally burrowed beneath the blankets, sleepy, satisfied, and full of hope for tomorrow. The potions had helped, they were together, and their mutual love gave them strength. Quinn sank into a dream-like trance, imagining bouncing a dark-haired girl on his knee as they faced Anna across a game board.

A pair of soft lips pressed against his shoulder. "I love you, Quinn Smith."

"Harper," he replied. "My name is Harper."

"Hmm? What was that, darling? I couldn't hear you."

He tried to answer, but the words again came out an incoherent mumble. Something about this was important, though his sleepy brain couldn't comprehend why.

Tomorrow, came his last thought before Morpheus swept him from the waking world. *I can tell her tomorrow.*

XXXIII

Domino Effect

"WELL, THAT WAS a lovely breakfast."

Anna set down the empty teacup and smiled across the table at Quinn. Today was the day. By now her message would have reached Rabbie MacAlaster at the distillery. They would sneak in to meet him, get answers to their questions, and hopefully put enough facts together to unravel Harper's crimes.

She was certain the distillery would jog more of Quinn's memories loose. He'd already shown marked improvement. He hadn't forgotten the events of last night and he'd spent most of breakfast reminding her of places they'd visited on their honeymoon. Her own memory seemed clearer this morning as well, though she couldn't say whether it was aided by Quinn's own recollections or by the drops of potion she'd licked from his lips.

"It was. I'm pleased to see you eating so heartily every morning. It worried me when you began every day ill."

"You remember that again?" Her smile grew bigger. "Oh, Quinn, I'm so happy to see how much you've improved!"

He grinned back at her. "Don't get too excited. I'm still a touch foggy. A number of things still elude me. Directions, places, names."

"Oh, if you want to see bad with names, you should talk to my brother. His is no typical habit of forgetting names. It's as if the name enters his ears only to be snatched up by a demon and whisked away to the darkest level of hell, never to be seen again."

Quinn laughed. "His name is Nick, correct? Lord Sharpe? I'll have one up on him then, when we meet again." He swallowed the last of his tea, then rose and offered Anna his hand. "To the distillery. Hopefully when we return we'll have a message from this notorious name-forgetter."

They donned their outerwear and headed for the door, where the hotel car would be waiting to drive them about for the day. As they passed through the lobby, Anna surveyed the area for signs of Harper or other suspicious persons.

"I'm wondering if they evicted him," Quinn said, following the train of her thoughts. "In that case, he might be watching the door."

"Yes. In a cab, even, waiting to follow us."

"Entirely plausible."

Outside, the waiting driver waved a hand at a massive black steam car. He opened the passenger door and set a step stool beside it. Anna had set a single booted foot atop the stool, when a shout made her jump.

"Mrs. Harper!"

Anna turned toward the frantic voice. A young man came racing to her, waving a slip of paper. He skidded to a halt beside her and tipped his cap. Anna studied him, a vague sense of familiarity nagging at her. Wide dark eyes. Warm, brown skin. A deep dimple in his left cheek. She couldn't place him.

"I have your telegram, Mrs. Harper!" The youngster held out the note to her. "I'm so sorry. It ought to have been delivered last night, even late as it was. When I saw this morning that it had arrived, I rushed to bring it to you. I know you've been asking after it."

"Thank you so much." Anna unfolded the paper, her hands

trembling with excitement. At last! Her answer from Nick. She read the brief words.

On overnight train. ETA 9:12 a.m.

"That's it? For heaven's sake, Nick, you are the worst communicator." She looked up at Quinn, whose blue-gray eyes watched her with undisguised curiosity. "He's arriving in just over half an hour. I need to go meet him. What are we going to do about the meeting with Rabbie? Could we risk sending another message and asking him for a later time? I don't want him getting caught and losing his job, or worse."

"I'll go alone. You meet with your brother."

Anna took Quinn's arm and drew him away from the others, glancing around for potential eavesdroppers. "I don't like that. What if Harper follows you? What if he means you harm?"

"I won't be alone. I'll be inside that hulking car with a driver to help me. And once I'm at the distillery, I'll have allies. I promise to be careful."

Anna bit her lower lip, her protective instincts warring with her investigative ones. "Fine," she agreed at last. She snuck one of the small pistols out of her pocket and slipped it into Quinn's coat. "Take this."

"I have one."

"I want you to have two."

"And what about you?"

"I'll have Nick."

Quinn nodded. "Gather back here when we've learned all we can?"

"Yes. Good luck." She kissed him, not caring that her behavior was scandalous.

Anna waited until Quinn was safely inside the steam car and it was trundling down the road before walking to the train station. The telegraph boy escorted her all the way, repeatedly apologizing for the delay in receiving her message.

"If I'd been the one there last night, I would have taken it right to you," he said. "But I work the day shift most days now. The new lad, he doesn't know you yet."

Anna's steps slowed. "You know me?"

The boy laughed. "Of course I know you, Mrs. Harper. You didn't think you and Mr. Harper could send as many telegrams as you do and I wouldn't remember you? And Mr. Harper always says, 'Thank you.' Most rich men don't bother."

"He does?" That didn't sound much like the self-absorbed Harper she knew.

"'Course he does." The young man frowned at her confusion. "Is something wrong, Mrs. Harper? It's peculiar for you to be staying at a hotel instead of at home. I'm sorry, it's not any of my business."

"No, no, you are quite right to be concerned, Mr...?"

"Smith—"

Anna almost groaned aloud.

"Field. Jack Smithfield."

"Well, that's at least a little different," she muttered.

"Pardon?"

"Tell me, Mr. Smithfield, do you know my address here in town? My real address, rather than the hotel."

"Of course."

"Wonderful. This may sound odd, but do you think you could write it down for me?"

"Sure can. I have paper and pen at the office."

"Excellent. That will be a great help. And would you happen to know which train arrives at 9:12 a.m.?"

"The overnight from London? Platform three."

"Thank you. I can see why they want you on the day shift. You have an excellent mind for details. Keep it up and they'll want you in charge of the whole office."

His grin showed off his dimple to great effect. "That's my plan."

"And an excellent plan it is."

"Thanks, Mrs. Harper. That's kind of you to say so." He ducked into the telegraph office and returned momentarily with a slip of paper with an address written on it. "Here you are. If you need to send any more messages or have any more questions, I'll be here most of the day."

"Thank you, Mr. Smithfield. I may yet return. But first I have to meet my brother."

"9:12 a.m. Platform three." He nodded to her. "Good day, Mrs. Harper."

"And a very good day to you as well."

Anna unfolded the paper with her address on it as she made her way to platform three. Great King Street. She knew the area. A pretty, upper-class neighborhood northwest of here, and not far from the distillery. Perhaps she could convince Nick to take a drive past the house. She wasn't certain if she wanted to go inside. If the staff were loyal to Harper, that could prove problematic. She sat herself down on a bench to mull the matter over.

The train arrived two minutes early. Anna recognized Nick the moment he stepped off the train: tall, broad-shouldered, dark-haired, and with a commanding presence born from years of life in the peerage. A woman with short blond hair wearing a pink overcoat hung on his arm. His wife.

Friend, Anna's memory told her, and this time the word brought nothing with it but a sense of genuine affection.

"Anna!"

Brother and sister raced towards each other, dodging other pedestrians before catching one another in a fierce embrace.

"Nick! I'm so happy you're here!"

Once-hazy memories crystalized in her mind. It was as if she'd never forgotten him. Not only did she recall childhood games, but now she could remember his entire house—including the linen closet. It was different now than when she'd lived there, because he had redesigned every room, from wallpaper, to drapery, to furniture. He had the best eye for aesthetically-pleasing decor of anyone she'd ever encountered. He'd even begun to make a business out of his talent. Peculiar for an earl, but she loved it.

She looked up into his amber eyes, remembering the way they had teared up as he'd handed her off to Quinn at their wedding. Then more tears at his own wedding, after she and Quinn had rushed to London to be there.

Nick released her and stepped back. "You look well. How are you? You were drugged? How is your memory? What can I do to help?"

"I'm fine, and the memory is returning in bits and pieces. I've recovered quite a lot simply seeing you and Berries." She looked at Lady Sharpe. "I'm sorry, I've forgotten your real name. You'll have to remind me."

"Ida." She held out a hand and Anna took it and gave her an affectionate squeeze.

"Ida. Of course. Perfumes by Ida. Your new business. The soap test has been a complete success. The rose scent lingers long after washing without being cloying. I can't wait to see the results of your handkerchief tests."

Ida beamed. "Thank you. Shall we find a cafe where we can sit and talk? Or would you prefer to go home? I'm sure you must have so many more questions than just my name. I'll try to answer as many as I can, and you must brief us on how this happened in the first place. Nick has been in an absolute panic since your message arrived. He was certain you were irreparably harmed or in danger of being sent to an asylum, but you seem entirely in command of yourself, and you look in perfect health. And your belly looks so cute! Can you feel the baby kicking yet? I'm so excited for you!"

Nick took hold of his wife's arm. "Ida, darling, I know you love to chat, but perhaps we can move the conversation off the train platform? Maybe somewhere with coffee? I hardly slept on the train and my head is pounding. Anna, you have coffee at your house, don't you?"

Anna gestured for the others to follow her. "We'll find a restaurant with coffee. We aren't going to my house. Not yet."

"Whyever not?"

"I'm not certain it's safe."

Nick stopped walking. "Seriously, Anna, what the devil is going on? Are we in danger? I would never have brought Berries along if I knew there would be danger."

Ida put her hands on her hips. "Excuse me?"

Nick sighed. "I would have tried to come alone and she would have insisted upon following me. Let's go get the damned coffee."

Anna led them to the Balmoral hotel, choosing the same corner table where she and Quinn had eaten dinner. Hot pots of coffee and tea arrived within moments and Nick's whole body sagged in relief.

"Thank God." He took a sip of the coffee and let out a satisfied sigh. "Now tell me what's going on, Anna. Why do you think your house isn't safe? And where in hell is Harper? I can't believe he would leave you alone at a time like this."

"I have no idea where he is."

Please not following Quinn. Follow me instead.

She scanned the room, hoping for a glimpse of him. She'd be thrilled to be spied on if it meant Quinn was safe.

Nick gave her a puzzled frown. "No idea? Have you forgotten? Was that part of the memory problem?"

"It's not a memory problem. I simply don't know."

Nick and Ida exchanged a look of confusion.

"That's not normal, Anna," Ida said. "You two have always been inseparable. Is something wrong? Is he forgetting to tell you things? Or is it only those strange troubles at the distillery?"

Anna shrugged. "I have no idea. I couldn't care less about his troubles. He won't be bothering me much longer. I've filed for divorce."

Nick spit coffee all across the table. "You've *what?*" he choked.

"Oh, no!" Ida clapped a hand over her mouth. "Oh, Anna, that's awful! You were so in love. What happened?" She blinked away a tear. "And now you'll have to raise your baby all on your own. Or will he take the baby away from you? Oh, Anna!"

"He has no claim on my baby. Mr. Smith is the baby's father and he and I will raise our child together, just as we were always meant to."

Nick had gone as pale as the white coffee cup clenched in his hand. He stared at his wife. "We need to get help. Right now. I don't know what she was drugged with, but she's completely off her head. I hope Harper doesn't believe any of this nonsense she's spewing."

Ida dabbed at her eyes with her napkin. "He must be absolutely devastated."

Anna set her teacup down with enough force to rattle the saucer. "I am right here in front of you, and I am *not* spewing nonsense. You both know full well that Quinn is the father of my child. We made the announcement at *your* house."

"I remember," Ida said. "But then who is Mr. Smith? Oh, Anna, you sound so confused."

"Quinn Smith," Anna replied confidently, though she felt anything but. "My first husband."

Nick and Ida exchanged another long, silent glance.

"Quinn *Harper*," Nick corrected. "Your *only* husband."

"Quinn Harper."

Anna's head swam. She grabbed hold of the table to steady herself as the memories fell like dominoes.

And why would you wish to teach me such things, Mr. Quinn Harper of Harper-Douglass Whisky?

Ha! Take that, Quinn Harper!

You are a naughty man, Mr. Quinn Harper.

I love you, Quinn Harper.

I am pleased to announce the engagement of Lady Anna Masterson to Mr. Quinn Harper.

I love you, Quinn Harper.

I win again, Quinn Harper.

I love you...

"Quinn. Oh, no. Oh, God, what have I done?"

Her brother took hold of her arm. "Anna, it's all right. Everything's going to be all right. We'll find Harper. We'll get you a doctor."

"I have to go. I have to fix this." She pushed herself up from the table. Colored lights danced in front of her eyes. The room tilted. Memories poured in, one atop the next, smothering her beneath the unending stream. "Have to fix..." She took two staggering steps. "Quinn..."

For the first time in the whole of her life, Anna Harper swooned.

XXXIV
Taking Ownership

"STOP THE CAR!"

The driver hit the brakes and turned to look at Quinn. "Sir?"

Quinn stared down the wide road at the handsome Georgian row houses. "I know this street."

"Aye, sir. Great King Street and Pitt, that's where we are, sir. Lovely neighborhood."

"Turn here. Left."

"Not the distillery, sir?"

"Later. I need to see something first."

"Very good, sir. Shall I drive slowly?"

Quinn nodded. "Aye. I'll let you know if I want to stop."

"Very good, sir."

The driver turned back to his duties and took the car in a wide turn onto Great King Street. Quinn peered out the window, watching each house pass by. He knew this neighborhood. He'd driven it. Walked it. Hit these very same bumps in the road.

"Here, right here. Stop." The driver pulled the car to the side of the road. "Wait here. I'll be back shortly."

"Aye, sir. Of course. Shall I open the—"

Quinn was out the door before the man could finish his sentence, bounding up the front steps of what he was certain was his own house. Or had been, once. There was only one way to find out. He rapped on the door.

The door opened promptly, and a gray-haired butler with rosy cheeks and a prominent chin peered out.

My butler, Quinn knew immediately, though the man's name escaped him.

"Mr. Harper!" the butler exclaimed. He swung the door wide to usher Quinn inside. "Please come in, sir. I'm sorry we didn't know you were coming. We will have the house ready in no time. Is Lady Anna not with you? Will she be arriving soon?"

Lady Anna. Mr. Harper.

The names rattled in his head for a moment, chipping away at some of the confusion that had been plaguing him the last few days. Names that had been right yet somehow wrong.

"Harper," he said, testing the name aloud. "Not Smith."

"We haven't forgotten, sir," the butler assured him. "We always use the name Smith with Lady Anna's clients. But she hasn't had any callers since she's been away."

"Good, good," Quinn replied distractedly. "But Harper is her real name. Harper is *my* name."

The butler's face scrunched up into a worried frown. "Yes, sir, of course it is."

"Quinn Harper." A feeling of intense satisfaction filled Quinn's chest. "Mr. Quinn Harper of Harper-Douglass Whisky."

Wispy memories began to coalesce. The day a solicitor had arrived at his tiny flat in Covent Garden to tell him he was now the proud owner of a whisky manufactory. The months—no, years—of research and study, learning the ins and outs of distillation and meeting with every expert he could find. The pride when people had at last begun to take notice of his hard work. Anna's very first tour of the distillery. The sense of betrayal when he'd discovered someone had been stealing from the company.

"Petersen," he snarled, his enemy's true name coming out before he had a chance to stop and think about it. "The scoundrel! After all I did for him. And trying to steal Anna from me, the bastard!"

"Sir?" Quinn's butler had taken several nervous steps away. "Is there something we can do to help you?"

Quinn shook his head. His memory still had gaps, and he was struggling to remember why Anna hadn't come along with him, but he knew what he had to do. He had to question Rabbie and the other employees. Stop Petersen for good. And discover whether Douglass had joined in the treachery.

"No. Please excuse me. Lady Anna and I will return later today, but I have work to do now." He turned and walked out the door to where the hotel car awaited him. "And I'll be damned if I'm going to sneak into my own bloody distillery!"

"Sir?" the driver asked.

Quinn climbed into the vehicle. "To the Harper-Douglass distillery, please. Front entrance."

"Mr. Harper, sir," a young voice hissed. Quinn turned to see Rabbie MacAlaster waving at him from behind a stack of crates. "Over here."

"Come on out, Rabbie," Quinn called. "I'd like to talk to you."

The young man's eyes grew wide, and he looked around nervously before darting to Quinn's side.

"Should we hide?" he asked. "The note said to be absolutely

secret. I was worried when you were late. Where is Mrs. Harper? Should we hide?"

"This is my company, and I'm not hiding from anyone."

The boy wrung his hands but nodded vigorously. "Yes, sir. Mrs. Harper said you had questions for me?"

"I did, but I think many of them have already been answered. Come along with me. I need to speak to Mr. Douglass."

"Which Mr. Douglass, sir?"

"Uh…" Quinn picked through his scattered memories of his business, trying and failing to put names with faces. "The Mr. Douglass who dislikes me."

"Och, aye. That'll be Hamish. But don't take it t' heart, sir. Hamish Douglass likes no one."

"Me least of all."

Rabbie shrugged.

Quinn gestured at what he thought was his office building. "His office is this way?"

"Aye, sir."

"Good." Quinn entered the building, following the path that felt right rather than trying to think his way through. He hammered on a door, and a moment later a brawny, dark-haired man opened it. His brown eyes grew round in surprise before narrowing into a scowl of utter disgust.

"Smith," he snarled.

"Harper," Quinn corrected.

The look of surprise flashed once more across Hamish Douglass' face. "So, you've remembered yourself, have you?"

"Aye, I have," Quinn replied, putting more certainty into his voice than he actually possessed. "And what I'm wondering is, why did you address me by a false name just now? One might think you wanted me not to remember."

Douglass answered with nothing more than a grunt and seated himself back behind his desk.

"What was Petersen's game? Are you a part of it?"

Douglass muttered something half in Gaelic. All Quinn could make out were the words, "bloody Englishmen."

"Are you?" Quinn demanded.

Douglass stared at him, stone-faced.

Quinn pounded his fist on the desk. "Answer me, dammit! This is my fucking company, whether you like it or not, and if you're trying to destroy it I will have you put down like a rabid dog!"

"Dinnae want…" Douglass mumbled.

"What?" Quinn demanded.

Douglass' head snapped up and he met Quinn's glare with one of his own. "I dinnae want to destroy the company! I'm nae a fool. But it should be mine."

"Uncle Owen left it to me. He had no children and my grandmother is his sister. I was the closest heir he had."

"You're nae in the male line."

"So?"

"It cannae pass through a woman! This distillery belongs to me. It shouldnae have your damned English name on it."

"That's woman-hating bullshit. He named me in his will. That's that."

"Your grandmother betrayed the Douglass name, running away with that Englishman."

"My grandmother lost her sight, she worked so hard and so long at a horrible, low-paying, grueling job to feed her family! She is a bloody astounding woman and worth a hundred of you! Now get your fucking arse off my property and never come back!"

Douglass didn't move.

Quinn drew one of the revolvers and pointed it at Douglass' chest. "Get. Off. My. Property."

Douglass rose slowly, shoving his chair so hard that it toppled over. "Rot in hell, Harper," he snarled, elbowing his way past Quinn to the door.

Quinn followed, determined to escort the man from the

premises at gunpoint if that's what it took. Douglass stormed from the building, only to stagger to a halt the moment he set foot outside. Quinn came within inches of crashing into him.

"Christ Almighty," Douglass swore.

The acrid scent of smoke stung Quinn's nostrils. He pushed past Douglass to see a narrow column of black curling up from the far side of the warehouse where his whisky was aged.

"Fire!" Douglass shouted. He raced toward the source of the conflagration. Quinn dropped the gun and ran after him. "Get water! Buckets! Form a line!" Douglass pointed and gestured at every man he saw, herding them into order. "Now, man! Now!"

Quinn laid a hand on the bigger man's shoulder. Douglass turned to look at him. "You gather everyone on this side," Quinn said. "I'll circle around back. We work together. Men first, then the whisky. Wood and bricks are replaceable. Understood?"

Douglass gave him a firm nod. "Aye."

"Back to work." Quinn bolted for the opposite end of the building, leaving Douglass to corral the workers into a makeshift fire brigade.

"Mr. Harper, sir," Rabbie said from somewhere behind him. "How can I help?"

Damn. Quinn had entirely forgotten about the boy during his screaming row with Douglass.

"Water. Buckets. Gather everyone you can and start filling and carrying. Make a chain. I'm going to make sure no one's left inside that building."

Rabbie's jaw dropped. "You can't go in there! You could be killed!"

"Mr. MacAlaster, I am the owner of this distillery, and I am responsible for every single man who works here. You'd better believe I'm going in there. Now get to work!"

"Aye, sir!" Rabbie raced off, shouting at men who were

standing around in shock and beginning to line them up just as Douglass had done. He'd make a good supervisor some day.

Quinn ran for the back door to the warehouse and yanked it open. A blast of hot air hit him in the face, making him rock backwards in shock.

"Is anyone in there?" he bellowed.

Silence.

"Anyone?" he called again.

A muffled groan came from somewhere inside.

"Goddammit!" Quinn yanked off his necktie and unfastened his shirt enough that he could pull it up over his nose and mouth. "Crawl for the door! I'm coming for you."

Forgive me, Anna.

He pressed his shirt to his face and plunged inside.

XXXV
A Sea of Troubles

ANNA HAMMERED HER FISTS against her brother's irritatingly hard chest. "Put me down!"

The front door of her townhouse swung open before he could kick it in, thank God, and Nick strode into the atrium with Anna wriggling in his arms.

"Summon a doctor," he commanded. "Lady Anna is unwell."

"I'm fine!" Anna hit him again, to absolutely no effect. "Put me down, damn you!"

Ida covered her mouth in shock. "Anna!"

Anna stopped squirming. "Haven't you ever heard a lady swear before?"

"No. Only… Well, only myself, and then only when I was very, very angry."

"She called me a 'bloody arse,' once," Nick said proudly.

"You *are* a bloody arse," Anna snapped. "Now put me down."

"Promise you won't swoon again?" He set her on her feet as gingerly as if she were made of glass, hands hovering, prepared to catch her if she fell.

She swatted him away. "I'm fine."

A footman raced into the hall, his hat askew, tugging on an overcoat as he ran. "I'll have the doctor here as soon as I can."

"Stop," Anna ordered. "I don't need a doctor. I'm perfectly well."

"Fetch the doctor," Nick said in that annoying I'm-an-earl-so-I-can-do-whatever-I-want voice of his.

"Right away, my lord," the footman replied before darting out the door.

Anna threw up her hands. "Even my own staff!"

Ida laid a gentle hand on her arm. "I know you must be frustrated, but you fainted dead away and the things you were saying didn't make any sense at all. You should have a doctor check you and the baby, to be safe. And with the Royal College of Surgeons here in town there are a great many excellent doctors available. You will have the very best care."

"Ugh!" Anna stomped toward the door. "I don't need the very best care. I need to leave. Now. I have to see the solicitors before the divorce becomes final."

"You have plenty of time, Anna," Nick replied. "It needs to go through the courts. A judge will need to hear your case and review it."

"I told them to expedite the process. Ugh! You would think they could have mentioned that his name was Quinn. But, no, it was just 'Mr. Harper' this and 'Mr. Harper' that. 'You wish to divorce Mr. Harper? I'm sorry to hear that, but I'm certain we can make the arrangements.' I should have asked. I should have said, 'What's my husband's name?' Then this would have been done with yesterday! But now it's all a wreck. I don't want to divorce Quinn. I wanted to divorce the false Mr. Harper who it turns out was never my husband in the first place, thank heavens. Because if I had had to sleep with that slimy, harebrained… Forget it. Forget all of it. I'm leaving to fix everything. Have fun chatting with the doctor."

She yanked open the door, jumping backward when she came face-to-face with a raised fist.

The man immediately dropped the hand that Anna belatedly realized had been about to knock on the door. "So sorry to startle you, miss. I have trunks from the Waverley hotel for Lady Anna Harper?"

Anna frowned over her shoulder at her brother. "You had my trunks fetched?"

"I'm not having you stay in some hotel when you have a perfectly good house here where you can recuperate."

Anna rolled her eyes and turned back to the man at the door.

"Leave them there. My brother can haul them inside." She shot Nick a triumphant look. "And then I'd like to hire your cab."

"Of course, miss."

Anna strode out toward the waiting vehicle, pausing when she spotted a thin tendril of dark gray standing out against the clear, blue sky.

"Is that smoke? Is something on fire?" She sniffed the air. Her gaze followed the trail toward the ground, estimating the location. "Oh, Lord, the distillery! Quinn! You! Cab driver! We have to go now! Hurry!"

"Anna!"

She leapt into the waiting cab before her brother could try to grab her. "No! You can't stop me! I have to go. Quinn could be in danger!"

Nick knelt beside her trunk, unfastening the latches and digging through her possessions, his face grim. "I won't stop you. But you should take this."

He tossed something at her, and she snagged it out of the air. Her little bear. Anna stared at the toy, remembering it fully now. Nick the girl bear looked as silly as ever in her crooked waistcoat and fluffy tutu. Small. Cute. Deathly fierce.

"Go help your husband," Nick said. "Ida and I will be right behind. With the doctor."

"Thank you." She turned to the driver. "The Harper-Douglass distillery. As quickly as possible."

The driver snapped the reins and the horses sprang into action. She slipped Nick the bear into a pocket. Her other hand found the cool metal of the gun.

"If you've hurt Quinn, you are a dead man, Wilhelm 'Harper' Petersen," she whispered. "You are going to rue the day you ever laid eyes on a bottle of whisky."

Flames leapt from the pile of rags and debris in front of the double doors that served as the warehouse's primary entrance. Arson. No bodies lay on the floor. No men cried out for help.

A trap. He'd walked into a goddamned trap.

Quinn heard a noise behind him just in time to spring to one side. An iron pipe surely intended to crush his skull landed instead on his shoulder. Pain blossomed all across the left side of his body. His vision blurred and he staggered, narrowly avoiding a second blow.

Clutching his left arm to his chest, Quinn ran deeper into the warehouse, weaving among racks of barrels to hide from Petersen's murderous wrath. Stinging tears ran down his cheeks and his throat burned.

Sunlight streaming in from above gave him hope. The narrow clerestory windows were left open to allow for the air to circulate in the building. Grabbing hold of the closest rack with his good hand, Quinn hauled himself up until his head was level with the window, bracing himself between the rack and the wall.

Gulping fresh air, he paused to assess himself. Now that he had stopped, his head was swimming with the pain. His left arm hung limply, his shoulder misaligned. Using his right hand to assist, he shoved his left hand inside his waistcoat to hold the arm still, like a bad caricature of one of those military portraits.

Quinn leaned his head against one of the eight-year-old barrels. His oldest whisky. He had a list of customers eager to purchase it two years from now. The first batch of ten-year Harper-Douglass. He had a small store of barrels in London, but even the astronomical price they would no doubt fetch if they became a rarity couldn't make up for the loss of the rest. If this warehouse burned down, his life's work would be obliterated.

Breathe, Harper.

Quinn filled his lungs with another deep breath of cool, clean air. All was not lost. The conflagration was in the clearest area of the building. The distillery sat right on the banks of the Water of Leith. His workers were even now hauling water from the river to douse the flames. If he could get out of this building, he could direct them to break down the doors and hit the fire at its heart.

If he could get out.

The front doors were a flaming mess. The high windows were too small to fit through. Petersen lay in wait somewhere between Quinn and the back exit.

Or had he ducked outside? Whatever scrap he had burned gave off great roiling clouds of smoke. He couldn't remain inside without some breathing apparatus. Even here by the window, the smoke stung Quinn's eyes and made him cough.

And it was growing worse. He was sweating profusely from the heat, and the pain in his shoulder caused his vision to blur. He needed to take the risk and run for the exit.

Quinn dug into the pocket of his coat with his free hand, wobbling precariously without the extra stability of his hand against the wall. His fingers found the handle of the second pistol. Anna had been right to send him with an extra.

He took one more breath of clean air, then dropped to the ground, wincing as the impact with the floor jarred his injured shoulder. He took off at a run, thanking God his restored memories included the ability to navigate the warehouse. He flew past rack after rack of barrels, gun at the ready, prepared to fire if necessary.

Petersen was nowhere to be seen. Quinn ran at the back door, ramming it with his good shoulder. A wave of pain shot through his entire body but the door remained firmly closed.

No.

Quinn tried again, but though the door shuddered a bit, it refused to swing open. Petersen had blocked it from the outside.

No!

Quinn aimed the pistol and shot out the door lock, then tried again, with no better result. In a panic, he fired the rest of the bullets straight through the door, wildly hoping that he might dislodge something, or even hit Petersen if he was obstructing the door personally.

Exhausted and choking on smoke, he rammed the door one final time before giving up. He was trapped. He sank to the floor, lying down where the smoke was thinnest, put the butt of the gun to the door, and pounded with all his remaining strength.

XXXVI
Anna to the Rescue

"THE WAREHOUSE!"

Anna raced toward the conflagration, her boots pounding on the packed dirt. All the buildings he could have set fire to, and that fool Petersen had chosen this one? Didn't he realize it would do no good to steal a company if the entire product base was destroyed?

No, he hadn't thought that far ahead. He'd chosen the building most often unoccupied and seized the opportunity. Now that she had her memories back, Anna could see the pattern in everything he'd done. Petersen was an inveterate gambler. Every time he lost, he raised the stakes in an increasingly desperate attempt to recoup. He was reckless, short-sighted, and capricious. And he was about to run out of options.

"Quinn!" Anna shouted, running toward the lines of men who were hauling water up from the river in buckets, barrels, bowls, pitchers, and anything else that could hold liquid. "Quinn, where are you?"

The acrid smoke stung her nostrils, and she instinctively put a hand to her belly. Standing in the foul air wouldn't be good for her or the baby. She needed to see Quinn. If she could only confirm that he was safe, she could retreat to a better location.

"Lines one and four, move in closer!" Hamish Douglass called to the men he was directing. "We've got it contained, now get everything on that front door!"

"Douglass!" Anna hurried over to the burly supervisor.

"We've got this, lassie," he said, not even looking at her.

"Where's Quinn?"

"Dinnae ken." He gestured at the firefighting workers. "Aye, that's it. Closer now!"

Anna yanked on his sleeve. "Where is he, dammit?"

"I dinnae ken, lassie. Went off to fight the fire, same as me."

"Mrs. Harper!" Rabbie jogged over from the line he was shepherding into place. Sweat trickled down his face, leaving clean streaks through the black soot that coated his skin.

"Rabbie. Where's my husband?" She grabbed the young man's wrist, panic clawing at her insides. "Where is he? He's not here. Why isn't he here?"

"He went around back, Mrs. Harper. To make certain everyone was out of the building."

Her hands clenched so tightly that Rabbie yelped in pain.

"And he hasn't come back to fight the fire? Did no one see him come back?"

Rabbie shrugged. "I dinnae ken."

"Oh, God, oh, God, oh, God." Anna let go of Rabbie and flew around the corner of the building, no longer caring about anything in the world except Quinn. Not the fire, not the whisky, not Petersen, not even the ridiculous divorce. She'd divorce Quinn a million times over as long as he was unharmed. She'd even marry someone else if that's what it took to keep him safe and alive.

Tears welled in her eyes. This was why Petersen's scheme had worked for so long. This was why she'd believed that through some drastic circumstance she could have left the love of her life. Because she could. She would. She would do anything. Absolutely anything.

She spun around another corner and almost stopped dead in her tracks. The back door was barricaded shut by a trolley laden with barrels.

"Quinn!"

No. No. Please, no.

He had to be inside. It was the only explanation for his absence. Petersen had deliberately trapped him in the burning building. Anna ran toward the door, her legs churning faster than she had ever thought possible, one hand clutched to her belly.

I'll save him, darling. I won't let you lose your Papa.

"Anna!" Petersen darted out from behind a stack of unused crates, some small vial or bottle clutched in his fist. "Anna, my dear, I'm sorry to have to do this to you, but you must be made to see reason. It's the only way."

Anna didn't even break stride. She whipped the pistol from her pocket and fired. Petersen dropped like a stone, and she ran past, not even bothering to look where the bullet had struck him. She didn't care.

Anna gripped the handle of the trolley and pulled. The vehicle didn't budge, but the shove sent her off balance. Her feet skidded on a pool of whisky that had leaked from a hole in one of the barrels, and she flailed.

"Dammit!"

Anna's hold on the trolley kept her upright, but the slip had cost her precious seconds. She adjusted her footing and tried again. These blasted heavy barrels weren't meant to be hauled around by a small woman, but what choice did she have? Smoke seeped from the cracks around the door. Quinn would be running out of air. With no one capable of helping within shouting distance, Anna was his only hope. She took a deep breath and put all her strength into it. With a mighty yank, she set the trolley into motion, stumbling backward as it rolled mercifully away from the entrance.

A blast of hot smoke assaulted her when she swung the door open, and she had to step back and wipe her eyes before she could peer inside.

She didn't have to look far. Quinn lay on the floor beside the entrance, motionless.

"No. Oh, no, oh, no."

Was he even breathing? Anna could hardly see through the smoke and her tears. She grabbed Quinn's arm and tugged, trying to drag him outside. He whimpered.

"Quinn!" she gasped. "Oh, thank God, thank God." She pulled harder and felt something pop in his upper arm or shoulder. Quinn jerked and whimpered again.

Oh, no. Was he injured? Had she injured him? She had no time to check. Grabbing him by both arms this time, Anna hauled him out the door and into the clean air.

She dragged him several yards more, then dropped to her knees by his side. His skin was pale, almost bluish, and his breaths came in tiny, shallow wheezes.

"Quinn. Quinn, can you hear me?"

He neither moved nor made any sound. She nudged the injured arm again, hoping for a response, but this time he didn't even twitch.

"Quinn, my love." She cupped her hand to his cheek. "Be strong, love. I won't let you die."

He had a store of healing potions in his office, bought to save lives in the event of a workplace accident. Had he ever thought that one day they might be used to save him? She certainly hadn't.

Anna glanced at Petersen. He was sitting up now, clutching his side and moaning. She'd only winged him. Damn. She couldn't dare leave Quinn's side as long as Petersen was even remotely mobile.

Petersen caught her looking and scrambled behind the

crates where he'd been hidden before. Anna's jaw clenched. Far, far too mobile.

She turned to the trolley. If she couldn't bring a potion to Quinn, she'd bring him to the potion. She shoved the leaking barrel off the trolley with minimal effort, but the second, full barrel was too heavy for her.

Smoke stung her eyes, but the gathering tears came from within as well. Quinn was in danger, her baby was in danger, she was in danger. And the man who had done this to them was still mobile, with who knew what horrible things in his spray bottles. She couldn't give up now.

Dropping to the ground, Anna braced herself against the building, put her feet to the barrel, and pushed. It inched toward the edge of the trolley, teetered, then toppled.

"Thank God," she gasped, scrambling back to her feet.

She grasped Quinn by both arms once again to drag him toward the trolley, but when she pulled he barely moved. Lord, he was heavy. Her arms and legs ached from her prior exertions. She had to do this. She *had to*. Gritting her teeth, she dragged him a few more feet.

"Mrs. Harper!" Rabbie's voice called from around the corner of the building. "Mr. Harper! We have the fire under control!"

"Rabbie!" Anna shouted. "Rabbie, help! Please hurry!"

The young man came running, skidding to a halt when he reached Anna and Quinn.

"Help me get him up on the trolley," Anna pleaded. "We must get him to his office at once."

With Rabbie grasping Quinn under the shoulders and Anna taking his legs, they managed to haul him up onto the bed of the trolley. Rabbie wheeled the small cart around and broke into a run. Anna raced alongside, helping Rabbie steer the trolley around and over ruts and bumps. The rough ride jostled Quinn in a manner that would surely have been painful had he been conscious. The fact that he didn't react in any way terrified Anna down to her very bones.

I won't lose you. I won't lose you.

They raced around the warehouse, past the hard-working men who were even now dousing the last, stubborn licks of flame, right up to the front door of the Harper-Douglass offices. Anna flung the door open, then she and Rabbie grabbed Quinn and dragged him down the hall into his office, where they stretched him out on the floor.

"Go for help," Anna told Rabbie. "Look for my brother. He should be bringing a doctor."

Rabbie tore off without another word.

Anna dove for the center drawer of Quinn's desk.

"Thank you, thank you, thank you for showing me this," she said, her hands feeling for the tiny latch at the back that would open the hidden panel. "Thank you for sharing everything with me. Thank you for encouraging me to go where I wanted and learn what I wanted. Thank you for trusting me with your work, your possessions, your heart, your life." Her fingers curled around the small key. "You've always believed I could do anything. And I'm going to prove it."

Tears overflowed as she lifted her trembling hand to the heavy safe built into the wall. The key slid into the hole and the lock clicked—a sound as beautiful as any Anna had ever heard. She shoved legal documents and stacks of banknotes aside, snatching the handful of small vials from the back corner.

She knelt beside Quinn and popped the cork from the first of the vials. Sliding one arm behind his neck, she tilted his head up and touched the bottle to his lips.

"Drink, love."

Liquid dribbled down his chin. Anna dipped a finger into the potion and stuck it into his mouth, determined to get some small amount into him. "Come on, love, you can do this." She tried again, and this time she felt a tiny bit of pressure as he sucked the potion from her leather-clad fingertip. "That's it. You can do it."

After a few more tiny doses he began to suck hard enough that she dared to pour the potion straight into his mouth. He gulped the liquid down until the whole bottle was empty. Anna clutched the other two bottles and gave him a quick examination.

No blood. No obvious injuries. The arm she'd been concerned about rested at a normal angle. His color already looked healthier, and his breathing was easing. She pressed two fingers to his throat to feel his pulse. Strong and steady. She would watch and wait and hold the remaining potions in reserve if he needed them.

She lay down beside him, pressing her body tight to his, one arm draped protectively across his chest.

"I love you, Quinn Harper," she murmured.

"Anna?" His voice was weak and hoarse, but the sound of it was the sweetest music Anna had ever heard. She clung to him, weeping in relief. "I'm sorry, Anna. Didn't know." A fit of coughing interrupted. "Was a trap."

"I know." She stroked her hand up and down his chest. "It's all right. Everything will be all right."

"No." His head rocked slightly side-to-side. "No. Building's burning. You shouldn't be here."

"Quinn." Anna sat up and stroked his cheek. "We're safe. We're out of the building. In your office."

"No, Anna. No, you have to get out. Fire. Petersen. He's the villain, Anna. He's not Harper. He's not your husband."

She squeezed Quinn's hand. "I know. I remember. Relax. Rest. You must get well."

"Rest. Yes." He frowned and shook his head. "No, can't rest. Danger. Fire. Need to rescue someone."

Anna glanced skyward, praying for patience. Her gaze dropped back to the potions in her hand. She uncorked one and pressed it to Quinn's lips. "Drink."

She let him drink about half of the potion, then recorked it and stashed it in her pocket. He sighed in relief and closed his eyes. Anna's shoulders sagged. As long as he could rest, he would recover. All she needed to do was sit here and guard him in case Petersen tried anything else.

Just when she thought he might be drifting off to sleep, he shot up, his blue-gray eyes wide and startled.

"Oh, my God! The warehouse! The fire."

Anna reached to soothe him, but he leapt to his feet and dashed for the door.

"I have to go. I have to help."

"Quinn, no, wait!"

Anna scrambled to her feet, cursing. As much as she adored his good heart and determined nature, right now she would have preferred a modicum of selfishness. He was in no condition to be running around, and certainly not to be putting himself anywhere near the fire.

She chased him down the hall and out the door, squinting and sneezing when the bright sunlight hit her eyes.

"Stop right there," a chilly voice commanded.

Anna froze. Petersen stood no more than five yards away, a pistol in one hand and a potion spray-bottle in the other. The right side of his coat was smeared with blood, but he remained steady on his feet. He aimed the gun straight between Quinn's eyes.

"Now be a good girl, darling, and throw down your weapon," Petersen instructed. "Or your 'Mr. Smith' will find more than a potion scrambling his brains."

XXXVII
Defensive Measures

"No, Anna, don't do it. Save yourself."

The pistol skittered across the ground, stopping mere feet away from Quinn's boots. Quinn's jaw clenched. He'd known Anna would never listen, but he'd had to try. He'd do all he could to keep her from harm. Anna and their child were all that mattered in the world, and right now Quinn had only two things to defend them with: his voice and his body. And his preference was to keep the latter intact.

Petersen waggled his gun. The gun Quinn had foolishly left lying on the ground when he'd run to see about the fire.

"Kick that gun over here, Smith," Petersen ordered.

"My name is Harper, you son of a bitch." Quinn stared down the man who had once been a friend. Petersen was disheveled, bloodied, and had clearly fallen so far that he'd lost whatever sense of reason he'd possessed.

"Oh, yes," Petersen sneered. "Quinn Harper of Harper-Douglass Whisky. Always doing good. Always helping others.

Always so pleased with himself for deigning to throw a crust of bread to us lowly commoners."

"What the fuck are you talking about?" Quinn said. Petersen had completely lost his mind. It was the only explanation. "I practically rebuilt this entire distillery with my own two hands. I know the name of every employee here—or did before you went and drugged me—and I've shared in every single one of their jobs. If that's not a working man, I don't know what is."

Petersen snarled. "Stop acting like you care. You've gone soft. Married an heiress. Bought yourself those fancy suits."

"Put the gun down, Petersen," Quinn said, trying to bring his voice back to a calm tone. "No good can come of shooting anyone. We can sit down and talk about this like civilized people."

Petersen shook the gun violently, and for an instant, Quinn was certain this was the end. When the pistol didn't fire, he sucked in a deep breath.

"There is nothing to talk about! You ruined my life!"

"What?"

"All I needed was a small advance on my pay. A little loan from a friend. But you wouldn't dirty your hands that way. Had to 'help' the way *you* wanted to. Shut me out from everything."

Quinn stared at him, no longer knowing what to say. He remembered—clear as day now—that night he'd found Petersen bloody and battered for failure to pay a gaming debt. He'd been a friend. Of course Quinn had helped.

And, yes, that meant shutting him out from the gaming houses. Quinn had also arranged for a portion of his pay to go straight to his creditors. Given him new assignments that required additional time and effort to help keep him occupied. Everything seemed to have gone so well. Quinn had no idea what had happened to cause Peterson to snap.

The crunch of gravel behind him almost made Quinn turn around. During the conversation, Anna had crept closer. Her hand brushed his back. Quinn spread his arms and legs wide to make himself the largest shield possible.

"Stop moving!" Petersen shouted. "I *will* shoot!"

"Let Anna go," Quinn commanded. "This is between you and I."

Petersen let out a short bark of laughter. "You think it's not about her too? It was always about her. From the first day you brought her here, walking around with your hands all over her. Flaunting your beautiful, rich, titled wife. Letting her befriend all of us. Taunting us with what we could never have."

The shouting had attracted attention. Hamish Douglass approached from the direction of the warehouse, where only a few gray wisps of smoke remained of the fire. Quinn kept his gaze on Petersen, possible scenarios running through his mind. If Douglass was truly on the side of that madman, Quinn was as good as dead and Anna would be mind-wiped.

Never. They will never harm her.

Anna's gun wasn't far away. Quinn could dive for it and try to shoot Petersen. If he could distract him enough, he might have the time. Or he could charge Petersen. He'd probably get shot for his troubles, but it would let Anna get to the gun and protect herself.

The best choice of bad choices, he decided. Protection for Anna and the baby was of utmost importance. He'd get Petersen off guard if he could, and then rush him.

"Do you know why you could never have a woman like Anna?" Quinn asked, taking one step forward. Petersen's gun hand steadied, the barrel aimed straight for Quinn's brain. Quinn froze and lifted his hands in the air in surrender. "Because she would never choose someone like you. Look at what you've done. Look at what you're doing. She would never want a man who behaved that way. She's not a prize. She's not something I bought or something I won. She is a gift I was given. *She* chose *me*. And no matter what you do, she will never choose you."

Quinn launched himself at Petersen, ducking low in the hopes that any gunshot would sail over his head. In the same instant, a large figure crashed into Petersen from the opposite direction, sending him catapulting into the air and leaving Quinn grasping at nothing. Douglass.

The gun fired. Quinn hit the ground hard, jarring his tender shoulder—which now that he thought about it had felt surprisingly better until that moment. Another shot fired. Quinn started to roll over, only to be crushed beneath a pile of skirts. Anna.

"Stay down," she commanded, pressing a gloved hand to his chest. Purple leather. One of her new pairs. If he were truly lucky, she might do wicked things to him with those gloves someday.

Her opposite hand clutched Nick the girl bear. She kept the toy with her at all times, he now remembered, but he couldn't recall why.

A third shot fired, then a fourth. Douglass and Petersen rolled across the ground, fighting for control of both guns. One of the pistols went off again, and Douglass collapsed, crying out in agony. Petersen scrambled to his feet and strode toward Anna and Quinn, a gun in one hand, and his spray potion in the other.

"That traitorous bastard," he snarled. "Even if he lives I won't split the company with him. When I marry Lady Anna I'll take the whole thing for myself. Now it's time to finish this, once and for all."

He walked toward them, the spray potion at the ready. Anna pointed her bear at him, wielding it like a weapon.

"Goodbye, Mr. Harper," Petersen mocked. "And hello, Anna Petersen."

Petersen sprayed his potion. At the same instant, Anna squeezed her bear. The head popped off, and a thunderous blast of air burst forth. The explosion lifted Petersen off his feet, flinging him backwards, sending Quinn and Anna tumbling in the opposite direction. Quinn's head bounced off the rough ground. Sparks of pain shot through his skull and stars danced in front of his eyes.

When at last he came to rest, he blinked up at the bright blue sky, dazed, his whole body aching. Some sort of wet droplets spattered his cheek, but before he could do anything about them, or even ascertain what they were, a gloved hand wiped them away.

"Quinn." A gorgeous, dark-haired woman sat beside him, gazing down at him in concern, her hand cupping his cheek. "Quinn, can you hear me? Do you know me?"

He stared at her for a long moment, taking her in. Memorizing her. His wife. His love. He'd know her anywhere.

"Anna," he breathed.

Tears of relief ran down her cheeks. "Drink this." She held a half-empty bottle to his lips and he gulped the potion down, his mouth puckering at the unpleasant, spicy taste. "Good. Now lie still and recover for a moment. I'm going to go give this last healing potion to Mr. Douglass."

"What about… What's-His-Name?"

"Petersen?"

"Yes. Him."

Her amber eyes turned rock-hard. "I hope he's dead."

XXXVIII

Forgiven and Forgotten

"Not dead, thank God."

Anna frowned down at her husband as he knelt beside Petersen's prone body and checked for a pulse. She huffed in displeasure.

"You disagree?" Quinn asked.

"He tried to kill you. More than once."

"I didn't say I forgave him. But I don't think he needs to die."

"You're too soft, Harper," Douglass growled. "Listen to your wee wife. She has the right of it."

Anna smiled at Douglass. His arm hung limply from the wound to his shoulder, but the potion had revived him enough that he was sitting up and scowling again. A positive sign.

"Thank you, Mr. Douglass. It's good to see you're a man who can learn from his mistakes. Perhaps now you will acknowledge that women are good for more than looking pretty and making babies."

"Says the woman making a wee Harper babe."

"I didn't say there's anything *wrong* with making babies. But we can do other things if we wish. Investigating crimes and stopping murders, for example."

"Aye, lassie," he sighed. "You did good."

"Thank you. And thank you for your assistance."

"You're welcome. Harper and I may ne'er see eye-to-eye, but I'd nae wish him dead."

"Nor I you," Quinn replied.

"I wouldnae have gone along with his plan, if I'd known he meant to kill you. He told me you'd lost your mind. Said you fooled around with recreational potions and ruined your brain. Thought you were someone named Smith."

Quinn raised one blond eyebrow. "And you believed him?"

Douglass looked down at the ground. "I *wanted* to believe him. He said he'd marry Lady Anna and share ownership with me. I figured he couldnae run the place, so it'd be all mine. I was a fool."

"Aye."

"I'll help clean up from the fire. Then you'll nae see me here again."

"No. I'd like you to stay."

Anna knelt beside her husband and took his hand. Lord, but she loved this man. Part of her wanted to shout that Douglass had betrayed him and didn't deserve a second chance, but she kept the words bottled up. This was who Quinn was. He sought the good in people, accepted them, quirks and flaws and all. It had earned him hard workers and loyal friends. And an adoring wife.

"You're a natural leader," Quinn continued. "The men listen to you. They work hard for you. You've been valuable to the company, and as Anna said, you have demonstrated an ability to learn from your mistakes. If you can accept that your place here is as an employee, I'd like you to stay. But if you challenge my ownership or try to turn any of the men against me, you will be dismissed at once. Understood?"

"Aye, lad. I accept."

The two men shook hands.

"You'd hate being an owner, anyhow," Quinn said. "You'd

have to live half your life in London, talking to snooty, rich Englishmen."

"Aye. I want no part of that. There's one of your Englishmen now. Look at him, with his perfect clothes and his nose-in-the-air walk. You'd think *he* owned the damned distillery."

Anna turned around. Nick and Ida strode toward them, accompanied by a handful of Quinn's workers and an unknown man who Anna guessed must be the doctor.

"That's my brother you're talking about," she said to Douglass.

"Well, lassie, I can't help that he looks to be a stuffy arse."

She laughed. "Only sometimes."

"Anna!" Nick rushed toward her. "Anna, how are you? How's Harper? Are you hurt? The doctor is here with me."

"I'm fine, and Quinn is doing well. The doctor should examine Mr. Douglass first. He took a bullet to the shoulder." She tossed a look at Petersen. "And I suppose someone ought to check on him as well."

"He's stirring a bit," Quinn said. "Sharpe, do you think you could send someone to the police? This man is an arsonist and attempted murderer. We don't want him wandering free."

"Of course," Nick replied. "Ida, love, could you stay with my sister in case she needs anything?"

Ida nodded. "She'll be fine, Nick. Small, but fierce, isn't that how you like to describe her?"

"Besides, I already have everything I need." Anna placed one hand on her belly, squeezing Quinn's hand with the other. "Right here."

Quinn leaned in and kissed her cheek.

"How's your memory?" she asked.

"Imperfect. Still trying to fill in the gaps. Why did Petersen go mad and try to take over the company in the first place? He'd stopped gambling, and his project starting the Esbjerg distribution site had gone so well. Why did he snap? Have I missed something?"

"He hadn't stopped gambling," Anna explained. "That's what I learned in my investigations. The gaming houses were closed to him, but he stumbled upon a gentleman's lunch club where the men placed high-stakes wagers on all sorts of things. He had a run of good luck, moved on to even larger wagers, and quickly found himself ruined."

"So he decided to steal whisky."

"He talked his cousin in Esbjerg into joining the scheme for a share of the profits."

"That man who chased you on the bike?"

"A Petersen. They believed they could get away with it, since they could work from both the Scottish and Danish ends of the distribution."

"Damn. And while I was off in Copenhagen, verifying the tainted whisky and trying to mitigate some of the damage with our clients, he decided he needed to wipe our memory."

Anna nodded. "Either he feared you were getting too close or he discovered I was on to him."

"And it only escalated from there. I think maybe he really is somewhat insane."

Anna shrugged. "Maybe."

Petersen groaned, his head rocking from side-to-side.

"Oh, are you waking up, Mr. Petersen?" Anna asked. "Good. You can explain to the police how you tried to burn down the warehouse with my husband inside."

"Who?" he mumbled.

"Quinn Harper, of Harper-Douglass Whisky. My true and only husband. I'm determined never to forget again."

Petersen groaned again and opened his eyes. His pupils were wide, his mouth twisted in confusion. "Where am I?"

"Lying on the ground at the distillery."

He frowned even more. "Wh-who are you?"

"Anna Harper. Have you forgotten me? I can't say I would be terribly upset if the blast potion from Nick the bear sprayed your own potion back at you."

Petersen blinked up at her, his head shaking once more. "Who am I?"

Quinn held up a hand to stop Anna before she could reply. "I'll take care of this." He leaned over Petersen. "Do you remember me at all?"

"No."

"Do you remember anything?"

Another head shake.

"And you don't know who you are?"

"No. Who am I? Tell me."

Quinn sat silently for a moment, then with a wry smile answered, "Smith. Mr. Wilhelm Smith. From Newcastle."

XXXIX

Tying the Knot

"YOU DON'T HAVE TO COME if you don't want to."

Quinn turned away from the house to look at his wife, who sat in the passenger seat of their pretty little steam car, inching toward the driver's side.

"I'm sure by the time I reach London I'll have gotten the hang of driving."

"If you want to drive, Anna, just say so. I don't mind."

"I don't want to drive in the city. Not yet. But I also don't want to make you come along when you're worried about the distillery and the repairs. Plus Petersen, and whether he'll be sent to prison or an asylum. I know these things are bothering you. You can stay here. I can make certain the divorce doesn't go through on my own."

Quinn checked that their trunks were securely fastened, then climbed into the driver's seat. "No, I need to come along. It's awkward at the distillery when I'm stumbling over names and forgetting where I put things. I need to see this…" He checked his notebook. "Elle Ainsworth person. Who did Rabbie say she was, again?"

"His cousin Henry's wife. Or maybe fiancée? Rabbie seemed a bit confused about the whole thing. His family is odd, he says, and there are almost as many MacAlasters as Mastersons. But no matter. The important thing is that Elle owns a potion shop and is said to be an expert mixer. If anyone can help you, she can."

"Good. Then I'm going. I want to see my mother and grandmother. And I want to have some time with just the two of us, now that we're ourselves again."

Anna's hand settled on his thigh, the purple gloves bright against his gray trousers. "We were always ourselves, Quinn. Even when we didn't remember. Everything you did was because of who you are, deep inside. My drive to investigate, to learn, to not let anything hold me back? That was me coming out, though I didn't remember myself. We never truly lost ourselves. And I think that's why we never lost each other. Somewhere inside, we knew."

Quinn nodded, the words he wanted to say not quite fully formed in his mind. If he couldn't find them by the time they stopped for the night, he'd simply do his best and stumble through.

He pressed on the throttle, and the car began to roll down the street. "I'll drive us out of the city, and then you can take over. I'll navigate while you practice."

Her brilliant smile erased any lingering doubts he had about leaving Edinburgh. Here was where he belonged. At her side.

"Quinn, this road doesn't look familiar," she remarked sometime later, when she had finally settled into the routine of driving. "Did you misremember something? I'm sorry I didn't say anything sooner, but I've been concentrating so much on the driving."

He patted the map spread across his lap. "Don't worry.

We're on the right path. Given what time it was when we set out, I knew we'd have to stop for the night relatively soon, and I'd rather not overnight in Newcastle, considering recent events. So I picked a different route."

Anna glanced away from the road just long enough to give him a suspicious frown. "I see."

"You *will* see. In another two hours or so."

"Hmm. Well, while we wait, we can discuss what we want to name our baby boy. Quinn Junior, perhaps?"

"Anna Junior. It will be a girl."

Two hours later, they had eliminated ninety-nine percent of all English names and a good many from other cultures as well. Quinn was nearly ready to give up and let Anna name the baby after him, though he didn't want to admit it.

"There's only one solution, love," he said, as she pulled the car to a stop. "We'll have to name the baby Smith."

"Quinn?" Her suspicious tone had returned.

"You were supposed to laugh," he sighed.

"Quinn, is this…" She twisted in her seat, scanning the little border town he had led them to. "You navigated us to Gretna Green!"

"Aye, love. I did." He wasn't certain if detouring to the famous elopement site was the most romantic idea he'd ever had or the silliest, but he forged ahead. "I know I loved you and married you in the past, but I wanted to show you how much I love you here in the present. And how I will continue loving you into the future. So, Present Anna, will you marry me?"

She did laugh, then, long and loud and joyously. "Yes, Quinn Harper, I will marry you. Today, tomorrow, and always."

Hand-in-hand they entered the blacksmith's shop, a simple, single-story structure that appeared unchanged from the days more than a hundred years before when weddings had first taken place here. A worn wooden bench and a lectern with an open logbook stood near the door. At the opposite end of the room, a grizzled old man pounded away at his latest creation.

"Write your names in the book and have a seat," he said, without even glancing up from his work.

Quinn and Anna scribbled their names in the ledger book that rested on a lectern by the door, then sat on the bench, watching the blacksmith at work. Anna tugged at her skirts.

"I should change," she fretted. "Do you think there's a place I could change?"

"A linen closet, perhaps?" Quinn offered.

She gave him a playful jab with her elbow. "I'm serious. I should wear my amber gown."

"The gown already had a special day. The day I realized nothing would stop us from being together. Not the false Mr. Harper, not my memory problems, nothing. If you really want it, I'll find you a place to change, but you don't need it, not on my account. I'd elope with you even if you were wearing a ripped, dirt-stained, traveling dress." His eyebrows twitched. "Or nothing at all."

She met his salacious grin with one of her own. "Maybe you're right. But I do need to change gloves. I'll be right back."

She darted out the door just as the blacksmith finished up and turned around, wiping his hands on his apron.

"Your lass decided not to marry you after all?"

"She's run out to fetch something," Quinn replied. "She'll be back in a moment."

The blacksmith sniffed in a way that made Quinn suspect he'd seen more than one prospective bride flee before the vows. "Either of you from around these parts? Won't be legal, otherwise. Twenty-one days, that's the rule."

"We have a residence in Edinburgh. But it's irrelevant, since we're already married."

"T' other people? I won't have any part of that."

"No. To each other."

The blacksmith looked at his book of names. "Harper and Harper, eh? Like the whisky?"

Quinn grinned. "Aye. Like the whisky."

"Did someone say whisky?" Anna appeared in the doorway, holding a bottle of five-year single malt, her hands now clad in the emerald green gloves she'd worn on the day Quinn had first met her. "I grabbed a bottle from the car. I thought it would be a good way to thank our, er, host? Minister? Wedding person? I'm sorry, I don't know what to call you."

"Ross."

"Ah. I'm relieved to know that you do not use your profession as your surname, Mr. Ross." She held out the bottle. "Here you are. Thank you for your services this evening."

He accepted the bottle and waved a hand at the anvil. "Stand over there. You need a rope?"

Quinn drew a narrow strip of Douglass plaid from his pocket. "I brought this."

Ross took the cloth and motioned Quinn and Anna into place. "Hold hands while I tie this around you. Then say whatever words you like and you'll be married. You might want to take those gloves off, lassie."

"I'd rather wear them, thank you," Anna replied. She held out her left hand. Quinn caught it with his right, giving her a squeeze.

Ross wrapped the scrap of plaid around their enjoined hands, knotting them together. "You take him to be your husband, lassie?"

"Yes," Anna replied.

"What about you, lad? You take her to wife?"

"Yes," Quinn answered.

"Any other words?"

"Anna," Quinn began, gazing into her eyes. "I fell in love with you the day we met. And I've fallen in love with you every day since. Over and over. Even when my mind went blank, my body and my heart called out for you. Nothing can keep me from you. Nothing can make me forget you. You are a part of me. Now and always."

Anna's eyes shimmered with unshed tears. "I love you, Quinn Harper. Don't ever forget it."

She had said those very same words to him, once. The night they'd first gone to bed together. The night he'd proposed. Those few words meant more to him than any flowery speech ever could.

"I remember," he whispered.

"Guess I'd better pronounce you man and wife," Ross said, "'cause you look like you're about to start winding her little ball of yarn. Done. You're married. Get on with you. I'm gonna go enjoy this whisky. There's a place down the road where you can stay the night."

"Thank you," Quinn replied.

He and Anna rushed out the door and down the street to the inn, leaving their belongings in the car, their hands still tied together.

"We'll send someone to fetch the trunks," he murmured.

Anna nodded. "We won't need them until morning. We're not going to be wearing any clothes tonight."

"No. Except maybe those sexy gloves of yours."

Quinn wasn't certain how they made it into the room without losing some article of clothing. His necktie and coat slipped off as he was reaching to lock the door. He had to pause to pull his hand out of the sleeve before he could turn the key. Fortunately, the proprietors of the small inn had made certain the bed was turned down and a warm fire crackled in the hearth. He and Anna could get directly to business.

"Someone's in a hurry," he teased.

"'Efficient' is the word you were looking for."

Quinn turned and caught her up in a passionate kiss. "Mmm. Aye."

Anna backed him into the wall. Her soft lips trailed across

his jaw and down his neck, while busy hands deprived him of additional layers of clothing.

"Ah, love," he sighed. "I wish I could say I remember every time we've done this, but I don't. I do, however, remember a few key instances."

"The closet. I know."

"More than that. Our wedding night."

"Yes." She pried his shirt open and placed a kiss directly over his heart. "It was so lovely."

"The very first time I made love to you. Our first kiss. Our first dance. The day we met. I may never recall every detail of falling in love with you, Anna, but I remember how it felt. How it still feels."

Her fingers drifted down to the fastenings of his trousers. "My darling, wonderful, precious husband," she murmured against his chest.

In an instant, she had dropped to her knees and freed his cock, letting her tongue run slowly from base to tip. Quinn groaned and dug his fingers into her hair, tugging the long, dark locks from their tidy knot.

Anna grinned up at him. "I love when you make those sorts of noises." Her tongue made a lazy, swirling motion, and he let out another groan, partly for her benefit and partly because holding it in would have taken too much effort.

"Oh, God, you're a tease."

And he loved it. Her lips kissed him. Her mouth moved over him, taking him deeper, bit-by-bit. Slowly, gently, then harder, faster, until he could hardly stand the perfect torment of her squeezing and sucking.

"Anna," he gasped, "you should…"

He lost the ability to speak. Lost the ability to think. And finally, blessedly, lost himself inside her. His entire body went limp, sagging back against the wall. She pulled away slowly, dabbed at her mouth with a handkerchief, and rose to her feet.

"I think you earned that."

"Christ, Anna." He let a long, silent moment pass while he caught his breath and regained his stamina. "You're a hell of a woman. What did I do to deserve you?"

Anna shrugged. "What you always do. Be yourself."

"Ah." He looked her up and down, enjoying her rumpled, partly unfastened dress, her tangled hair, and her flushed cheeks. "Well, right now, *myself* has decided he needs to return the favor."

He lunged for her, catching her by the waist and sweeping her off her feet as she giggled in delight. He loved that noise. Few people, he was certain, could make Anna giggle, and none as often as he could. Best of all, he was the one man in the entire world with the privilege of hearing her wicked giggle, usually followed by her happy, satisfied giggle.

He laid her down, not on the bed, but in front of the fireplace, stretching out beside her and taking his time removing her dress, kissing each bit of skin he exposed. Shoulders, arms, breasts, belly. Kneecaps. Her creamy, white thighs. Slowly he kissed and sucked, inching ever higher as she squirmed and sighed.

"Quinn, please," she begged. "You're torturing me."

"I know love." His tongue made a slow circle over her clit, and her lips parted on an exhalation of delight. "But you started this game, and I know you always want me to play my absolute best."

"Yes. Oh, yes."

Quinn kept up his methodical pace, relishing every noise Anna made and every undulation of her body, until at last she broke apart, crying out in relief and rapture. He moved to lay beside her, holding her close and breathing her in.

"I love you, Anna."

"I love you too." He pressed his cheek to hers. "More? Or sleep? And stay here or move to the bed?"

"More and here. But fetch some blankets so it's cozier."

"Right away, my lady."

Quinn built a snug little nest by the hearth, and they cuddled inside and made love until the fire had burned down to a handful of glowing embers.

"Fire's going out," he said, before she could nod off in his arms.

Anna snuggled closer. "I'm not worried. You always keep me warm."

He scooped her up and carried her to the bed, tucking them both in beneath a mound of soft bedding. "Happy second wedding night, my love."

She kissed him. "We should do this every year."

"Mmm. But maybe without the memory loss and almost being burned alive."

"Agreed."

Quinn placed a protective hand over her belly. "And remember, next year we'll have a little one with us."

"Which will make it all the more scandalous and exciting when we elope."

He laughed and kissed her again. "This, my love, is exactly why I married you."

"And don't you forget it."

Quinn draped an arm around her, molding their bodies together, feeling their two hearts beating as one.

"I won't."

Epilogue

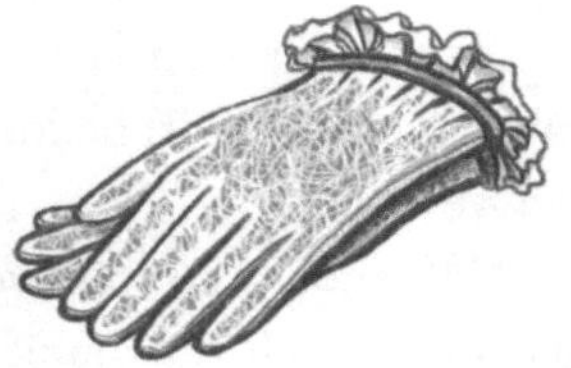

Anna grunted in pain. "I am never doing this again."

"Not much longer, now, love," Quinn soothed.

She glared at him. "This is all *your* fault."

He was a decent enough man to look guilty about it. "I hope you don't intend to divorce me again."

"It never went past the preliminary hearing." She grunted again and adjusted her position a tiny bit. "No—ugh—damage done."

"Ah, but the scandal sheets still went wild. Between the almost-divorce and the fire we had the biggest sales spike we've ever had."

"Don't move, Mrs. Harper," said the calm voice of a professional who had done this hundreds of times. "Relax. Breathe easy. Look at me. Perfect. Now smile." The photographer snapped the photo. "Excellent. I think we've got it. You can set that prop down."

Anna lowered the enormous bottle to the ground and rubbed her aching arms. Nearly an hour she'd been here, twisting and turning and posing. "I don't know what I was thinking, agreeing to this. Seven months gone with child and

I'm standing around holding giant whisky bottles until my arms fall off. I ought to be sitting down."

Quinn stepped up behind her and took over the massaging of her sore muscles. "You never sit down. Besides, just think how incredible this advertisement is going to look. When we colorize your eyes and the dress and the whisky, it will catch every eye in the country."

"It will scandalize every stuffy matron in the country. They will say I'm supposed to be knitting baby clothes, not flaunting my belly in whisky advertisements."

Quinn kissed her cheek. "And we have already established that scandal makes for excellent publicity. We'll run the ad in all the more salacious papers and periodicals. Maybe we can even put it in the back of the next episode of *The Daring Debutante*."

"If you ever write it."

"I did write it. You need to edit it."

"I haven't seen it. Did you leave it at our Edinburgh house?"

Quinn sighed. "Probably. I swear I leave something every time we come to London. I'll cable Rabbie and have him send it. We can release it once we're past this ten-year whisky madness. Did I tell you I'm having to hold an auction for the bottles from the fire-damaged barrels? I've had dozens of requests because someone said at a party they thought it would be the most unique flavor to have come from Scotland in a century."

"I'm not going to complain if anyone wants to pay exorbitant prices for our products. But save a bottle for us so we can test if there really is any difference."

Quinn pulled out his notebook. "I'll make a note of it. Shall we go home? The stew has been simmering since lunch and we still have a child and potions to fetch before we can eat."

"Yes, let's. We've been away quite long enough, and Elle can't enjoy having an extra toddler running around her shop."

A short cab ride brought them to a fashionable shopping

district, lined with stores that were dousing lights and closing their doors for the night. Elle's potion shop was locked tight, and a sign reading "closed" had been set in the window, but light glowed from behind the curtains. Anna rapped on the door.

It swung open a moment later to reveal a blond man in a severe, black suit wearing a mischievous smile.

"Good evening," Henry Ainsworth greeted Anna and Quinn, waving them inside. "Come to select a small beast? I'm afraid we're nearly sold out today. We have this one." He gestured at the blond, freckled toddler that clung to his pant leg, frowning suspiciously at the strangers.

The little girl said something that might have been a French swear. Anna grinned. Good on her.

"I don't recommend her," Henry continued. "Fathered by some scoundrel. You might like that little dark-haired one, though. Quiet, but determined. Likes to chew on books, I'm afraid."

Penny looked up from the book she was clutching, spied Anna, and raced across the room on her chubby little legs. "Mama!"

Anna picked her up and gave her a kiss.

"Boo," Penny declared, brandishing the heavy tome she carried.

"Book, yes." Anna settled the little girl on her hip as best as she could manage with her round belly. She peered at the book. "*Great Expectations.* A bit long for your age, don't you think?" She pried the book from Penny's fingers, causing the toddler to wail in protest. Anna held the book out to Henry. "It looks a little soggy on the corners. I'm sorry."

"She can keep it," Henry said. "I have three copies at home, and she seems to have taken to it. She climbed the shelf half-a-dozen times trying to get to it. Eventually she pushed a chair clear across the room so she could climb up and reach."

"Boo!" Penny cried. Anna returned the book to her and she hugged it happily, gnawing on one corner.

Anna cringed. "I'm glad you love books, sweetheart, but maybe you could not eat them? This is why we have cloth books for you at home."

Henry motioned toward the back room. "I believe Elle is ready for you, and I'm sure you want to put Miss Dreadful the Book-Eater to bed." He scooped up his daughter. "I know Hannah is getting sleepy."

Hannah mumbled her naughty French word again.

"Exactly."

The potions workshop was a small, but tidy room with two floor-to-ceiling bookshelves, a long work table, and cabinets stocked with tools and ingredients. A few toys lay scattered across the floor. Elle sat at a stool, her tiny baby strapped to her chest, carefully packing vials into a small, wooden box. Her warm brown eyes flicked to the newcomers.

"Hello, Mr. and Mrs. Harper. I have your potions ready." She handed a large vial to Quinn. "I didn't change your dosage at all, but based on our conversation I lowered the potency. I don't think you'll ever need anything beyond a mild recollection potion ever again."

"That and a notebook," Quinn replied with a lopsided smile.

Elle nodded. "So many malicious potions in such a short time would do anyone permanent damage. You've made an excellent recovery."

"And you'll never be as bad with names as Nick is," Anna added.

Quinn laughed. "Truth."

Elle tucked one last potion into the wooden box. "I put your childbirth kit together," she said to Anna. She closed the lid and flipped the latch on the front. "I know you have another month or two to go, but it never hurts to be prepared."

Quinn took Penny from Anna's arms to allow her to pick

up the box and take a peek. Potions for pain relief, stamina, healing, and more were neatly arranged and labeled. A sheet of instructions had been glued to the lid.

"I love these. You've improved the design since Penny was born. You must sell hundreds of them."

"They are popular," Elle admitted. "And I enjoy making them. We mothers ought to support one another."

"Thank you," Anna said. "I greatly appreciate your expertise. And thank you for letting Penny play. It's so nice for her to know a girl her own age."

"Thank Henry for that. He watched them most of the time."

"I'm thinking of starting a new career as a child-rearer," Henry said, sounding entirely serious. "I'm certain there is great demand for a male nanny who will teach children bad habits."

"Only in our house, love," Elle replied.

Anna laughed and thanked her friends once again before departing.

"Let me know when you have a free evening and we'll have you over for dinner," Quinn offered as they paused by the door to say farewell. "I'll even make something fancier than stew."

"We'd love that," Elle replied. "Have a good night!"

Penny fell asleep on the ride home. Anna tucked her into bed, then settled down in the dining room for a quiet dinner with her husband. She filled her belly with stew and some leftover lemon tarts that Quinn had made for her the day before.

"It was a lovely dinner, Quinn," she said as they walked together to their bedroom. "Thank you."

"You're most welcome, love. I will never tire of cooking for you." He checked his watch. "Are you sleepy? It's been a long day, and I'm willing to go to bed if you are. Or we could play a game before we turn in. We haven't played backgammon recently, or we could play cards. I'm open to anything, really."

Anna thought for a moment, considering what games she had available and what variations they might play. Her husband watched her silently, his pretty eyes gleaming with happiness and desire.

"I have an idea."

Quinn's eyebrows twitched. "Does it involve kissing?"

"My best ideas always do."

"Aye." He grinned and held the bedroom door open for her. "I remember."

The End

About the Author

AWARD-WINNING AUTHOR CATHERINE STEIN believes that everyone deserves love and that Happily Ever After has the power to help, to heal, and to comfort. She writes sassy, sexy romance set during the Victorian and Edwardian eras. Her stories are full of action, adventure, magic, and fantastic technologies.

Catherine lives in Michigan with her husband and three rambunctious girls. She loves steampunk and Oxford commas, and can often be found dressed in Renaissance festival clothing, drinking copious amounts of tea.

· · · ❧ · · ·

Visit Catherine online at
www.catsteinbooks.com
and join her VIP mailing list for a free short story.

Follow her on Twitter @catsteinbooks,
or like her page on Facebook @catsteinbooks.

· · · 🖑 · · ·

Thank you so much for reading.
If you enjoyed the book and are so inclined, I would love for
you to leave a review. Happy readers make an author's day!

I love hearing from readers,
so feel free to contact me on social media, or email:

catherine@catsteinbooks.com